Those Roguish Rosemonts

*Three brothers with rakish pasts
find love where they least expect it*

Three brothers, three young men from a privileged,
aristocratic background. All are expected to uphold
the Rosemont family name—which means giving
up their roguish ways and marrying well. But
are they ready to make convenient marriages
where love is second to duty? That is when they
each meet a woman who challenges them
and convinces them that love is the
only way to find true happiness.

Read Ethan's story in
A Dance to Save the Debutante

Jake's story in
Tempting the Sensible Lady Violet

Luther's story in
Falling for the Forbidden Duke

All available now!

Author Note

Falling for the Forbidden Duke is the final book of the Those Roguish Rosemonts series. It features Luther Rosemont, the Duke of Southbridge, who has avoided being captured by husband-seeking debutantes for the past ten Seasons. Then he meets Georgina Daglish, the illegitimate daughter of a former courtesan. He's immediately smitten, but just as immediately aware that she is wholly inappropriate as a duchess. Especially as Georgina has plans of her own, ones that do not include a man or marriage.

Luther and Georgina's story was a fun one to write as they are equally feisty and equally determined not to fall in love. I hope you enjoy reading *Falling for the Forbidden Duke* as much as I enjoyed writing it.

I love hearing from readers and can be reached through my website, www.evashepherd.com, or on Facebook, www.Facebook.com/evashepherdromancewriter.

EVA SHEPHERD

Falling for the Forbidden Duke

HARLEQUIN®
HISTORICAL™

ISBN-13: 978-1-335-72373-4

Falling for the Forbidden Duke

Copyright © 2023 by Eva Shepherd

For questions and comments about the quality of this book, please contact us at CustomerService@Harlequin.com.

Harlequin Enterprises ULC
22 Adelaide St. West, 41st Floor
Toronto, Ontario M5H 4E3, Canada
www.Harlequin.com

Printed in U.S.A.

Recycling programs for this product may not exist in your area.

After graduating with degrees in history and political science, **Eva Shepherd** worked in journalism and as an advertising copywriter. She began writing historical romances because it combined her love of a happy ending with her passion for history. She lives in Christchurch, New Zealand, but spends her days immersed in the world of late Victorian England. Eva loves hearing from readers and can be reached via her website, evashepherd.com, and her Facebook page, Facebook.com/evashepherdromancewriter.

Books by Eva Shepherd

Harlequin Historical

A Victorian Family Christmas
"The Earl's Unexpected Gifts"

Those Roguish Rosemonts

A Dance to Save the Debutante
Tempting the Sensible Lady Violet
Falling for the Forbidden Duke

Young Victorian Ladies

Wagering on the Wallflower
Stranded with the Reclusive Earl
The Duke's Rebellious Lady

Breaking the Marriage Rules

Beguiling the Duke
Awakening the Duchess
Aspirations of a Lady's Maid
How to Avoid the Marriage Mart

Visit the Author Profile page
at Harlequin.com.

To my two oldest friends, both called Susan:
Sue L and Susie K.

And by "oldest," I mean time served,
not your ages.

Chapter One

Somerset, England, 1892

Luther Rosemont, the Eighth Duke of Southbridge, had endured a staggering ten London Seasons and had still not found his bride. Some would say he was being overly picky. Luther would not.

There was no denying he had exceedingly high standards, but if a duke couldn't demand the highest of standards, then who could?

He came from a long, illustrious line of dukes who stretched back to the Tudor era. He was honour-bound to marry a woman with the same impeccable breeding as himself, one with a pedigree that marked her out as a duchess. This was a lesson that had been drummed into him by his father from the moment he had been capable of understanding, or, knowing how dogmatic his father had been, probably since his time in the cradle.

While it was not essential, Luther also wished his duchess to be intelligent, cultured and of a pleasant disposition. And, as her primary duty would be to produce the next duke, and preferably a spare or two, a level of mutual attraction would be advantageous. After all, the act of procreation should be more than just a duty for them both.

He did not expect love. That was a luxury to which lesser men could aspire and was another lesson that his father had never ceased to drill into him. Dukes put their duty to the family first and were above such petty concerns.

His two brothers, Ethan and Jake, had both married for love, and for that Luther was pleased. But he was neither the spare, as Jake was, nor the spare's spare, as was the case with Ethan. He was the Duke.

Finding the perfect duchess was just one of his many duties, along with managing the Rosemont estates, caring for the extended Rosemont family, which contained more first, second and third cousins than he could count, and ensuring the welfare of his tenants and servants.

And yet it was *that* duty that pressed down on him like a heavy burden.

Luther continued to stare out of the window at the Rosemont Estate, with its trees bare of foliage, the garden pruned back and waiting to burst forth in spring, and the grey winter sky, while contemplating this seemingly insurmountable task.

He could put it off no longer. Whether he liked it or not, this Season he had to find a duchess.

He squared his shoulders, lifted his chin and adopted the imperious pose of his ancestors, whose portraits lined the walls of Rosemont House.

As the Duke of Southbridge, he was expected to face every challenge with fortitude, strength and stoicism. His father had pointed out, repeatedly, that his predecessors had shown such strength of character when leading men into battle. It was now up to Luther to follow in their exalted footsteps and do nothing that would bring shame on his venerated ancestors.

He released a loud exhalation of frustration and his shoulders slumped. No one was asking him to lead troops into battle. All that was expected of him was to find a damn wife.

He just wished that attending the London Season and facing the twittering debutantes and their ambitious mothers wasn't so excruciatingly dull. His first few Seasons had been almost tolerable. He'd done a quick assessment of the available debutantes. Once he'd established that none had what he was looking for in a potential duchess he'd been able to escape to more enjoyable pursuits, knowing that there was still plenty of time, and that there'd be another Season next year and another crop of debutantes.

But with each successive Season the ordeal was becoming more tedious. Year after year, a seemingly interchangeable stream of debutantes was presented to him. They were all starting to look the same, sound the same, until they merged into a swirl of pastel silk gowns and constant smiles.

He'd almost prefer to be dressed in heavy armour and wielding a sword on Bosworth Field or facing down the French bowmen at Agincourt, as previous dukes had done, than endure yet another Season.

It wouldn't be so bad if the debutantes didn't seem to be getting younger and more mindless with each passing Season. He knew that wasn't true. They remained eighteen, the traditional age at which a young woman made her debut. It was he who was getting older. Now he was a man of twenty-nine, those innocent young women were starting to make him feel positively ancient.

He moved from the window to the sideboard, poured himself a glass of brandy and swirled the amber liquid around the bottom of the balloon-shaped glass. It was a bit early in the day, but he needed something to assuage his grim mood, brought on by his mother's announcement over the breakfast table.

She had got it in her head that Luther need not wait the three months before the next Season began, as she had found his bride and invited her for the weekend.

According to his mother, Lady Olivia, the only daughter of the Earl of Dallington, was now of age and reputed to be perfect in every way. That was yet to be seen. After all, his mother had made that claim before, on more occasions than Luther could remember. But hopefully, this time she had not exaggerated the young lady's virtues and Lady Olivia would meet his expectations.

He threw back his brandy, looked over at the decanter, thought better of it and placed his empty glass on the nearest table.

'Show some fortitude, strength and stoicism, for God's sake. You're a duke, so act like one.'

He heard his father's gruff voice. The man had been dead for twelve years, and yet his voice often rang clear in Luther's mind, reminding him constantly that he had not yet performed this one, simple duty expected of him.

As the daughter of the Earl of Dallington, Lady Olivia's had a lineage almost as long as the Rosemonts', and if she was as pretty, sweet-natured and intelligent as his mother claimed, then perhaps this weekend would be an enjoyable one, and not the waste of time he was expecting.

He needed to be positive. If she was the one, then his quest would come to an end. Not only would he have done his duty but he would also never have to face another Season.

He shuddered at the thought, relented and poured himself another brandy, then drank a toast to Lady Olivia, hoping with all his heart she would indeed prove to be his perfect duchess.

Georgina Daglish knew she should be grateful and most of the time she was. Although, on some days showing constant gratitude demanded more forbearance than she believed herself capable of. Today was one such day.

Lady Dallington was on the rampage. And when such moods took her, Georgina was inevitably in her firing line. To stop herself from exploding and telling Lady Dallington what a silly, irrational and downright irritating woman she was, Georgina did what she always did and reminded herself to take pity on the lady.

She closed her eyes, drew in a calming breath and recited all the reasons why she should be tolerant of Lady Dallington's all but intolerable behaviour.

It could not be easy for her. Every day she was confronted with evidence of her husband's infidelity. Every time she saw Georgina she was reminded that her husband had kept a mistress. The Earl of Dallington had known Georgina's mother before he married Lady Dallington and continued to visit her at her Bloomsbury home after his marriage, a home which he had bought for her, and the liaison only ending with the untimely death of Georgina's mother just over four years ago.

Now the child of that union was living in Lady Dallington's house as her husband's ward. Georgina knew that her mere presence was an insult to Lady Dallington, and a constant reminder that, despite being a countess, she was just as powerless as any other woman, and had to do exactly as her husband demanded.

If it was up to Lady Dallington, Georgina would have been tossed out onto the street to live in the gutter, which was where the Countess believed she belonged. Instead, the Earl, her father, had accepted her into the family and treated her with the same aloof affection with which he treated his legitimate daughter, Lady Olivia.

'Why on earth did you drag my daughter out for a walk in such inclement weather?' Lady Dallington barked as Georgina and Olivia shrugged off their thick woollen cloaks. 'And today of all days. Oh, my goodness, Olivia, your hair,' she squawked. 'You have to look your best and now the rain has made it frizzy.' She turned to face Georgina. 'My daughter's hair is frizzy and it is all your fault.'

'It was my idea,' Olivia interrupted the tirade. 'I needed to get out and feel the fresh air on my face before getting cooped up inside all weekend.'

'Cooped up inside? How can you say such a thing? You'll be spending the weekend at the most well-appointed home in England, and in the company of a duke, no less.'

She stroked back her daughter's blonde hair and turned to Georgina with a disapproving glare. 'I know this was your idea and my lovely daughter is just trying to protect you, yet again. Unlike some people, she at least knows how to act like a lady.'

Georgina clenched her teeth tightly together to stop herself saying that the only person present not acting like a lady was Lady Dallington herself.

'Oh, but ladies take walks, don't they, Mama?' Olivia said, nudging Georgina and giggling.

'Not when they're expected to get ready for the most important journey of their lives. I impeach you, when we are at the Duke's home, do not let Gina influence you or sabotage your chances of making such an advantageous marriage.'

Lady Dallington could never bring herself to use Georgina's full name, not when it was so similar to her husband's given name, George. But at least she had actually used a name this time. Usually Georgina was merely referred to as *You there*, or *Girl,* and they were among the more polite terms.

Olivia was about to say something else, but Georgina gave her a small nudge. Lady Dallington might be at her most annoying, but she was right. Olivia did need to get ready, look her very best and prepare herself for what might be a life-changing visit. Hopefully, by the end of this weekend a duke would be courting her, or, better still, would have offered her his hand in marriage.

That was possibly the only area in which Georgina and Lady Dallington were in agreement. They both wanted the best for Olivia, and Georgina knew that such a marriage was what her sister wanted.

Although why women wanted marriage so desperately was something Georgina could never quite understand. From observing the life of Lady Dallington, it seemed she was no less dependent on the good graces of a man than Georgina's mother had been. Lady Dallington had respectability and status, but in all matters she had to defer to her husband as if she were a child with no mind of her own.

That would never do for Georgina, but Olivia wanted to marry, so if she was to do so it would be wonderful if she reached the very pinnacle of society and married a duke.

Where Georgina differed from Lady Dallington was that she only wanted that marriage for Olivia if the Duke was a kind man who treated his wife with the utmost respect. She would wish this for all women, but Olivia deserved it more than most.

Georgina loved her sister, and her happiness meant everything in the world to her. From the moment she had joined the Dallington household, Olivia had treated her with nothing but kindness. She had been sixteen when her mother died, and Olivia thirteen. The Earl had kindly taken his illegitimate daughter into his home as his ward, something many men in his position would not have done.

While Lady Dallington had made it abundantly clear that she was not wanted, Olivia had been excited by her arrival, telling Georgina she had always wanted a sister and they would always be the best of friends.

And they had been. While Georgina had to feign gratitude towards Lady Dallington, there was nothing false about her eternal gratitude to Olivia for her sweetness and generosity of spirit. The death of her mother had left her bereft, and Olivia had seen her through those dark days and continued to bring light into Georgina's life.

She deserved to become a duchess and deserved to marry a man who would love and cherish her. If the

Duke was such a man, then Georgina would do everything she could to encourage the match.

'I believe your mother is correct, Lady Olivia,' Georgina said. 'We should get ready for the journey.'

'Now, go and get dressed for the trip,' Lady Dallington said, as if Georgina had not spoken. 'Both of you,' she added. 'Although why we have to take Gina with us, I'll never know.'

Because your husband said so, Georgina would like to have said, and that means, as his wife, you have to do as you're told.

Olivia lifted her chin in defiance. 'Because if Georgina doesn't come with us, I'm not going either.'

Lady Dallington sent Georgina a furious look, as if she had been the one who had spoken.

'Well, she *is* going, so you don't need to do her bidding. She's got her wish even though I believe it's a big mistake. What will the Duke think of us when we turn up with...' Lady Dallington's frown became more pronounced and her nostrils flared as if she could smell something unpleasant '...with my husband's ward?'

'He'll think how lucky I am to have such a lovely sister,' Olivia said, smiling at Georgina.

'She is your father's ward,' Lady Dallington all but shouted. While everyone knew Georgina's true parentage, this was never openly discussed. A pretence was maintained that Georgina had just sprung from nowhere, with no parents or background, and for some unknown reason the Earl had decided to make her his ward. Everyone knew this to be a falsehood, but no one said differently.

'Perhaps we should do as your mother says and ready ourselves for the journey,' Georgina said quietly.

With her chin still in the air, Olivia turned and walked off towards the stairs. Georgina made to follow, but her progress was halted when the Countess grabbed her arm.

'I want none of your tricks this weekend,' she seethed into Georgina's ear. 'You are to stay in the background at all times. You will do nothing to attract the Duke's attention. Do you understand me, girl?'

Georgina bit her tongue to stop herself from saying what she was really thinking. She had never given Lady Dallington reason to think that she was like her mother. She did not perform *tricks* and would never do anything to hamper Olivia's chances of becoming a duchess. Yes, her mother had educated her in the expectation that she too may choose to find a wealthy man to support her, just as she had herself. But Georgina was most emphatically not her mother.

She had seen what that life was like and wanted none of it. Georgina would forge her own way in life without a man. Nor would she be chasing after marriage. All marriage had given Lady Dallington was the status of being an earl's wife, but in every other way she was little different from Georgina's mother. Her husband came first. He ruled the family, made all the decisions, and his happiness always had to take precedence over her own.

That was what Georgina wanted to say to the Countess. Instead, she lifted her chin so Lady Dallington would know she would not be cowed and replied, 'Of course, my lady.'

Lady Dallington stared at her through narrowed eyes, as if not entirely believing her. 'Make sure you do.' She released Georgina's arm. 'Now, make yourself useful for once and go and help Lady Olivia get dressed, and do something to mend that frizzy hair.'

Georgina recoiled in surprise.

'Olivia's frizzy hair, you stupid girl. No one cares what *your* hair looks like.'

Maintaining her composure and squashing down her rage, she walked up the stairs. Not much longer, she repeated to herself. Soon she would be free. In another four months she would come into her trust fund, start her business, escape from Lady Dallington and live her own life without being dependent on anyone, ever again. But before that happened, she would love to see Olivia achieve her dreams and marry a good man. And hopefully, after this weekend, Olivia would have the happiness she deserved.

Chapter Two

A carriage bearing the Duke's crest, and with a driver and footman in the Duke's livery of gold and purple, was waiting for them when they arrived at the train station, along with a second carriage to carry the servants and a third for the luggage.

While Lady Dallington tried to steer Georgina towards the servants' carriage, the Earl took her arm, making it clear she would be travelling with the family, something which surprised Georgina.

Riding in the carriage was a small thing, but one that made a big statement. Her father had taken her into his home, knowing how it would scandalise Society. By including her in this visit and having her arrive in the same coach as his legitimate daughter, he was sending out a message that she was part of the family, and he expected other people to treat her as such.

She tilted her head in thanks towards her father, who sent her a small smile as he helped his wife into the carriage. Since joining the Dallington household, such exchanges were the only acknowledgement she received from the man she had once called Father. He had made it clear that out of respect for his wife and his legitimate children, she was now to be his ward, and they would conduct themselves accordingly. But, on occasions such as today, he made these gestures that told her he did still consider her to be his daughter.

While she missed the open, easy familiarity they had once shared, Georgina had sympathy for her father, who had risked much by taking her into his household. She would be grateful to him for ever, and tried hard to show her gratitude by not upsetting his wife, no matter what the provocation.

But right now Lady Dallington was upset. While the Earl was comfortable with Georgina's riding with the family, it only increased his wife's state of agitation. As they drove through quaint villages and along country lanes towards the Duke's estate Lady Dallington's anxiety became increasingly palpable, until her nervous energy seemed to fill the enclosed space and ripple out to include the other three passengers.

'Are you sure you packed enough gowns?' she asked Olivia, not for the first time.

'Yes, Mama,' Olivia said with a sigh. The following coach was testament to that. While Georgina had a small suitcase and a carpet bag that contained sufficient clothing to see her through the two days of the visit, Olivia's trunks were packed with enough changes of clothes for a year-long voyage.

'And you have clothes for riding, for taking walks, and any other activity the Duke might suggest, along with enough day dresses as well as evening gowns?'

'Yes, Mama. Please, stop worrying.'

'I'm your mother. It's my job to worry.'

Georgina smiled to herself, remembering her mother

saying something similar. Her smile became a choked-back sob. Now there was no mother to worry for her. No one to care what became of her. She sat up straighter and lifted her chin. But at least her mother had taught her to be strong, so that she could survive on her own, and that was what she would do.

Lady Dallington pulled her gloves off then put them back on and clenched her hands tightly together. The Earl reached over and placed a calming hand on his wife's. 'Olivia is correct, my dear. You worry needlessly. Your daughter will be a triumph, of that I am sure.'

She gave her husband a nervous smile. 'I'm sure you're right.' She looked back at Olivia, her eyebrows drawn tightly together as her teeth nibbled on her lower lip and inspected her daughter's appearance.

The carriage turned off the lane and drove through black and gold wrought-iron gates at the entrance of the Duke's estate, then travelled up the long gravel drive-way, bordered by tall elm trees.

'Take your cloak off. We're nearly there,' Lady Dallington said, reaching forward to undo the button at Olivia's neck.

Olivia swatted her mother's anxious fingers away. 'I can do it, Mama.'

Both Georgina and Lady Dallington had travelled in dark clothing, aware that steam trains could leave smuts on one's clothing and permanently damage light-coloured fabrics. The cold weather meant all three women were also wearing thick woollen cloaks.

Despite the temperature and the mode of transport, Lady Dallington had insisted that Olivia wear her ice-blue silk gown made by the prestigious French fashion designer The House of Worth. It had been bought for

Olivia's debut when she was to be presented to Queen Victoria. With its low neckline and thin straps, which left much of the arms bare, it was hardly suitable for a cold winter's day, but Lady Dallington had said that first impressions were vitally important, and the dress would highlight Olivia's blonde hair and blue eyes and give her a suitable look of innocence.

On that, Georgina had to agree. Olivia looked stunning and, with the other two women dressed in drab colours, when the Duke saw her she would shine out like a bright star in the dark sky. Georgina did not, however, see the sense in dressing Olivia in a manner so unsuitable for the season, and did not think shivering in the Duke's presence on arrival would make the intended good first impression. But Georgina knew better than to contradict Lady Dallington.

And Olivia *was* shivering, either from the cold or nerves, or perhaps both.

'You look beautiful,' Georgina said, smiling in reassurance. 'I wouldn't be surprised if the Duke fell at your feet and proposed immediately.'

Olivia giggled and put her nose in the air. 'If he does, then I will make him beg and grovel for my attentions.'

'You will do no such thing,' Lady Dallington squawked. 'Don't let Gina put such foolishness into your head.'

'Georgina merely complimented Olivia,' the Earl said, with a quick smile in Georgina's direction, causing Lady Dallington's lips to draw tightly together.

'All I'm saying is, at all times you will act like a duchess,' Lady Dallington said, her voice deliberately controlled.

'That's why I've got my nose in the air. I'm behaving

like a true duchess,' Olivia said with another giggle, causing Lady Dallington's lips to tighten further.

They turned a corner and the Duke's home came into view.

With as much discretion as possible, all four looked out of the windows at the magnificent house at the end of the driveway, and the eyes of all four grew large as they took in the grandeur.

When Georgina had first arrived at the Earl's house she had been overwhelmed by its size and opulence. The home she had shared with her mother had been comfortable and cheerful but the entire downstairs of their house could have fitted into the Earl's drawing room. The Earl's magnificent estate might be daunting, but its size was dwarfed by the Duke's home, which was decidedly palatial.

Surrounded by a large topiary garden, the three-storey house, with its two wings and crenellated towers, dominated the landscape. The pale ochre of the stonework stood out against the grey winter sky like a bright beacon.

A river ran beside the house, spanned by a picturesque stone bridge. A large, tranquil lake was adorned with fountains, and the lands surrounding the house stretched as far as the eye could see. Statuary of Greek and Roman gods lined up in front of the house, giving the illusion that they were about to enter an enchanted world.

Everything was designed to impress and the occupants of the carriage were certainly that. As one, they sat back on the lush upholstery and stared straight ahead, as if all were trying to take in what they had just seen.

'The Duke is obviously a man of wealth and discernment,' Lady Dallington said, breaking the silence. 'You will need to make a good impression on him from the moment we arrive and continue to impress him throughout the weekend with everything you do and say.'

She reached over and moved the straps of Olivia's gown, patted her hair, pulled up her white gloves and brushed down her skirt.

While her mother fussed, Olivia looked back out of the window and seemed to crumple under the weight of expectation that had been placed on her young shoulders.

Georgina sent her an encouraging smile. 'When you become the mistress of this estate it will be no less than you deserve, and the Duke will be lucky to have such a beautiful, accomplished and lovely young woman as his bride. You do not need to be intimidated by the Duke's wealth. You are just here to assess whether he is worthy of your hand.'

Lady Dallington opened her mouth to speak, but the Earl raised his finger, so her mouth slammed shut.

'You're quite right, Georgina,' the Earl said. 'Any man who marries a daughter of mine should count himself lucky, even if he is a duke, and even if he is as rich as Croesus.'

'Thank you, Papa,' Olivia said, smiling at her father, who had turned back to look out at the house. 'And my God, the man is wealthy,' he muttered.

The carriage came to a halt in front of the entrance.

Lady Dallington adjusted Olivia's gown once again. 'Right. Your father and I will get out first. Then you wait a few seconds so you can make your appearance.' She stood up, then sat back down. 'Or would it be better if Olivia gets out first so she is the first person the Duke sees?'

'Oh, for goodness' sake, woman,' the Earl said, standing up, throwing open the door and stepping down. 'Olivia,' he said, extending his hand.

Olivia descended from the carriage, and she did actually place her nose in the air as befitted a duchess, causing Georgina to smile at her cheekiness.

'You remain here until the introductions have been done,' Lady Dallington said. 'We don't want you trying to take attention away from Lady Olivia.' She looked Georgina up and down. 'You should not be with the family anyway. You should have been in the servants' carriage, where you belong.'

Georgina couldn't help an annoyed sigh from escaping. She *was* family, whatever this woman might say, but she would do as instructed, for Olivia's sake. She hoped the Duke was not like Lady Dallington, and many members of Society, who condemned the offspring of illicit liaisons, as if they were somehow to blame for the parent's behaviour, and had no reservations in showing that disapproval. If he was, then that alone would show he was not good enough for Olivia. However, she fully intended to stay in the background throughout the visit so that the presence of the Earl's notorious ward caused no distraction.

After giving Georgina yet another look of admonishment, Lady Dallington put on her brightest smile and descended from the carriage to meet the man she hoped would soon be her son-in-law.

Georgina resisted the temptation to peek out of the window. She had no doubt that Olivia would conduct herself in the manner befitting a future duchess, but she was anxious to see the Duke, so she could assess whether he was worthy of Olivia.

After what she hoped was sufficient time for the family to introduce themselves and for the Duke and Olivia to make an initial evaluation, Georgina pulled up the hood of her cloak and opened the carriage door.

She kept her eyes lowered, knowing that Lady Dallington would prefer it if Georgina did not even look on the Duke's illustrious face, but curiosity soon got the better of her. She couldn't resist taking a quick glance at the man who might become her sister's husband.

Slowly, she lifted her head. She froze, her foot suspended over the bottom step of the carriage. Her heart seemed to leap as her breath caught in her throat. No one had warned her that the Duke was so handsome, although handsome hardly did him justice. With tousled black hair, serious dark eyebrows over deep brown eyes, and olive skin, he was simply magnificent. The wind caught his slightly overlong hair, tossing it over his high forehead, and thoughts of Heathcliff striding across the moors sprang to her fanciful mind.

'Miss?' the footman said quietly.

'Oh, yes,' she muttered, realising she was still standing in the door of the carriage, her foot poised in mid-air, while the footman held her hand.

What on earth had come over her? It must have been the surprise of seeing a man so young and so manly. She had expected the Duke to be of a more mature age and, if she dared admit it, stuffy and somewhat foppish, in the way of so many aristocratic men.

She descended the last step and told herself that this was all for the best. Olivia was a very lucky young woman. She took another quick look at the Duke, at the broad shoulders and long, slim legs of his athletic body. Fighting to ignore the strange fluttering sensation deep inside her, she repeated to herself that her reaction was simply because she was so pleased for Olivia.

Luther was impressed. So far Lady Olivia was living up to everything his mother had said about her. She was pretty, and her ready smile suggested a sweet disposition. She also gave every indication of having a modicum of intelligence, which was more than he could say for most debutantes he had met.

She was, however, rather young, and of course there was an innocence to her, but that was to be expected. Debutantes *were* young, and their mothers made sure their innocence was preserved until their marriage. For most men, that was part of their appeal, and it *should* be for Luther as well. Only a virtuous young woman of unsullied reputation could be the Duchess of Southbridge.

The mother was a bit of a strain, he had to admit. She was still prattling on about something, the train journey, or the weather, or complimenting him on his house. He was hardly listening, but the mother was not Lady Olivia's fault and should not be held against her.

'Ah, here's Georgina, my ward,' the Earl said, interrupting the Countess and drawing everyone's attention to the young woman who had just alighted from the carriage.

Luther had heard about the Earl of Dallington's ward. Indeed, all of Society had, even if it was only discussed behind closed doors. While he admired the Earl for taking on the care of his mistress's daughter, he was surprised that she had been included in this visit.

The young woman in question lowered her hood, revealing lustrous auburn hair, woven with shades of gold and copper and pulled back into a tight bun behind her long, graceful neck.

'Your Grace, may I present Miss Georgina Daglish?' the Earl said, smiling at his ward and waving for the young woman to join them.

Luther bowed and made a formal greeting.

She curtseyed and looked up at him. Heat radiated through him as he met her eyes. He knew that reaction well. It was lust. But it had never before hit him so hard, so suddenly and in such an inappropriate setting.

She was breathtaking, but it wasn't just her beauty that was causing his reaction. There was something about her, something elusive, something that had reached within him, tightly grabbed his heart and caused a raw, primal reaction to surge up within him.

Although only a few years older than her legitimate sister, those dark brown eyes were worldly, as if she had seen and knew much more about life than most women ever would.

And those lips—when had he ever had such an immediate and powerful reaction to a woman's lips? The full, bow-shaped top lip seemed permanently pursed, as if in expectation of his kisses. He drew his gaze away, as a torrid image entered his mind of those lips exploring much more of his body than just his lips.

'Your Grace,' she murmured, her light, feminine voice containing a husky undertone.

Miss Daglish's mother was reputed to have been one of the most sought-after courtesans of her time, and many a man was said to have been envious of the Earl when he secured her as his mistress. If she was anywhere near as captivating as the daughter, he could see why she had been in such demand.

But this weekend was not about finding a mistress. It was about finding a wife, a woman who would become the next Duchess of Southbridge. And when he did find that elusive woman, he was determined to honour his wedding vows, settle down and not be like so many other men of his class and keep a mistress or two on the side. He had seen the pain his father's infidelities had caused his mother, and he would put no woman through that torment.

He nodded one more time at Miss Daglish and turned his full attention back to Lady Olivia.

'Shall we?' he said, offering her his arm. She smiled prettily, placing her arm through his, and he led her up the stairs and into a house that one day might be hers.

The Earl and Countess followed behind him, the mother twittering the entire time about how grand the entranceway was, how splendid the portraits adorning the walls, how enchanting the stained-glass dome. Luther could almost hear her mind assessing his wealth. He was tempted to ask her if she would like to peruse the estate finances so she could get a full account of what he was worth.

Meanwhile, Miss Daglish walked several paces behind, and kept her head lowered. Deference was not what he had seen when they had locked eyes. He suspected it was a manner she adopted to satisfy her guardians, one that was not her true character.

The servants helped the guests out of their cloaks, and despite his best intentions Luther couldn't help but take a quick look in Miss Daglish's direction. Unlike her half-sister, she was not adorned in a pretty gown, but wearing a drab, greyish brown dress, with no lace, ribbons or the other paraphernalia women liked to drape themselves in. Had she been deliberately dressed in a costume that would make her look as unattractive as possible? If that had been the intent, it had failed. Nothing could fully disguise that lush, curvaceous body. Her full breasts appeared to strain against the jacket, as if just waiting for some man to set them free, and her tiny waist accentuated the sensual curve of her hips. It was a womanly body, one that Luther could not help but admire. He quickly looked away and smiled down at Lady Olivia, hoping no one had noticed his appalling lapse in good manners.

If Miss Daglish was going to continue to be such a distraction, he could only hope that he saw as little of her as possible this weekend. He had to focus on his task, getting to know Lady Olivia and deciding whether she had the qualities he was looking for in a duchess.

He escorted the party further down the entranceway and stopped at the foot of the stairs. 'The housekeeper will show you to your rooms. If you're not too tired from your journey perhaps you would like to join my mother and me in the main drawing room before we dine.'

'That would be delightful,' the Countess answered for them all.

Luther remained watching as the two young women walked up the staircase. They linked arms and chatted together quietly, and he fought not to watch the gentle sway of Miss Daglish's hips.

He forced his gaze away, and turned back to the Countess, who continued to look around as if taking an inventory of all that she saw, while the Earl smiled approvingly.

'If you'll excuse me,' he said, bowing to the Countess before she had a chance to once again engage him in conversation.

The Countess curtseyed low, while the Earl bowed. Once they had disappeared up the stairs, he turned and headed for the drawing room. His mother had preferred not to meet their guests on arrival, the day being rather chilly, but had insisted that Luther give her a full report immediately on what he thought of Lady Olivia.

He paused at the doorway and took one last look in the direction of the stairs, wondering what the young women had been discussing so quietly. He suspected it was him. He had little doubt that Lady Olivia would have been impressed. Debutantes were trained to be impressed by dukes, but, given Miss Daglish's background and all that she must have seen, he suspected she took a more objective view when assessing men.

Before the footman could open the door, Luther gave the handle a quick turn, as if such a forceful action would clear his mind. It mattered not what Miss Daglish thought of him. All that mattered was whether Lady Olivia would measure up and be worthy of becoming his duchess.

Chapter Three

The door of the bed chamber closed behind the sisters, allowing them to be completely themselves. Olivia immediately grabbed Georgina's hands, her eyes wide, and jumped up and down like an excited child.

'This house is the biggest I've ever seen.' She threw her arms wide as if to encompass the entire estate. 'Did you see that entranceway?' Georgina merely smiled in answer to the rhetorical question.

'All those arches and domes, that painted ceiling, and rows and rows of marble pillars. It makes our home look decidedly shabby,' Olivia rushed on. 'I can see why Mother wants me to marry him. This is everything she has ever wanted.'

'And what of you, Olivia? Is it everything you've ever wanted?'

'It certainly is magnificent, and who wouldn't want to live in a home such as this?' She stopped smiling and became thoughtful. 'But what I really want is to marry a man whom I love with all my heart and who loves me in return. That's worth more than all the grand houses of England.'

'And do you think the Duke could be that man?'

Olivia's brow crinkled. 'Perhaps. He certainly is handsome, in a broody sort of way. I wonder if he ever smiles, but he is polite, of course, and that's to be expected from a duke, I suppose.' She shrugged one shoulder. 'To be honest, I don't know what to think yet. I've only just met him. Once we've had some time together without Mother doing all the talking, I might be able to tell you what I really think. But I have to say my first impression is favourable. But what did you think?'

Georgina paused, as if giving herself time to consider Olivia's question, and tried to compose an answer that would give away nothing untoward. 'I agree that he is indeed handsome, and I think you are sensible to wait until you have spent time together before you pass judgement.'

'I might have a word to Mother to suggest that she let you chaperone me. With Mother as chaperone neither of us will get a chance to speak and I'll never know what he's really like.'

Georgina merely smiled at this suggestion. She knew that Lady Dallington would never agree, and for that she was pleased. The Duke had affected her in a way that was unacceptable, and particularly in these circumstances. The less time she spent in his company this weekend the better.

Hopefully, she was worrying unnecessarily. While on first seeing him it had been as if the ground had moved beneath her feet, leaving her disorientated and confused, he had probably hardly even registered her presence. Why should he? To him, she was merely the Earl's ward. A woman of no account whose clothing marked her out as little more than a servant, rather than a member of an aristocratic family.

And hopefully, while Olivia's regard for the Duke grew, her own strange reactions to him would diminish until he no longer affected her. Then her initial consternation would merely be an uncomfortable memory best forgotten.

Olivia tugged on the bell pull to summon her lady's maid to help her dress for dinner, and continued to discuss the beauty of the house, while Georgina smiled and nodded.

Molly, Olivia's lady's maid, rushed in with a pale lemon satin gown draped over her arm, followed by a maid carrying a blue and white China bowl and a large jug of water. Georgina had seen Olivia wear that gown when she was having her fittings with the dressmaker. It was charming, with intricately embroidered butterflies in a slightly darker shade of lemon and woven with small seed pearls. Olivia would look stunning tonight. The Duke would be unable to resist her, would know that she was perfect for him, and all would be right.

'Your mother also suggested you wear the diamonds tonight, my lady,' Molly said.

Olivia and Georgina both raised their eyebrows, knowing what that meant. Lady Dallington loved those diamond earrings, necklace and tiara, which had been bequeathed to her by her mother-in-law and had been in the Dallington family for many generations. She only wore them when wanting to show off the family's wealth and standing.

Tonight, Olivia really would look like the Duchess she hopefully would soon be.

Leaving Olivia to her dressing, Georgina retired to

her own room. Unlike her sister, she had not been hired a lady's maid by Lady Dallington to take care of her dressing, but one of the Rosemont maids had left a bowl and jug of water on her washstand, and she was more than capable of dressing herself.

Once finished, she joined Olivia in her room.

'Oh, why does Mother dress you like that?' Olivia said when Georgina entered, taking in the plain dark brown gown. 'It's as if she wants you to be invisible.'

Georgina merely smiled. That was exactly what Lady Dallington wanted, or, better still, for Georgina to disappear altogether.

'It matters not how I look, but you, Olivia... I have never seen you look more attractive.' Georgina shook her head in wonderment, walked around Olivia and admired her from every angle. 'You look exactly like a duchess should. If the Duke doesn't propose this weekend, then the man is a fool and does not deserve you.'

Olivia giggled and gave a little twirl, the embroidered train swirling around her feet.

'Right, shall we go and astound the Duke with your grace and beauty?' Georgina said, linking arms with Olivia.

The two young ladies descended the stairs, paused at the bottom and looked up and down the hallway at the multitude of doors, then giggled. 'Which drawing room did the Duke say?' Georgina asked, still spluttering with laughter.

'I've no idea. Do you think we should try every door until we find them?'

'That could take all night. I can see there are definite disadvantages to having a house of this size.'

Olivia giggled again. 'But it might be fun to explore

all the rooms.' She opened the nearest door. 'No, not that one.'

They ran to the next door, opened it together, peered in, then, giggling, shut it and rushed to the next.

A passing footman halted in the hallway, stood to attention, his face expressionless, as if finding lost, giggling young women was a perfectly normal occurrence. 'The Duke and Duchess are waiting for you in the green drawing room. Please allow me to escort you.'

Still smiling, they followed the liveried man down the long hallway and entered the drawing room, where Lord and Lady Dallington were already waiting, along with the Duke and Duchess.

Georgina immediately stopped smiling, lowered her eyes and remained a few steps behind Olivia as they entered the room. At the sight of the Duke, once again, her stomach clenched and her heart seemingly fluttered inside her chest. She could only hope that her presence would be ignored by all and she could get through this evening without revealing how seeing the Duke was affecting her.

'There you are, my dears,' the Earl said. 'I was beginning to think you had got lost.'

Olivia laughed and looked at Georgina, who would have joined in with her sister's merriment if she wasn't so distracted by the man watching them from across the room. He was now dressed in evening wear, of black swallow jacket, white shirt and tie, and an embroidered grey waistcoat. While the clothing was formal, there was still something wild and untamed about his appearance that Georgina couldn't help but react to.

The Duchess approached and took Olivia's hands and smiled. 'It's lovely to meet you again, Lady Olivia.'

Olivia bobbed a curtsey and greeted the Duchess.

'It must be two years since I last saw you,' the Duchess continued. 'I must say, you have grown into a lovely young woman.' She sent a pointed look at her son, who bowed his head in agreement.

'Miss Daglish,' the Duchess said, turning to Georgina.

'Your Grace,' Georgina murmured as she gave a low curtsey. The Duchess bowed her head in acknowledgement, and the grip of Georgina's tense nerves released ever so slightly. She had detected no look of disapproval in the Duchess's expression. Since she'd joined the Earl's household, she'd had to endure countless people glaring at her down their raised noses while they frowned at her in disgust.

One of the many lessons her mother had taught her was to always remember to keep her dignity, no matter how people treated her. But it seemed the Duchess, unlike so many other of her class, had not prejudged her and was graciously accepting her into her home.

'You must sit by me, my dear,' the Duchess said, leading Olivia to a chair that was between hers and the one at which the Duke was standing.

Georgina followed on behind and looked around for a chair where the Duke would not be visible to her, and she would be removed from the party. As she did so she was able to take in the room's grandeur. The green embossed silk wallpaper that lined the walls gave the drawing room its name, and a magnificent crystal chandelier suspended from the high ceiling sent soft candlelight over the room. Several lit fireplaces, surrounded by engraved marble mantelpieces, ensured the large space was warm and comfortable, and the portraits that adorned the walls declared that this was a well-established family that had been among the rulers of English Society for countless generations.

'Georgina, you can sit next to me,' the Earl said, patting the sofa beside him and smiling at her tenderly, as if aware of her discomfort, even though he would have no awareness of the real reason.

She forced herself to smile in thanks. She appreciated her father's gesture, but tonight it might be better if he followed his wife for once, and consigned Georgina to her role as outside the family circle, where her reactions to the Duke would not be tested.

With much rustling of silk and satin, the ladies sat, followed by the gentlemen. Georgina once again lowered her eyes, intending to take no part in the conversation.

'I was just saying, before you arrived, Olivia, that this is a magnificent room,' Lady Dallington said. 'The Duchess informed me that parts of the house were originally built in the Tudor era and successive dukes have added to it over the centuries.'

Lady Dallington continued chatting, oblivious to the fact that she was monopolising the conversation and preventing the Duke and Olivia from getting to know each other better, which was the entire point of this visit.

Despite the obvious impatience on Olivia's face, and the polite boredom on the Duke's, Georgina could not completely condemn Lady Dallington's behaviour. It was nerves, that was obvious in the constant shuffling of her fan and the way she kept playing with the buttons on her gloves.

When the gong rang for dinner, Georgina almost heard sighs of relief. The Duke stood and offered his arm to Olivia. She smiled up at him and took his arm. The Earl took the Duchess's arm, and Georgina followed at a discreet pace behind the line-up as they walked down the hallway to the dining room.

Lady Dallington turned to her with a false smile. 'Sit as far away from the Duke as you can,' she whispered.

'Yes, my lady,' Georgina replied. Such a demand would usually irritate Georgina. She would be tempted to point out to Lady Dallington that men were perfectly safe in her company. Georgina's mother might have had a reputation for seducing husbands away from their wives, but Georgina was not her mother. But the unexpected effect the Duke was having on her made her wonder, was she, in some small way, more like her mother than she was willing to admit?

They entered the dining room, which was just as grand as the drawing room. The large oval table, covered with a crisp white cloth, was laid with cream and gold plates, bearing the Southbridge crest. Silver candelabra in the centre of the table sent out an intimate light, and glittered off the highly polished silverware and crystal wine glasses.

Name cards indicated where each guest would sit, and it became immediately apparent that Lady Dallington would not get her wish. The Duke was seated at the head of the table, Olivia on his right, Georgina on his left.

'Your mother was telling us before you arrived that you are an accomplished pianist and have a delightful singing voice,' the Duke said to Olivia as he pulled out her chair. 'Perhaps after dinner you would like to play for us.'

A stricken look passed over Olivia's face. Of all the

things on which Lady Dallington could compliment Olivia, her musical ability was not one of them.

'No, Georgina is the talented one,' Olivia said, sending an appealing look in Georgina's direction. 'If anyone should play for us, it is her.'

The Duke turned towards her. 'Then I look forward to hearing you play, Miss Daglish,' he said, moving behind her and pulling out her chair.

Georgina took her seat and tried not to register that his jacket had lightly brushed against her arm, or that she had been unable to avoid inhaling his musky masculine scent.

'I believe Olivia overstates my ability,' she said quietly, catching Lady Dallington's eye and seeing the disapproval.

'She most certainly does,' Lady Dallington said with an obsequious smile directed at the Duke. 'My daughter is always too generous in her compliments and downplays her own talents. Her music teacher said she has a rare ability, so she simply must play for us.'

Olivia's eyes grew wider and she gave a small shake of her head, seen only by Georgina.

'Perhaps if I play it will allow the rest of the party to converse,' Georgina said, looking in Lady Dallington's direction.

'No, Olivia will play,' the Countess said, smiling with clenched teeth.

Olivia looked to Georgina, her expression desperate, as if she had just been told there was no more room on the last lifeboat. An expression that was missed on no one, except the Countess.

'Georgina is right,' the Earl said. 'She should play this evening, so the rest of us can converse.'

Olivia breathed a sigh of relief.

'Of course, you are right, my dear.' Lady Dallington smiled at her husband, then sent Georgina a frown of disapproval, as if this was all her fault.

The footmen served the soup course, and the Duke turned to Olivia.

'You'll have to hear my daughter play at some other time, Your Grace,' Lady Dallington said before he had time to speak. 'She really is very talented. And you must see her wonderful watercolours. The painting master said they were unlike anything he had ever seen in all his years of teaching.'

This comment elicited a small laugh from Olivia, which she covered with a light cough.

'And as for her embroidery, it is unsurpassed.'

Georgina wanted to throw her bread roll at Lady Dallington and tell her to stop trying so hard to sell her daughter.

'In that case,' the Duke said to Olivia, 'I look forward to seeing your unsurpassed embroidery and your paintings that are unlike any other.'

Olivia blushed slightly and smiled in gratitude at the Duke, causing Georgina to relax slightly. The Duke was not affronted by Lady Dallington's boorishness, and she was pleased to see him and Olivia exchange a delightful moment.

'And Olivia is such a keen rider, and a wonderful horsewoman,' Lady Dallington continued.

Both Georgina's and Olivia's spoons froze halfway to their mouths, and Olivia sent Georgina another stricken look.

'I'm pleased to hear that, Lady Olivia,' the Duke said.

'I too love to ride and have a large stable of horses. Perhaps we could ride out tomorrow.'

That *would* have been an excellent idea and would give the Duke and Olivia a chance to spend time away from the Countess's constant interruptions. Except for one major problem. Olivia had a fear of horses and had not ridden since she'd fallen off her pony when she was a child. Georgina had to wonder whether the Countess was blind to her daughter's problems, simply stupid, or a combination of the two. Or was she so determined to capture the Duke for Olivia that she would say or do anything, even tell outright lies?

'Perhaps,' Olivia murmured.

The Duke gave her a curious look then turned to Georgina. 'And do you ride, Miss Daglish?'

'Yes,' she said, knowing that to elaborate would not only incur the wrath of Lady Dallington but would also take the attention away from her sister. Georgina's mother had insisted she become an expert horsewoman, along with taking lessons in painting and piano. She had also been taught to converse in French, Italian and German. These were all skills her mother had deemed essential if she was to one day become the mistress of a wealthy and influential man.

'Then you must feel free to avail yourself of the horses whenever you choose.' He smiled at both Georgina and Olivia. 'I will let the stable hands know.'

'Thank you,' Georgina said quietly, keeping her enthusiasm to herself. It would be wonderful if she could escape this stifling atmosphere, get some time alone and once again feel the wind through her hair.

The Duke turned his attention back to her, and she realised that, despite her attempt to maintain an impassive expression, she was smiling. She quickly looked down and focused on the next course of crumbed sole.

Stop looking at me, she wanted to cry out.

His attention should be fixed exclusively on Olivia. Not just because she hoped they would be compatible and Olivia would find her ideal husband, not just because any attention he showed her would elicit the anger of Lady Dallington, but mainly because each time those dark brown eyes fixed on her it caused disconcerting feelings to ripple throughout her body. A feeling that would be inappropriate at any time, but never so much when seated at a stilted dinner party.

His attention remained on her for a second or two longer, before he turned back to Olivia. Georgina briefly placed her hand on her stomach and quietly released a held breath.

'And will the Rosémont ball be the first of the Season again this year?' Lady Dallington asked, interrupting the quiet conversation between the Duke and Olivia.

'It will, and we're hoping to make this one special,' the Duchess said. 'It will be your first ball, won't it, Lady Olivia?'

'Oh, yes, and I'm so looking forward to it. Aren't we, Georgina?'

'Gina will not be attending,' Lady Dallington cut in. 'It is for debutantes only.'

The Duke's jaw clenched slightly at the Countess's lack of manners, and he turned to Georgina. 'Will you not be having a coming out?'

'Wards do not get presented to the Queen,' Lady Dallington answered for her.

The Duke's grip on his knife and fork tightened and he looked down the table at Lady Dallington. 'I had assumed that, despite not being a debutante, Miss Daglish would be allowed to answer questions when asked.'

Georgina bit her lip to stop herself from smiling. This exchange was going to draw enough ire from Lady Dallington as it was, so her smiles would only intensify the woman's wrath.

'Of course she is, Your Grace.' Lady Dallington sent the Duke a fawning smile. 'Gina, answer His Grace when he asks you a question.'

'No, I will not be coming out,' she said. 'As Lady Dallington said, debuts are for debutantes. I am no debutante.'

'But she'll be attending the balls as my chaperone,' Lady Olivia added.

'Then it will be a delight to see you both at the Rosemont ball,' the Duke responded before Lady Dallington was able to speak.

Instead, the Countess snapped her mouth closed, her lips becoming pinched. Georgina had little doubt that Lady Dallington was about to inform the party that Georgina would not be attending. But that decision had been taken from her. The Duke himself had all but invited her to the Rosemont ball. Lady Dallington would not defy a duke, particularly one she hoped would marry her only daughter.

It was kind of Olivia to include her, and she did take some satisfaction in the Duke's standing up for her and putting Lady Dallington in her place, but Georgina had no desire to attend the Rosemont ball or any other.

She knew exactly what would happen if she did. The women would shun her, seeing her as a threat, while the men would take the opportunity to openly assess her, wondering whether they should attempt to take her as their own mistress. Everyone would know her background and would make the assumption that she would eventually make her living in the same manner as her mother.

She hoped that the Duke did not see her in that way. She would never be any man's mistress and most certainly not the mistress of the man who would hopefully marry Olivia.

But it *was* nice to see Lady Dallington's expression when he had defended her, even if Georgina needed no one fighting her battles. She had swallowed Lady Dallington's insults for the last five years. She could continue to do so for a few more months, before she got her freedom.

Conversation resumed, and fortunately no more attention was paid to Georgina through the remainder of the dinner, but the Duke's attempts to make conversation with Olivia were constantly thwarted by Lady Dallington's unwanted interruptions.

Seated next to him, Georgina could sense the Duke's increasing frustration.

He said nothing, and outwardly did nothing, but his long fingers gripped his knife and fork more tightly each time Lady Dallington spoke, while the edges of his lips curled down into a slight frown.

Georgina wished she could take control of the conversation and direct it away from Lady Dallington. Instead of constantly praising her daughter, Lady Dallington should be trying to find an area that would engage both Olivia and the Duke in conversation, without all this strain.

Making people comfortable, especially men, was one of the many accomplishments at which Georgina's mother had excelled. Her dinner parties had been lively affairs, where people conversed, laughed and enjoyed themselves, including the Earl. Whereas tonight the Earl was sitting at the end of the table, looking as uncomfortable as everyone else.

There had never been this tension, this awkwardness at her mother's dinner parties. Once again Georgina had to pity Lady Dallington. She was trying so hard and failing so dismally.

Finally the tedious meal came to an end, and they retired back to the drawing room. The Duke led Olivia to a settee and sat beside her. Georgina hoped that Lady Dallington had the sense to sit at a discreet distance from the couple. But no, she placed herself in the chair opposite and continued talking.

Olivia and Georgina rolled their eyes at each other, expressing their mutual frustration, as Georgina took her place at the grand piano.

While she played, she watched the others interact. This really was hopeless. Olivia sat in silence while her mother continued chatting. Even the Duchess, the Duke and the Earl eventually conceded defeat and sank into silence, the Earl looking around as if wishing he were somewhere, anywhere else, while the Duke and Duchess politely listened to Lady Dallington.

Poor Olivia was looking exceedingly tired, more so than could be simply the result of being bored by her mother. This really was becoming an excruciating ordeal for her sister.

When she sneezed Georgina stopped playing and crossed over to her, even though she knew such interference would incense Lady Dallington.

'Are you all right?' the Duke asked, also standing.

'She's perfectly well,' Lady Dallington answered, just as Olivia sneezed again. 'There's no need to fuss,' she said, flicking her hand at Georgina in dismissal.

'I'm fine,' Olivia said, dabbing her nose with her lace handkerchief. 'Georgina, please, continue playing. It's lovely.'

Georgina waited, to ensure Olivia was quite well, then returned to the piano. Perhaps she *was* fussing too much. It was just a few sneezes, but Olivia also looked fatigued and she knew Lady Dallington would not notice that she was putting her daughter under a great deal of pressure.

But the Duke did notice. 'After your journey I am sure you would all wish to retire early,' he said, taking Olivia's hand and helping her to her feet.

Georgina cast a glance at the clock ticking away on the mantel. It was just gone eleven o'clock, much earlier than they would normally retire, but he was the Duke and nobody was about to argue with him.

The others stood up and said their goodnights. The moment they left the drawing room, Olivia had yet another sneezing fit. 'Are you sure you are quite well?' Georgina asked.

'I told you not to fuss,' Lady Dallington said. 'It's just nerves. And you're not helping, monopolising attention with your piano playing and making my daughter look bad. Why couldn't you say you didn't know how to play the piano?'

'I believe Georgina did Olivia a great service by playing,' the Earl said before Lady Dallington could admonish her further. 'You had somewhat overstated your daughter's musical abilities.'

Lady Dallington's lips pursed tightly, but she said nothing.

'And it does look like Olivia could use an early night,' the Earl added. 'So, let us retire.' With that, he took his wife's arm and hurried her away.

Olivia sneezed again and giggled. 'At least my sneezing got us out of that,' she said, pointing at the drawing room.

'But you do look tired, Olivia. Perhaps an early night would be best,' Georgina said.

'But not before you join me in my bedchamber. We need to discuss the Duke. You still haven't told me what you think of him.'

'I believe we should leave that until tomorrow, as you need your rest.' Georgina was taking the coward's way out. She did not want to discuss the Duke, tonight or at any other time. She would rather not even think about him, and most certainly did not want to tell her sister that when he looked at her it was as if the temperature inexplicably went from that of winter to that of a scorching summer's day.

No, she most certainly would not be telling Olivia any of that.

Luther collapsed back into his chair the moment the guests left and frowned at his mother.

'Lady Olivia is lovely,' she said. 'Do not let the mother put you off. If every man who didn't like his future mother-in-law failed to wed, the world would be full of bachelors.'

Luther laughed and stretched out his legs in front of him, finally feeling as if he could relax. If nothing else, it had certainly been an interesting evening. He had not

expected to spend it listening to the daughter of a courtesan play the piano so sublimely. Nor would he have
expected a young woman from such a background to
be so demure and ladylike. Although that demureness
always appeared to be one of deliberate control. It was
as if a flame was smouldering beneath the surface, one
which she was preventing from igniting into an inferno
by sheer will power.

'So, the unfortunate mother aside, does she meet with
your approval?'

'Yes,' was his immediate answer as he thought of
Miss Daglish's confident expression as her long, elegant
fingers swept over the piano keyboard. He could not remember when he had heard Bach played so exquisitely.

'Good, I thought she would. She's so pretty and
sweet.'

Sweet? Luther shook his head and almost laughed
at his mistake. How could he possibly have thought
his mother was asking about Miss Daglish? And sweet
was not a word he would use to describe her, nor his
reaction every time he looked at her. Sweet, that most
certainly was not.

'I'm so pleased that finally a debutante meets with
your approval. I think you should propose as soon as
possible because she's going to be quite sought after
this Season. Wouldn't it be wonderful if we could make
the announcement of your engagement at the Rosemont
ball? What a glorious start that would be to the Season.'

'Hmm,' Luther gave as a non-committal answer. It
would be good to avoid yet another Season being chased
by those competing debutantes, and he had no objections to Lady Olivia. She appeared to have every attribute he sought in a future wife. Breeding, a pretty

countenance and she was most certainly agreeable. He could imagine the man who married her would find he had a companionable wife and it would be a most satisfactory arrangement. And, as Lady Dallington had mentioned several times, she had four younger brothers, and the women on both sides of the family were known for producing large families of sons.

Luther usually found it easy to fault the debutantes who were paraded before him each Season, but he was finding it hard to fault Lady Olivia. She was delightful and, while it was obvious she was trying to make a good impression on him, there was none of that annoying desperation he often saw in debutantes.

'You can't deny, she would make an ideal Duchess of Rosemont.'

His mother's statement drew another *hmm* from Luther.

'Or would you rather go through another Season?' She gave him a knowing smile, which he acknowledged with a grimace.

His mother was right. He should be more enthusiastic. Lady Olivia was indeed an ideal future Duchess of Southbridge. He should make his approval clear, court her, marry her, produce the requisite heir and spare, and his duty would be done.

Unfortunately, it was hard to concentrate on Lady Olivia's finer points when he was constantly distracted by the other young lady's presence. He was sure if she was not accompanied by Miss Daglish, he would be more enthusiastic about this arrangement.

This was all wrong. He was supposed to be courting the respectable debutante, not having lustful thoughts about her illegitimate half-sister.

'I was surprised the Earl brought his ward with him,' Luther said.

And I wish to hell he hadn't.

'Yes, but the two young women do seem to be very close.'

'Almost like sisters.'

His mother said nothing, but raised her eyebrows, which spoke volumes. The true relationship between the Earl and Miss Daglish's mother was obviously not lost on her.

'The Earl is to be commended for his generosity in making her his ward.' His mother's statement contained more than it said. Luther's father was also known to have more than one mistress. He had even bragged about it to Luther. It was something about which Luther was certain his mother knew and had no choice but to accept.

A man's right to a mistress was yet another lesson his father had tried to instil in him. The wife of a duke must be respectable, but that did not mean he could not have fun with other, less respectable women. And a well-trained wife of an aristocrat knew her place and accepted that men had their needs, or so his father said.

Luther had always abhorred his father's attitude. As a young boy he had witnessed his mother begging her husband not to leave again. His father's lack of compassion for his distraught wife had shocked Luther to the core. Instead of relenting he had told his wife to remember her place, then disappeared for one of his protracted visits to London.

His mother had eventually *remembered her place*, accepted the situation and thrown herself into caring for her three sons. But the stricken look on her face was etched into Luther's memory. Despite what his father had told him, he would never do that to any woman.

While he couldn't admire the Earl for his indiscretions, he did have to respect him for taking responsibility for his illegitimate offspring. Perhaps it reflected the high regard in which he held Miss Daglish's mother.

'And whatever Miss Daglish's origins might be, it is hardly the fault of the child,' his mother continued. He heard the note of pain in his mother's voice as she no doubt wondered how many other children her husband had fathered and abandoned.

She leant forward in her chair, her brow furrowed. 'I hope you're not judging Lady Olivia harshly because of her association with Miss Daglish.'

'No. Never,' Luther shot back, affronted by the accusation. 'I agree with you entirely that one should not be judged by the actions of one's parents, and if anything I admire Lady Olivia more for her obvious friendship and affection for her half…for her father's ward.'

'I should hope so.' She sat back in her chair. 'Now, let's forget all about Miss Daglish and her unfortunate origins. It is Lady Olivia you need to focus on.'

Luther nodded but suspected that forgetting all about Miss Daglish was not going to be as easy as his mother seemed to assume.

'I'm sure once you get to know her better, once you have spent time with her away from her mother, you will see just how perfect she is for you. Or would you rather go through another Season in the hope of finding an even more perfect Duchess of Southbridge?'

She smiled as Luther rolled his eyes. 'Good, so no more talk of Miss Daglish. Focus all your attention on wooing the lovely Lady Olivia.'

Chapter Four

Luther awoke the next day with a sense of purpose. He had two more days to spend with Lady Olivia. He would ignore all other distractions and dedicate that time to discovering more about her so he could assess whether his search for a duchess had finally come to an end.

Joining his guests at breakfast, he merely gave a polite nod of greeting to Miss Daglish then turned his undivided attention to Lady Olivia. 'I'm planning on taking my horse out for a ride this morning. Perhaps you would like to accompany me, with your mother's permission, of course.'

There were few things Luther enjoyed more than riding round the estate, no matter what the time of year. If he could avoid the London Season entirely and spend his time in the country, enjoying the changing colours of nature, he was sure he would be a happy man. He could only hope that Lady Olivia shared this passion, and it would be one of the many pursuits they could enjoy together.

As expected, Lady Dallington smiled her approval at his invitation, but the reaction from Lady Olivia was not so enthusiastic. She gave a quivering smile, then a little cough, looked at Miss Daglish as if in appeal then turned back to him.

'Perhaps a stroll round the gardens would be more enjoyable,' Miss Daglish said, answering for her half-sister, who seemed to have lost the ability to speak for herself.

'Nonsense,' Lady Dallington said, her politeness containing an underlying admonition of Miss Daglish, forcing Luther to suppress his annoyance. 'The Duke wishes to ride, not walk in the garden.' She smiled at Luther, as if they were in complete agreement.

'Which would you prefer?' he said, turning back to Lady Olivia.

'I would prefer to walk, if that is all right with you.' She gave another little cough and took a quick sip of her tea. 'Georgina and I were saying when we arrived how much we would love to see the gardens.'

'Then it will be my privilege to escort both of you.' His smile included Miss Daglish. If he was to dedicate himself entirely to Lady Olivia, it would perhaps be best to avoid her company, but he couldn't help but take some perverse satisfaction in knowing the invitation would irritate Lady Dallington.

'I believe we had talked about playing cards today,' his mother said, cutting Lady Dallington off before she had a chance to speak. 'I'd be delighted if you joined me in the blue drawing room after breakfast for a round or two.'

Luther sent a thankful smile towards his mother, who responded with a knowing nod.

'Of course, Your Grace, thank you,' Lady Dallington said. 'Olivia's lady's maid can act as my daughter's chaperone.'

'Oh, that won't be necessary,' Lady Olivia replied. 'Georgina will make an excellent chaperone. After all, she is nearly twenty-one and she's like a sister to me.'

Everyone paused in what they were doing, teacups froze on lips, forks stopped halfway to mouths, as they registered the *like a sister* comment. Only the Earl seemed unaffected and continued to read his newspaper as if oblivious to the conversation.

'I'm sure Gina would much rather play cards,' Lady Dallington said, her jaw tense.

Luther looked at Miss Daglish to hear her response. The poor young woman looked as if she had just been given an invitation to her own execution. He could not help but take pity on her.

'That's settled, then,' he said, as if Lady Dallington had not spoken. 'I shall meet Lady Olivia and Miss Daglish at the entranceway after breakfast.'

Lady Dallington somehow managed to both smile at Luther and send a look of disapproval towards Miss Daglish, which had to be admired if only for its display of facial dexterity.

Conversation slowly resumed, and by the end of the meal Lady Dallington's voice was once again dominating, giving Luther yet another reason to want to escape with Lady Olivia into the garden.

Once breakfast was over and he had changed into clothing suitable for a walk, he waited for the young ladies at the top of the stone steps and looked out at the garden. Rosemont Estate was reputedly at its best in every season except winter, but Luther loved its stark beauty at this time of year. The leafless trees stood out in sharp relief against the sky, the subtle colours of the grass, moss and lichen soothed the eye and the air held a crisp freshness that you only got in the colder months.

The two young women arrived, dressed for the conditions in warm cloaks, hats and gloves. As was their way, they had linked arms and were talking and laughing together. They really were as close as sisters and Luther could not help but wonder what that would mean if he did marry Lady Olivia. Presumably his wife would want her half-sister to visit regularly. There was also a possibility that she would expect her unmarried sister to live with them, as it was most unlikely that Miss Daglish would find a husband. Few, if any, members of the aristocracy would want a wife who had such a questionable background.

This was undoubtedly a dilemma for Luther. How would he cope with having such a woman in his house, a woman who caused him to have inappropriate thoughts every time he looked at her?

But that was a dilemma for another day. For now, he needed to get better acquainted with Lady Olivia.

He extended his arm towards Lady Olivia's, and another immediate dilemma presented itself. Should he also escort Miss Daglish? Manners dictated that he should, so manners won, and he extended an arm to her as well.

She shook her head slightly, much to Luther's relief. 'I believe Lady Dallington would prefer it if I walked behind.'

'And do you always do what Lady Dallington says?' he replied before he had time to think.

'When she is correct I do.'

Despite the way she often lowered her eyes in a deferential manner, he had seen a boldness in them and the spark of an independent spirit. He suspected she only obeyed Lady Dallington when it was to her advantage to do so. Did that mean, in this instance, she was declining his offer to escort her for her own reasons? Was she as reluctant to be close to him as he was to her? And was it for the same reason?

But now was not the time to contemplate those questions. In fact, there should never be a time when it was necessary to think of such things.

They walked down the garden path, through the formal topiary garden, past the roses, pruned back almost to ground level so they could cope with the winter, and past trees denuded of their green foliage. All the while, Miss Daglish followed behind, far enough away to give them privacy but close enough so she could ensure nothing inappropriate happened. An irony that was not lost on Luther, given his inappropriate thoughts about Miss Daglish.

'The estate's garden in winter is not to everyone's taste,' he said. 'Once spring comes it has more appeal and is rather magnificent. Hopefully, you and your family will be able to visit us again then.'

'Oh, that would be lovely. Winter is a bit dull, isn't it? Although it is nice to be outside in the fresh air. Shall we walk along the river? We passed over a pretty stone bridge when we arrived and I'd love to see it again.'

'Certainly.'

They turned and headed along the gravel path towards the river, then stopped when they reached the centre of the curved bridge.

'This is such a romantic spot,' Lady Olivia said as

they looked down at the gently flowing river. 'Really, quite…'

Whatever she was going to say was cut off by a coughing fit.

Miss Daglish was immediately at her side. 'Oh, Olivia, are you all right? Should we go back to the house?'

Lady Olivia's coughing fit finally came to an end and she smiled at Miss Daglish. 'I'm afraid I seem to have caught a bit of a chill. I believe it might be best if I do return to the house.'

'Of course,' Luther replied.

'No, no. You two go on. I know Georgina hates being stuck inside and I wouldn't want to ruin your day, Your Grace.'

'Nonsense,' Miss Daglish said with more force than was necessary. 'The Duke can continue his walk, but I will return to the house with you.'

Luther couldn't help but raise his eyebrows. As a duke he was rarely told what he should do, and certainly not by a woman, and most certainly not by a woman with no status.

'No, you won't,' Lady Olivia said to Miss Daglish with as much certainty as her half-sister. 'If you return to the house you know what will happen, don't you? My mother will make you play cards with her, and it would be cruel to inflict that on you.'

Miss Daglish grimaced, causing Lady Olivia to laugh, which ended in a cough.

'Oh, Olivia, I must look after you. You really are unwell,' Miss Daglish said, all but ignoring Luther's presence.

'I'm not that unwell. It's just a bit of a cough and I don't need your help. Go for a walk round the gardens and make sure you're away long enough for my mother to forget that she expected you to join her.'

Miss Daglish looked back at the house and grimaced yet again. She had his sympathy. He could think of few things worse than being cooped up inside with Lady Dallington, having to listen to endless chatter over the card table. He really did owe his mother a debt of gratitude for keeping the Countess busy and out of his way, and at least he could save Miss Daglish from that dreadful fate.

'I would be honoured to show you the garden,' he said to Miss Daglish.

She looked from her half-sister to him, then back to her half-sister. 'Are you sure, Olivia?'

'Yes, I am. You want to walk as well, don't you, Your Grace?'

'Well, I… It depends on Miss Daglish.'

'Or would both of you rather play cards with my mother?'

It was his turn to grimace, causing both young ladies to smile.

'Off you go, then,' Lady Olivia said. 'I'll see you back at the house later, Georgina, and you can tell me all about how glorious the gardens are, even during the dullness of winter.' With that, Lady Olivia walked away briskly, as if to prove she was not seriously unwell and would put up with no further objections from him or Miss Daglish.

Miss Daglish continued to stare at her departing half-sister. 'I do hope she is not coming down with anything serious.'

'If it reassures you, I will ask the doctor to call and assess her condition.'

'Oh, yes, thank you.'

To that end he walked over to a gardener, clearing away some fallen branches, and asked him to head into the village to summon Dr Campbell, then he took Miss Daglish's arm and found himself doing exactly what he had been determined not to, being distracted by the beautiful ward.

How on earth had this happened? If Georgina didn't know better, she'd almost suspect that Olivia had deliberately arranged it. But that of course was nonsense. Olivia could not arrange to get a cough. And Olivia wanted to be courted by the Duke. Perhaps all it showed was how much Olivia trusted her. Unlike Lady Dallington, Olivia did not suspect Georgina of being the type of woman who would lure a man away. While Lady Dallington thought Georgina was just like her mother, Olivia saw her as the best of all possible friends.

And that was exactly who Georgina was. She loved Olivia with all her heart. She was her sister, her closest friend, and the one person Georgina could always rely on. She would never do anything to hurt Olivia. Never. With that firmly in mind she turned to face the Duke.

All they had to do was take a quick turn of the garden, exchange a few pleasantries then return to the house. She could do that. Despite what Lady Dallington thought, she could be trusted in his company, and she most certainly could trust herself to keep any wayward thoughts and feelings firmly under control.

He nodded and offered her his arm.

Tentatively, she placed her arm through his. Keeping those wayward thoughts and feelings under control would be a lot easier if he weren't so close. It would be easier if she weren't once again breathing in his scent, the one she had got a hint of when he helped her into her chair at last night's dinner. Musk, leather and bay, all so decidedly masculine.

Stay calm. The Duke does not know what effect he has on you. Do nothing that will reveal it to him.

As if under a control of its own, her body moved slightly closer to his as they strolled over the stone bridge and along the edge of the river.

She should be admiring the delightful surroundings, but all her awareness was focused on the man who was mere inches from her. She couldn't help but register the strength of his muscles in his arms, nor the breadth of his chest.

Think of Olivia.

'Perhaps we should just take a quick stroll to satisfy Olivia, then return to the house,' she said.

'As you wish.'

Georgina was sure there was relief in his voice. He wanted to be away from her and back with Olivia, for which she should be grateful, and yet the pain in the middle of her chest did not feel like gratitude.

'There is not much to see, I'm afraid,' he continued. 'Once spring arrives there will be flowers, the trees will be in blossom and Rosemont Estate really shows off in a grand manner.'

'I'm sure it does, but I rather like gardens in winter. I love the colours of lichen on the trees and the moss on the paths and the way the light plays on the bare branches. There is a dramatic beauty in the starkness, which is almost more enticing than the more obvious beauty of spring and summer.'

He stopped walking and looked at her, his eyebrows

raised in question, and she wondered if she had said something wrong.

'You are right. There is much to be said for unadorned beauty,' he murmured.

'But please, don't let me delay you,' she rushed on, disconcerted by his gaze. 'I'm sure you have much to do back at the house.'

Georgina was familiar with the assessing gaze of men. When walking with her mother she had seen the way men looked at her, even though her mother had kept her head high and refused to acknowledge their interest. Georgina had almost been able to read the lascivious thoughts going through the men's minds. And as she'd grown older those looks were no longer confined to her mother, but included her. She hated those men for looking at her like that, as if she were theirs for the taking.

But the Duke was not looking at her as if she was just a desirable object to be possessed. He was looking at her as if he really saw her, but that made it no less unsettling.

He looked away, as if he too was disconcerted. 'I have no plans. I cleared my schedule once I was informed we would be entertaining this weekend.'

'And instead of entertaining as you expected, you're stuck here with me.' She gave a small laugh to let him know it was said in jest.

His full attention returned to her. 'I wouldn't describe walking around the garden with an attractive woman as being stuck.'

Georgina inwardly kicked herself. Why had she made that joke? He would be thinking she was being flirtatious and seeking compliments, which she most certainly was not.

'But the wrong woman.'

'Lady Dallington would certainly think so.'

Despite herself, she laughed. 'I'm sorry. I shouldn't laugh. My presence is very stressful for Lady Dallington.'

'Perhaps the lady could be a bit more restrained in expressing that stress.'

'Mmm, perhaps.' While she had appreciated the Duke's defending her last night, she had no desire to turn him against Lady Dallington. She did not deserve that, and after all, he needed to see the woman who would hopefully be his future mother-in-law in a kinder light.

'Lady Dallington does try, but I more than anyone am aware that it is a bit much to expect a woman to accept the daughter of her husband's mistress into her home and treat her as if she were her own child.'

He halted, and she could see she had shocked him.

'I'm sorry to be so blunt, but we both know that is why Lady Dallington treats me the way she does.'

'You have nothing to apologise for. Your candour is rather refreshing and I hope you feel you can be blunt with me.'

'I'm afraid I tend to be blunt with most people, unless I believe such bluntness will cause them real harm.'

'Then I am pleased you don't consider me so delicate that you can harm me.'

She looked at him, saw he was joking, and laughed. 'I suspect you are made of sterner stuff.'

He smiled at her, and she both wished he wouldn't and was pleased he had. Olivia had said he was handsome in a brooding manner, but there was nothing brooding about that smile. His face changed entirely as if he was being lit up from inside, and the thought that she had made him smile sent a strange, warm sensation rippling through her.

A curl fell over his forehead and her hand lifted, with the intention of pushing it back. Thank goodness he brushed it away himself before she embarrassed herself and revealed too much of what she was thinking.

She turned away from him and stared in the direction they were walking.

Remember Olivia, she admonished herself.

It was something about which she should not need reminding, and if she was a better person she would be able to ignore all other thoughts, all other reactions, and focus on that alone. She just wished that she actually was a better person.

'You and Lady Olivia do seem to be close,' he continued, as if he too was reminding her that she should be thinking of her sister.

'Olivia is the best friend anyone could have.' *Something I should never forget.* 'I know we're only supposed to say good things about her to you, and you probably think we're all trying to sell her to you, but she really is the most wonderful young woman.'

'Then without trying to sell her, tell me why Lady Olivia is so wonderful.'

'Oh, that is very easy. From the moment I joined the household she has treated me with nothing but kindness. On that first day, she took me by the hands and told me how pleased she was to have a big sister, and that we would always be the best of friends, and she has been true to her word. She was only thirteen at the time, and I was sixteen. She was so sweet-natured, honest and open, and she still is.' She stopped walking and looked at him. 'Once again, I'm going to be blunt and say there is no one who would make a better duchess and an ideal wife.'

'And what about you, Miss Daglish?'

Georgina's stomach clenched as if she had taken a physical blow. 'I don't want to be a duchess and I would not be an ideal wife.'

He smiled. 'I meant, are you also sweet-natured, honest and open?'

Shame rushed over her and heat flushed her cheeks. Georgina could not remember a time when she had ever blushed, but she was blushing now at her absurd and humiliating mistake. 'I'm not... I mean, no, probably not. Well, I hope I'm honest and open but I think it would be stretching things a bit to say I'm sweet-natured.'

His smile grew wider and Georgina found herself smiling back at him. He was not mocking her, but seemingly amused by her honesty. 'I'm definitely not duchess material for so many reasons.'

They looked at each other and the unspoken words hung in the air. A woman from Georgina's background might become a duke's mistress, but she would never become his wife.

'I believe Lady Dallington will have finished playing cards by now and I am safe to return to the house.' Whether that was true or not Georgina did not know, but what she did know was it would be unwise to spend any more time in the Duke's company than was entirely necessary.

'I suspect you will never truly be safe from Lady Dallington.'

'I will one day, but not this weekend, I'm afraid. But we should return. We've satisfied Olivia's insistence that we take some air, and I do want to see for myself that she is not unwell.'

'Of course.'

He turned and led her back across the bridge and up towards the house. They paused at the entranceway. He made a formal bow and she curtseyed. Then they remained standing in the entranceway, as if both were reluctant to leave.

Think of Olivia, she reminded herself, made another quick curtsey, turned abruptly and rushed up the stairs, away from the Duke and towards her sister's bed chamber.

Chapter Five

Olivia was sitting up in bed drinking a cup of tea when Georgina entered.

'How was your walk?' Olivia asked. 'What did you and the Duke talk about? Tell me all about it.' Her voice was slightly croaky, but she otherwise looked quite healthy.

'That can wait. How are you feeling now? Are you better? Worse?' Georgina placed her hand on Olivia's forehead. 'You're a bit warm.'

'I'm all right. It's probably being in this stuffy room and drinking hot tea. But Molly seemed to think I should rest and far be it for me to argue with my lady's maid,' she said with a laugh as she placed her cup on the bedside table. 'So, what do you think of the Duke?'

'I think he's very nice and will make you a wonderful husband, but you need to get better so you can spend time with him and he can see what an ideal wife and duchess you will make.'

'What did you two talk about?'

'You.'

Olivia's lips turned downwards. 'That must have been a boring conversation.'

Georgina laughed. 'On the contrary. Are you sure you're well? Your face is rather flushed.'

'I'm fine—there's no need to fuss. So, where did you and the Duke walk to?'

Before she could answer the door opened and Lady Dallington walked in without knocking. 'What's this I hear about you cutting your walk with the Duke short because you were feeling unwell?'

'I had a bit of a cough, that's all, Mama.'

Lady Dallington edged Georgina out of the way, sat on the bed and put her hand on her daughter's forehead. 'You seem all right now. Do you think you will be well enough to come down for dinner? We're only staying one more day. It would be such a shame if you spent it shut away up here.'

'I'm sure I'll be fine. It was just a bit of a cough and I feel much better now.'

'Excellent. Wear that pink gown tonight. It shows off your lovely complexion and we want the Duke to see you at your best.'

'Yes, Mama,' Olivia said, followed by several coughs that did not sound at all good to Georgina.

'This is all your fault, you know,' Lady Dallington said, turning to face Georgina. 'If you hadn't insisted that the two of you go for a walk before we left home, then my daughter would not be in bed now.' Her eyes narrowed and she cocked her head to the side. 'I'd almost suspect that you did this deliberately to ruin my daughter's chances of a successful marriage.'

Georgina drew in a deep breath through flared nostrils and stared at Lady Dallington. The woman was being ridiculous and Georgina fought not to respond to her baiting.

Lady Dallington blinked repeatedly, as if suddenly aware that she was pushing Georgina too far.

'The walk was my idea, Mama. Georgina was actually opposed to us going out in such weather.'

Lady Dallington turned back to her daughter and smiled. 'You're always so loyal, even if your loyalty is undeserved.' She looked at Georgina, then quickly back at her daughter. 'You really will make a gracious duchess. Just make sure you get better as soon as possible so the Duke can see that for himself.'

A knock at the door drew the attention of all three. Georgina opened the door to a man dressed in a dark grey suit and carrying a black leather bag that showed him to be a doctor.

'Good afternoon, ladies. I'm Dr Campbell,' he said with a gentle Scottish burr. 'The Duke summoned me and said there was a young lady who needed to be attended to.'

'No need,' Lady Dallington said, waving towards the door. 'You've had a wasted journey. My daughter is not really ill, she's just a little over-excited about all that has happened. She should be up and about in no time.'

'I believe, madam, I will be the judge of that.'

He approached the bed and raised his eyebrows at Lady Dallington. With a huff of annoyance she lifted herself off the bed and stood beside it, glaring at the doctor.

'It's Lady Olivia, isn't it?' he asked. Olivia nodded and smiled at him. 'I'm Dr Campbell and have been treating the Rosemont family for many years. So how are you?'

'I'm well, thank you. As my mother said, I'm probably just over-excited.'

'Well, let's have a look at you. Open your mouth, please.'

Olivia did as requested. The doctor peered down her throat and made the familiar, non-committal '*Hmm*' noise that all doctors seemed to make. Then he removed a stethoscope from his leather bag and placed it on Olivia's chest, which caused some disapproving rustling from Lady Dallington. He then asked Olivia to lean forward and placed the stethoscope on her back.

'You have a bit of a chest infection but nothing too serious. Stay in bed for a day or two. I'll call in again tomorrow to see how you're faring.'

'I'll look forward to it,' Olivia said with another smile.

'A day or two? That is out of the question,' Lady Dallington said. 'We are guests of the Duke. He expects to spend time with Lady Olivia, and we are leaving the day after tomorrow. She can't stay in bed the entire time.'

'I would recommend that she does, and unless she makes a rapid improvement I would advise against travelling until your daughter is well, particularly in this weather. She merely has a chill at the moment, but you would not want it to get any worse.'

Olivia gave a small cough, as if to underline what the doctor had said, then sent him another smile.

'Oh, very well. You can take your meal up here tonight, and you, Gina, can also dine in Olivia's room.'

'Yes, my lady,' Georgina said. She had intended to spend the rest of the visit with Olivia, whether Lady Dallington suggested it or not.

The doctor said his goodbyes.

'I don't think much of him,' Lady Dallington said, frowning at the door.

'He's the Duke's doctor, Mama. That must mean he is an exceptionally fine doctor.'

'Hmm,' Lady Dallington said, in much the same non-committal manner the doctor had used. 'You, girl,' she said, pointing at Georgina. 'Make yourself useful and look after my daughter. She has to get better as quickly as possible. If she doesn't, I will hold you personally responsible.' With that she bustled out of the room.

'He's rather handsome, isn't he?' Olivia said as soon as the door shut.

'The Duke? Yes, I suppose he is.' Georgina could hear the falseness in her voice. Anyone who looked at the Duke could not be struck by how devilishly handsome he was. So handsome he made her forget herself and everything she held dear.

'You find the Duke attractive, do you?' Olivia's voice held a teasing note and Georgina feared she had exposed the full extent of her admiration for the Duke.

'I'm just pleased he meets with your approval.' In her consternation her voice had taken on an unfamiliar primness.

Olivia tilted her head, and her smile gave every appearance of smugness, although what Olivia had to be smug about, Georgina had no idea.

'Anyway, I wasn't talking about the Duke. What did you think of the dashing doctor?'

Georgina looked towards the door through which Dr Campbell had departed, trying to remember what he looked like. 'Oh, yes, I suppose so. But let's hope he's a good doctor as well.'

'The Duke is hardly likely to employ a second-rate

doctor,' Olivia said as if she had been personally insulted.

Georgina made no comment, but picked up a chair and moved it to the side of the bed.

'It looks like I'll have to stay in bed for a day or two, but that doesn't mean you have to be stuck here as well,' Olivia said. 'I don't want you getting bored.'

'I would never be bored by your company. So, what shall we do? Would you like me to read to you? Or should I get your embroidery?'

'No, I want to hear all about what you and the Duke talked about. And don't leave out a thing.'

It was not a topic of conversation that Georgina would have picked, but of course Olivia would want to hear all about the man she hoped to marry. 'We didn't really talk about much at all. He showed me some of the garden. He asked about you, of course, and I told him of all your fine qualities. And then we came back to the house, and that's it, really.'

Georgina hoped that would satisfy her sister's curiosity.

'Did he not ask you anything about yourself?'

'Why would he want to know anything about me?'

Olivia shrugged. 'I just thought he might.'

'Well, he asked about our friendship. And I told him about how you had been so welcoming when I first joined the Dallington household and how you had never treated me as anything other than a sister.'

'Well, of course, why would I not?'

Georgina had never discussed her origins with Olivia, and never quite knew how much she had been told. She always called her sister, but Georgina did not know whether she knew how true that was.

When Georgina had been taken into the Earl's home, he had made it clear that out of respect for his wife's feelings, and to preserve his legitimate daughter's innocence, she was to always act as a ward, never his daughter.

Georgina had always abided by his wishes, and in return he treated her with kindness and respect, if not the affection she would have wanted. Sometimes she suspected Olivia knew, but her sister knew little of the world and how men behaved. She loved her father, and Georgina would do nothing to temper that love. Olivia did not need her innocence and trust destroyed by being informed that her father had had a mistress with whom he'd spent as much time as he had with Lady Dallington.

'Not everyone would be as kind as you,' she said instead.

'I did it all out of selfishness. I wanted a sister so much, and instead all I got was brother after brother, but then you came along and I was so happy.' She took Georgina's hand and gave it a squeeze. 'You were an answer to my prayers and for that reason I have only ever wanted happiness for my sister.'

Georgina smiled and gently squeezed Olivia's hand in response. 'And that is all I wish for you as well. So we need to get you healthy again so you can spend time with the Duke. Becoming a duchess is no less than you deserve.'

Olivia smiled at her, and Georgina wished with all her heart that her kind thoughts weren't tinged by the pain gripping her stomach. How could she be such a terrible person that the thought of the Duke with her sister should make her jealous?

It was wrong to be jealous for so many reasons,

not just because Olivia deserved to be the Duchess of Southbridge. Even if he was not interested in marrying Olivia, she still had no right to think of him in the way she did. Men like him did not marry women like her. He would never consider her as a future wife—mistress perhaps, wife never.

Georgina closed her eyes briefly. Would being the Duke's mistress be such a bad thing? Her eyes shot open. Yes, it would be. Even if he did not marry Olivia, Georgina would never be any man's mistress, not even the Duke's. She would not be a kept woman. She would never be like her mother, dependent on the good will of a man. How she could even think such a thing was beyond her.

'Right. That's enough chat about men. If you don't want to do your embroidery, then I'll read to you.' She picked up the book from the bedside table, pulled it open and focused on the words, determined to put any irrational thoughts out of her head.

Georgina remained in Olivia's room for the rest of the evening, reading and chatting. Meals were delivered to the bed chamber on trays and eventually Olivia dozed off. The coughing and wheezing in her sleep suggested her chill was getting worse, so, rather than retiring to her own bed chamber, Georgina chose to remain in Olivia's room. She would hate for her sister to wake to find herself alone in the middle of the night in a strange house feeling unwell.

Despite the discomfort of the chair, Georgina eventually drifted off to sleep, but was awoken by a loud hacking cough and wheezing breath.

'Oh, Olivia. You poor thing,' Georgina said, puffing

up her pillows so she could sit up and get some relief in her chest. She passed Olivia a now cold cup of tea, which she drank with relief.

'It looks like that handsome doctor is going to have to visit again tomorrow,' Olivia said with a laugh, which turned into another cough. 'That's some consolation, I suppose.'

'I'll fetch you a bowl of hot water. The steam will hopefully ease your congestion.'

'You really are a wonderful sister,' Olivia said, patting Georgina's hand.

'Nonsense. I'll be back soon.'

With that she rushed out, hoping it would not be difficult to find the kitchen.

The moment dinner was over Luther excused himself and retired to the library, determined to remain there until the household retired for the night. He would make it up to his mother for being such a coward and leaving her with Lady Dallington, but he had seen being a coward as the safest option. His well-trained mask of politeness had already slipped during dinner, and if he had remained in that woman's company a minute longer there was the danger it would fall off entirely and his true thoughts would be revealed.

Despite being free from her, he still could not shake off his irritation.

Once again he perused the shelves for a book, one that would capture his full attention and stop the conversation with Lady Dallington from constantly running through his mind.

How dared she suggest that Miss Daglish was responsible for Lady Olivia's condition? It was outrageous.

'My daughter is usually of robust good health,' Lady Dallington had said with that annoying simpering smile she always adopted when addressing him. *'I'm sure if Gina had not insisted that Olivia take a walk in the cold weather she would not have been forced to take to her bed.'*

Luther had responded with an apology and a reminder that it was he who had suggested they take the air this morning, and that the horse ride he had originally suggested might have done even more damage to Lady Olivia's health.

That had caused Lady Dallington to increase the level of her simpering and yet again blame Miss Daglish.

'Oh, no, Your Grace,' she had said, smiling at him. *'You have done nothing wrong. I am referring to a walk they took before leaving home. It was then that Olivia caught this chill.'*

'If that was the case, would she not have shown signs earlier?' he had wondered aloud. *'And perhaps it would have been best if she had not travelled in a light silk dress, then remained standing outside in the cold on your arrival. Everyone else had been wearing warm cloaks and no one else became unwell.'*

This had caused the Earl to nod in agreement. *'Quite right, Your Grace,'* he had said, sending his wife a look of admonishment. *'I believe I said at the time it was too cold to wear such a garment, but you insisted.'*

Lady Dallington had fortunately changed the subject and did not try to blame Miss Daglish for the attire in which Lady Olivia had arrived, or the weather.

He drew down a book, scanned the cover, returned to the leather seat and settled down to read. But once again the words swam in front of his eyes. He slammed it shut and placed it on the desk.

Damn that woman and damn her unfair treatment of Miss Daglish. That young woman was defenceless. She was living in Lady Dallington's home, with no other means of support and unable to stand up for herself.

He picked up the book and stared unseeingly at the cover. Although Miss Daglish did take the constant criticism with a stoicism that was admirable. He gave a mirthless laugh. Stoicism was one of the many attributes his father said a duke should possess. Although his father would condemn him for even thinking about Miss Daglish in such a manner. He should not be wasting his time on a woman of no account, not when he was supposed to be focusing on doing his duty and finding a suitable duchess. Luther also knew what his father would say about stoicism in a woman. While dukes must display that admirable quality, it was not an attribute demanded of a duchess. They needed to be innocent, sweet, compliant and able to provide future dukes. These were qualities that Lady Olivia appeared to possess. When it came to women, his thoughts should be on her and her alone.

He opened the book and flicked through a few pages. It was Lady Olivia he should be admiring, not Miss Daglish. And yet, Miss Daglish did have so many admirable qualities, not least of all her virtuosity on the piano. Her musical accomplishment was undeniable. That was presumably why Lady Dallington did not want her to play. That, and the fact that she looked almost transcendent as she performed, as if transfixed by the music. Perhaps music was her escape from the constant badgering from Lady Dallington.

And she really did need to find a way of escaping, hopefully one that was more permanent than music could provide. But that was not his problem, and, given Miss Daglish's obvious beauty, her talents and her strength of character, she was sure to find a man to support her, just as her mother had done.

He slammed the book shut and threw it onto the table as angry bile surged up within him. He should be no more thinking of Miss Daglish becoming some loathsome man's mistress than he should be objecting to her treatment by Lady Dallington. Neither of these were his concerns.

Movement in the hallway thankfully distracted him from his thoughts and he looked towards the open doorway. Everyone had gone to bed some time ago, including the servants, and it was unusual for anyone to be up and about at this early hour of the morning. He placed the unread book back on the shelf and headed towards the door. Investigating the noise might be what he needed to occupy his mind. Reading certainly wasn't working.

He followed the sound of feet rushing along the hallway, down the back stairs and towards the kitchen. It must be a servant, although why one should be up at this late hour he could not imagine. They worked long hours and only something important would bring them back to the kitchen after they had retired for the evening. His curiosity turned to concern.

He entered the kitchen to find Miss Daglish kneeling in front of the coal range, inserting kindling into the fire box and blowing on the ashes.

'Miss Daglish?' he asked.

Her head turned rapidly to face him, her eyes startled.

'I'm sorry,' he said, taking a step towards her. 'I did not mean to give you a fright. I was merely curious as to what you were doing.'

She stood up, brushed down her skirt and gave him a quick curtsey. 'My apologies, Your Grace. Lady Olivia's chill appears to be getting worse. She's having trouble sleeping so I wish to take a bowl of hot water up to her to try and ease her congestion.'

He looked towards the door, frowning. 'And you didn't call for a servant?' That, of course, was apparent, but it was unusual to find a guest in the kitchen and even more unusual for a guest to know how to light the stove.

'It's late. I didn't want to disturb them, and I thought it would be quicker if I got it myself. After all, I am capable of boiling water.'

Luther raised his eyebrows at this surprising admission. 'Does Lady Dallington expect you to do the work of a servant?' Nothing would surprise him when it came to that woman.

She smiled. 'No, things aren't quite that bad, but I do know how to cook.' She gave a little shrug, then sent him an assessing look, as if judging how much she should reveal to him.

'And why is that?' he encouraged.

'My mother knew that if I followed the same path as her, I would need to be able to look after myself. She knew that such a life could be somewhat insecure, so believed it essential that I knew how to survive if I could no longer afford to employ servants.'

'I see.' Luther was tempted to ask if she did intend to follow the same path as her mother but knew that question to be entirely inappropriate.

'I suppose you are aware that before my mother became my father's mistress she was a courtesan.'

He nodded, keeping his face impassive.

She drew in a long breath and exhaled slowly before continuing. 'Her mother was also a courtesan, and it was a life my mother had been trained for, and that alone. She was beautiful and intelligent and was never without the support of a man, but that was not the fate of some of her friends, particularly once they passed the first flush of youth.'

She gave a small shudder and he was tempted to take her in his arms and comfort her, but suspected the last thing she wanted was for him to touch her.

'And so she trained you in cooking and cleaning, so you would be prepared for such a fate?'

She gave a small shrug of her shoulder. 'But that was not the only training she gave me.'

Luther fought to keep his face expressionless and not to wonder as to what that training had entailed.

'She wanted me to have options and encouraged me to be as self-sufficient as possible so I would never be solely dependent on the good graces of a man. Along with learning how to cook, I was taught dressmaking. I can do double-entry book-keeping and have even mastered one of those new typewriting machines.'

He could hear pride, almost defiance in her voice.

'All admirable skills, I am sure.' He walked over to the stove and picked up some kindling from the wicker basket. 'And you might be surprised to hear that I also have a few unexpected talents. I too can cook.'

'You?'

He smiled at her shocked expression.

'I jest not. When I was a young boy, I used to spend

a lot of time in the kitchen. It was always warm and lively and lots of fun. I repeatedly begged the cook to let me help, until she finally gave in. I'll have you know I make the lightest, fluffiest scones you'll ever taste, even if I do say so myself.'

This caused her to laugh. It was a delightful, musical laugh. One he would like to hear again, often.

'And I still sometimes come down to the kitchen when I'm up late at night,' he continued. 'Those lessons mean I can prepare myself a drink and something to eat without disturbing the household.'

He knelt down in front of the firebox and placed the kindling strategically so it would reignite the fire. 'So let me prove to you that I'm not a helpless aristocrat and I know how to light a fire.' He blew on the embers, which had been banked up and left to smoulder so the scullery maid could light the fire first thing in the morning.

While he was doing that, Miss Daglish removed a ceramic bowl from the shelf and filled a large copper kettle with water. He took the kettle from her and placed it on the stove top. 'How long have you been living with the Earl and the Countess?'

She frowned slightly. 'Just over four years. Since my mother died.'

'I'm sorry,' he murmured. 'That must have been hard for you.'

She nodded in acknowledgement. 'Yes. Despite what everyone thought of her, she was a loving mother and I miss her terribly.' She sent him a sweet smile. 'She was a proud, dignified woman, and I believe she had genuine affection for my father.'

'But she wanted a different life for you?'

She held his gaze. 'She was never ashamed of the life she lived, but it was a life chosen for her, and she did not want me forced into that life if it was not for me.'

He should not ask, but she was such a forthright young woman, he was sure she would not be offended by his own bluntness.

'And is it a life you will choose?'

She held his gaze, and he watched as a gamut of emotions crossed her face. He could see that for her this was not an idle question, but one that went to the heart of who she was, and what society expected of her. He should retract the question, but he desperately wanted to know the answer. And he wanted her to say no, it was not the life she wanted. If he was being honest, it would not be for reasons of morality, or because he wished to save this lovely young woman from such a fate, but because he could not bear the thought of her with another man. Once again bile rose up his throat. His hands clenched into fists, as if desperate to cause harm to this imaginary man.

'Whatever decision I make about my life, it will be mine alone,' she said with that now familiar defiance, leaving him none the wiser.

A whistle from the kettle drew her attention back to the stove. He continued to watch her, admiration swelling within him. Her life had been so different from those of the women he met during the Season. She was worldly, forthright and had an underlying strength that was formidable. He could talk to her like an equal, something he had never been able to do with the debutantes.

More steam came out of the kettle spout and the

whistle grew louder. She picked up an oven cloth and placed it on the handle.

'Here, please, allow me,' he said, reaching for the cloth and lightly touching her hand.

Heat vibrated up his arm, as if he had placed his hand directly onto the boiling kettle.

Her fingers lingered a mere second or two, but for Luther there was something so intimate and tantalising about the experience it almost left him breathless. He coughed softly at the ridiculousness of his reaction. He was expected to marry an innocent young woman from a good family. He was not seeking a mistress. Miss Daglish could never mean anything to him.

He carried the kettle over to the bowl sitting on the table and poured in the steaming water. She placed a cloth over the top and wrapped another round the outside so she could carry it.

'Please, allow me to carry it up to Lady Olivia's bed chamber for you.'

She nodded and he could see colour tingeing her cheeks, which could not be explained solely by the heat of the stove. Had his touch affected her as well? That was a reaction he would expect from an innocent debutante, not a woman who had seen all that Miss Daglish had.

'I hope Lady Olivia is not too unwell.' That was what Luther should have been talking about. Not asking Miss Daglish about her past, not overreacting to accidental contact and certainly not experiencing jealousy over other men.

'The doctor expects her to be better in a day or so as long as she remains in bed.'

'That is reassuring.'

'But this is most unusual for her,' she rushed on. 'She's usually in such robust good health. I believe she caught a chill when out walking before we left the Dallington estate. There's nothing she enjoys more than a good, vigorous walk, and even inclement weather won't stop her.'

She waited for his response. He smiled in reassurance, to let her know that one slight illness had not ruined Lady Olivia's chances of becoming a duchess. 'It never fails to amaze me how, when people are trying to convince me of a young woman's eligibility, their descriptions often sound as if they're selling me a prize animal. Robust good health, enjoying vigorous exercise, impervious to weather conditions… It sounds like I'm seeking a brood mare. Lady Dallington said much the same over dinner.'

He expected her to return his smile, or, even better, that he would be treated to another delightful laugh, but her brown eyes narrowed, as if a storm was brewing. 'Is that any wonder? After all, aren't you looking for a woman who will provide you with…?' She stopped, took in a deep breath and lowered her eyes. 'Forgive me.'

'There is nothing to forgive. I know what you were going to say and I agree entirely. The Season at times does have the appearance of a marketplace, albeit one with a very attractive veneer. But if it's any consolation, I too am placed on the market, with my wealth, titles and ancestry being assessed and weighed up by every mother with a daughter of marriageable age.'

'Yes, except you get to do the choosing, while the debutantes have to strut and perform for you.' She bit her top lip as if that condemnation had escaped before she had a chance to stop herself. 'Once again, I'm sorry, I shouldn't have said that.'

'You are saying nothing that isn't the truth, so there is no need to apologise.'

'Except the truth is not something young ladies, or, indeed, anyone in Society, is encouraged to speak.'

'Perhaps, but sometimes the truth is kept hidden to protect the innocent,' he said quietly.

'But does it protect the innocent if everyone knows that truth, and while they don't discuss it publicly they talk about it in private where the innocent can't defend themselves?'

He nodded slowly. It was obvious they were no longer talking about the unfairness of the Season, but her own situation. 'But at least by not discussing it openly, the child is not put in the position of defending the sins of the parents.'

He had meant to offer consolation, to let her know he did not blame her for what her mother had been, but her reaction was not that of gratitude. Her chin lifted and those big brown eyes fixed on his, burning with intensity. He was reminded of a leopard he had seen at the zoological gardens. Despite being confined by a cage, he too had stared out with strength and defiance.

'Sometimes those so-called sins are committed because the parent has no choice. Sometimes people, especially women, have to do things because it is the only way they can survive in a world where the odds are stacked against them.'

She had put him firmly in his place, and he should be focusing on how she had chastised him, but all he could think was how stunning her eyes were when they blazed with anger.

'And it's been my experience that, no matter what, it is always the woman who is seen as the sinner,' she continued. 'Men can do as they please without being condemned by society. And when it comes to noblemen,' she huffed out her annoyance through flared nostrils, 'nothing tarnishes their reputation, and often the more so-called sins they commit the more they are admired.'

'I meant no offence.'

She continued to glare at him, all pretence at humility now gone. She really was magnificent, formidable, but he did not want to argue with her. She was doing more than just stating an opinion, she was defending her mother. This was a personal issue for her, and no doubt a painful one. No matter what he thought of women who became courtesans, no matter his opinion on women who were kept by married men, his views should remain his own.

And if he did express an opinion, what could he say? That she was wrong? That it had been perfectly all right for his father to keep mistresses or to visit courtesans? Would he tell her that he had been raised to believe that a man such as a duke is entitled to have a wife and a mistress? Should he tell her that, despite all his father had said to him, he had never agreed with the way he had deceived his mother?

'Perhaps we should take this up to the patient before it gets cold,' he said instead, looking down at the bowl in his hands.

'Yes, yes, of course,' she said, rushing towards the door. 'This way.'

He had to smile. He was, after all, familiar with the layout of his own home.

He followed Miss Daglish through the silent house, up the stairs to Lady Olivia's bed chamber.

She opened the door and took the bowl from him. 'I must apologise, Your Grace,' she whispered, looking down at the bowl now in her hands. 'Sometimes I speak before I think.'

'As I said, Miss Daglish, you have nothing to apologise for and I admire your frankness,' he said equally quietly to avoid waking the patient. 'And please, wish Lady Olivia a speedy recovery.'

She bobbed a quick curtsey and disappeared into the room, leaving him standing in the hallway, staring at the closed door.

Chapter Six

Georgina had done nothing wrong. Yes, she had been alone with the Duke, but that was hardly her fault. She had not flirted, and no one could accuse her of having any intent towards him. And yet, guilt wracked her.

Perhaps it was because she had revealed more of herself than she intended, but what did that really matter?

She had told the Duke nothing he didn't already know, and presumably did not care about. After all, everyone in Society knew her mother had once been a courtesan, and that the Earl of Dallington was her father, and despite that the Duke had still invited Olivia to his house for the weekend.

Perhaps he hadn't expected to have to play host to the illegitimate daughter, but neither he nor the Duchess had given any indication that they judged her, and had been nothing but welcoming.

No, she had done nothing wrong by reminding him of her background, and it would not affect Olivia's chance of marriage. If noblemen only married young women who did not have illegitimate half-siblings, few debutantes would ever make it up the aisle.

That alone would not hinder Olivia's marriage chances. Perhaps she should not have been so brusque with him. Although the Duke did not appear to be the sort of man that would be offended by a bit of straight talking, particularly from a woman who meant nothing to him.

She placed the bowl on the desk.

Perhaps it had been remiss of her to become annoyed when he had talked of the sins of the parents, but how could she not? While he had appeared sympathetic, he really knew nothing of what women had to do in order to ensure their financial security and their children's future. She puffed out her held breath, knowing that she was trying to justify her behaviour and that she really should have kept her opinions to herself.

She was a guest in his house for one reason only, because of his interest in her sister. The Duke did not need to be given lessons on the unfair way society treated women from the likes of her.

Olivia roused herself and tried to sit up. 'You should get some sleep,' she said, or more accurately, snuffled.

'I'll sleep later. I've brought a bowl of hot water. The steam will hopefully bring some relief.' Georgina usually told Olivia everything, but she did not wish to tell her that the Duke had helped her light the fire and boil the water. Nor did she want to share details of their conversation. Why she wanted to keep that to herself she was unsure. After all, she had done nothing to be ashamed of, and yet she still could not prevent self-reproach from once again clenching at her chest.

'You're so good to me, Georgina,' Olivia said with a small cough.

Olivia was most certainly not at her best. Her blonde

hair was damp and matted, her nose was red and her breathing laboured. The dull pain in Georgina's chest intensified, and this time it was guilt over her own good health. If Olivia were not stuck in this bed she would be laughing and flirting with the Duke. He would not be spending time with Georgina and she would not be having these confusing emotions and thoughts.

'Now, let's get you better, shall we, so the Duke can court you?' Her words sounded false in her ears, and for a moment she struggled to breathe. What on earth was happening to her? She could not be jealous of Olivia. Guilt and shame were bad enough, but jealousy, that would be unforgivable. Olivia's happiness was something she wished for with all her heart. The Duke would make an excellent husband. He was handsome, charming, intelligent, caring, everything she would hope her sister's husband would be. No, she was not jealous. To be so would make her the worst of all possible women.

She pushed those thoughts away as she helped Olivia out of bed and to the desk and chair in the corner. Olivia obediently leant over the bowl of hot water, and Georgina placed the cloth over her head to make a steam tent.

Some mumbled words came from under the cover.

'Sorry, what did you say?' Georgina asked, leaning down close to the cloth.

Olivia lifted up a corner and peered from underneath. 'I said I heard voices outside the door and it sounded like the Duke.'

Georgina placed the cloth back over Olivia's head so she would not see her blushes. 'Yes, he found me down in the kitchen boiling water and helped me carry the bowl to your door.'

But that was all, she wanted to add. *Nothing happened between us.*

Although it didn't feel like nothing. For some reason their conversation felt decidedly intimate, and when their hands had touched it had been unlike anything Georgina had experienced before. She clasped her hands together, remembering how the touch of his fingers had sent tingling heat radiating up her arm.

No, Olivia did not need to know any of that. Georgina could hardly bear to think about it herself, but one thing she knew to be true. She was attracted to the Duke. It was a foolish, pointless attraction but she could no longer deny its existence, even though she knew it was an attraction that could go nowhere.

Georgina collapsed into the nearest chair, wishing she had never met the Duke. Life had been so much easier before she laid eyes on his handsome countenance, before these turbulent emotions welled up inside her.

After a few minutes Olivia lifted up the steam tent and smiled.

'Do you feel any better?' Georgina asked.

'A little, thank you.' She climbed back into bed and Georgina fluffed up her feather pillows and placed them behind her head.

'But I think I'm going to need to see the doctor again tomorrow,' Olivia said as she lay down and closed her eyes.

'Yes, of course. He did say he would make another visit to check on your progress, and hopefully you'll be better tomorrow and you and the Duke can get back to courting.'

Olivia was already drifting off to sleep and thankfully did not hear the way her voice had quavered when she had mentioned the Duke.

* * *

The next morning it was obvious that Olivia would have to remain in bed all day. Even Lady Dallington had to concede that fact. When she entered the bed chamber after breakfast, she rushed to Olivia's side, worry etched into her brow. 'Oh, this is dreadful,' she said, placing her hand on Olivia's forehead. 'The Duke cannot see you like this. You have to stay in bed until you look more presentable.'

'Yes, Mother,' Olivia snuffled.

'I suppose I'll have to do my best to convince the Duke that, despite this illness, you really are exactly what he's looking for in a wife. I'll emphasise how you're usually so healthy and remind him once again that I've had four sons, and your father has three brothers.'

Olivia gave a small laugh. 'I'm sure the Duke will appreciate being told that yet again. But if I'm to get well as quickly as possible, I think I need my rest now.'

'Certainly, dear.' She stood up, her brow still furrowed. 'I'll look in on you again later. Hopefully, you might be well enough to join us all for dinner tonight.'

Georgina looked at her sister, at her flushed cheeks, her reddened nose and bloodshot eyes, and assumed it had to be wishful thinking on Lady Dallington's part.

'Perhaps,' Olivia answered before another coughing fit took over.

'The Duke has kindly arranged for the doctor to visit again this afternoon. I'll ask him if there's anything he can give you that will get you out of bed quicker and mend your...' She circled her hand around Olivia's unfortunate appearance.

Again, Georgina assumed that was wishful think-

ing on Lady Dallington's part, as such a miracle cure
for the cold did not exist.

Lady Dallington left, and through her coughing
Olivia laughed. 'Poor Mama, I think I might have ruined all her hopes of becoming the mother of a duchess.'

'Nonsense. You just need to spend some time with
the Duke and I'm sure the two of you will find you have
much in common and that there is a mutual attraction.'

Olivia sent her a long, considered look, causing her
to blush as brightly as her sisters. Did Olivia know of
her attraction towards the Duke? To hide her consternation she once again fluffed up Olivia's pillows and
straightened the bedcover, although her actions were
entirely unnecessary.

Once that was done, Georgina sat down in the armchair beside the bed and picked up the copy of *Pride
and Prejudice*. It was a book they had both read before, on several occasions, and both took comfort in
the enjoyable journey towards true love for Elizabeth
and Mr Darcy.

The day passed pleasantly enough, with the two
young women chatting and laughing together, and taking their meals in the bed chamber on trays.

In the early afternoon, the doctor arrived to examine
Olivia. Lady Dallington insisted on being present and
interrogated the doctor on what he could do to hasten
Olivia's recovery.

'There must be something you can give her,' she repeated, and Georgina almost expected her to take him
by the lapels and shake him, such was the strength of
her frustration.

'The best thing the patient can do is have plenty of
bed rest, nourishing food and fluids,' the doctor said,

something that elicited a *hmph* of disapproval from the Countess.

When the doctor left, Lady Dallington also departed, and the sisters could hear her haranguing the poor man as they walked down the hallway.

Fortunately, Olivia did as the doctor said, and slept through the night, with Georgina dozing beside her in the armchair.

The next morning Olivia was slightly better. Her breathing was less laboured, her sneezing less frequent, but her cheeks and nose were still bright red, and her usually clear blue eyes remained bloodshot.

When Lady Dallington marched into Olivia's bed chamber, followed by the Earl, they were both dressed in their dark travelling clothes.

Olivia's parents stood by the bed and stared down at the patient, who had abandoned her tray of toast and tea and was now lying back on her bed.

'I'm pleased to see your appearance has improved, but you must do as the doctor says and remain in bed,' Lady Dallington said, taking her daughter's hand.

'I will. I am starting to feel a bit better and Georgina is taking such good care of me.'

'Lady Rosemont has said you can remain until I return in ten days.' She paused, her frown deepening as she turned to her husband. 'I do think I should stay. While Olivia is still confined to her bed,' she nodded towards Georgina, 'other people will be free to do as they please.'

Georgina bristled. What did Lady Dallington think she was going to do? Take the opportunity while Olivia was ill to seduce the Duke, perhaps convince him that she could become his mistress? It was an outrageous idea, but Georgina had to stifle her fury.

'You will not be staying,' the Earl said.

'But…'

He held up his hands to stop her arguments. 'In case you have forgotten, my dear, you have invited your entire family to visit on our return from the Rosemont Estate. I will not be entertaining your family alone. You will be returning with me.'

The Earl had not said so, but everyone in the room knew that Lady Dallington had extended the invitation in the expectation that she would be proudly announcing that her daughter was being courted by a duke, or, more hopefully, engaged to be married.

Lady Dallington's brow furrowed more deeply in consternation. 'Well, Gina will have to come back with us as well.'

'No,' the Earl said. 'Olivia said that Georgina has been a great help to her. She can remain and nurse Olivia.'

'But…'

The Earl sent his wife a stern look.

'Now, I believe we should say our goodbyes and depart,' he said, leaning down to kiss Olivia on the forehead. 'Stay in bed, stay warm, and do whatever the doctor tells you to.'

'Yes, Papa,' Olivia snuffled.

He smiled at Georgina. 'And I'm sure you will be an admirable nurse.'

Lady Dallington leant over Olivia and also kissed her on the forehead. 'I'll return once my family has left. It was so kind of Lady Rosemont to allow you to stay until I return. She obviously has high expectations for you and the Duke. Just make sure he doesn't see you looking the way you do now. And once you're better make sure you only wear your prettiest gowns at all times, even if you're going for a walk. And tell Molly to style your hair in that new French manner, and…'

'Come along, my dear,' the Earl said. 'Unlike coaches, trains do not wait for anyone, even countesses.'

She stood, sent Georgina another disapproving look and was about to speak when her husband coughed in irritation, so she took his arm and left the room.

Once they had gone, Georgina and Olivia smiled, exchanged sighs of relief, and spent the rest of the day chatting and reading.

At mid-afternoon, Olivia's lady's maid entered the bed chamber to inform them that the doctor had arrived.

'Oh, has he? Pass me my mirror, please,' Olivia said to Molly, sitting up in bed and adjusting her nightdress. 'And can you tidy up my hair, please?'

Georgina smiled at her vanity. 'I'm sure the doctor has seen people in worse condition than you.'

Olivia ignored her and continued fussing with her hair.

'While the doctor's here you should take a break,' Olivia said. 'Molly can chaperone me.'

'No, I'm content to stay with you.'

Olivia flicked her hand towards the door. 'You've hardly left this room for the last two days. I will feel terrible if you don't get out for a while. Please, if you don't take a break for yourself then do it for me so I don't feel so guilty.'

'I believe the Duchess is taking afternoon tea in the drawing room,' Molly said as she drew Olivia's long hair up into a bun on the top of her head.

'There you are. Go and have afternoon tea with the Duchess.'

Still Georgina waited. 'Are you sure?'

Olivia didn't appear to hear, as she was staring at herself in the hand mirror and instructing Molly to free a few locks, so the bun did not look so severe.

Turning to the mirror above the dressing table, Georgina also attempted to tidy her dishevelled hair, but there was little she could do about the tell-tale signs of tiredness under her eyes, caused by sleeping the night in an armchair.

She shrugged, said goodbye to Olivia and Molly and left. What did it matter if she did look bedraggled? After all, there was no one she wished to impress.

Chapter Seven

Luther had released a sigh of relief as Lord and Lady Dallington entered the carriage and drove off towards the train station. Lady Dallington had used their farewells as yet another opportunity to regale him with a seemingly endless list of Lady Olivia's attributes and was only stopped when her husband reminded her that they had a train to catch.

He had promised the Countess that their invitation to the Rosemont ball would be the first to be dispatched. He had also assured her that, once Lady Olivia was back to her usual good health, they would spend plenty of time together getting to know each other.

Now he could relish being free of the Countess and her constant chatter. She would be back in ten days, and that was not a date he was looking forward to.

In the meantime, he had the house back to himself. He had not seen Lady Olivia for two days and had seen nothing of Miss Daglish since their encounter in the kitchen. The two young women had taken their meals in Lady Olivia's room, and he suspected they would remain there until Lady Olivia recovered.

Not long after Lord and Lady Dallington's departure, the doctor's gig had turned the corner at the end of the driveway. Luther couldn't help but wonder whether the timing was deliberate. Poor Duncan Campbell had been on the receiving end of Lady Dallington's displeasure yesterday. She had insinuated that it was the doctor's fault that Lady Olivia was not recovering at the rate Lady Dallington expected.

After a brief conversation with the doctor, who assured Luther that Lady Olivia was an otherwise healthy young woman and should be recovered from her chill in a day or so, Luther joined his mother in the drawing room while the doctor disappeared upstairs.

'What did the doctor have to say?' she asked as she handed him a cup of tea.

'He believed Lady Olivia would soon recover. Apparently, he agrees with Lady Dallington that Lady Olivia is in robust good health. Although he didn't take the opportunity to remind me of how many brothers she has or uncles on both sides of the family.'

His mother smiled slightly, then adopted a more serious expression. 'We should not make fun of the Countess. I know how hard it is to marry off sons. I can't imagine the pressure on a mother trying to find a suitable husband for a daughter.'

'If I remember correctly, nature took its own course when it came to the marriages of your other two sons.'

'Well, with Lady Dallington now gone, once Lady Olivia is well again, you will be able to spend time with her and hopefully nature will take its course once again.'

'Perhaps,' was all Luther was prepared to add on that topic.

The footman opened the door and Miss Daglish entered. 'I hope you don't mind,' she said, her eyes lowered. 'Lady Olivia suggested I take some time away while the doctor is attending to her.'

'How lovely of you to join us,' his mother said, pointing towards the chairs. 'Please take a seat. And Luther, pour Miss Daglish some tea.'

The young lady took the seat closest to his mother and continued not to look at him. This was not the bold woman he had met in the kitchen, or who had walked with him in the garden. Once again she was acting the part of the meek ward. And an act he was sure it was. The real woman was the spirited, defiant one he was coming to admire.

As he poured the tea, Luther ran through all the instructions he had given himself after he had left her at the door of Lady Olivia's bed chamber. When they had been alone together in the kitchen, he had allowed his attraction for her to run rampant. That should not have happened, but it had. To deny it would only mean he was deceiving himself.

Of course he was attracted to her. That was a logical reaction from any red-blooded man in the company of a beautiful woman. But experience had taught him that attraction faded. He'd had many women in his life, all of them beauties in their own way, and he had found that, with time, that initial desire began to wane. He was sure the same would be true of Miss Daglish. If he did marry Lady Olivia, he was certain that he would eventually see Miss Daglish as just another pretty young woman among many.

Unfortunately, at present the pull of attraction was

just as powerful. But it would fade. He just had to keep reminding himself of that fact.

'How is the patient today?' he asked as he handed Georgina a cup of tea.

'She seems a little better. I'm sure she'll soon make a full recovery.'

'Yes, that is what the doctor said.'

'Well, I'm very pleased you can join us for afternoon tea,' his mother commented as Luther took his seat.

Georgina smiled at her, then once again lowered her eyes.

'So tell me, Miss Daglish, what does your future hold?' His mother was never one for skirting around a subject. 'Lady Dallington mentioned that she was hoping to find you a post as a governess or a lady's companion. Is that what you are hoping for?'

Miss Daglish took a sip of her tea, and that defiant look he found so appealing flitted across her face. It was as if she was in constant conflict with herself, trying to decide whether to play the humble ward or to reveal the real Miss Daglish.

Luther was also interested to hear her answer. He could not imagine her in the role of a demure governess or keeping some elderly lady company. But would she follow in the profession of her mother? She hadn't answered when he had asked a similar question when they were alone in the kitchen. Would she be bold enough to answer this time?

'My mother left some money for me in trust which I will get when I turn twenty-one,' she said. 'Then I intend to buy one of those new Singer sewing machines and start a business making ready-to-wear dresses.'

Mother and son exchanged surprised looks, causing Miss Daglish to smile. 'It's not as outlandish as it sounds. Olivia's dressmaker uses patterns produced in France from the top clothing designers. They're all hand-stitched in the finest fabrics, with intricate hand embroidery and bead work. I intend to use the same patterns but to produce the dresses by machine, rather than by hand, and in less expensive fabrics. Then more women will be able to afford to wear the latest fashions.'

His mother stared at her with wide eyes. Luther doubted she would be more shocked if she really had said she was looking for a wealthy man to keep her. 'But won't that upset members of the aristocracy, to see women of the lower classes wearing clothes that were previously exclusive to them?'

Miss Daglish's smile became almost wicked. 'Upsetting the aristocracy is not something that unduly worries me.' Then she bit her lip. 'I'm sorry, Your Grace. I should not have said that.'

His mother waved her hand as if to say she was not offended.

'But I don't believe aristocratic women will be unduly upset,' Miss Daglish continued in a more conciliatory manner. 'If anything, I believe they will feel proud to be setting the style for other women to follow.'

The Duchess nodded slowly, considering this piece of information. 'I think that is a capital idea. Don't you agree, Luther?'

They both looked at Luther. He knew little of women's fashions and was merely pleased that Miss Daglish's plans to upset the women of the aristocracy involved clothes, and not luring away their husbands, as her mother had done. 'I'm sure it is, but will you be able to make a sufficient living with just one sewing machine?'

Or will you be subsidising that income in another manner?

'My plan is to build up my clientele. Then I will be able to hire other women to make the gowns.' He could see excitement sparking in her eyes. 'Not only will it mean the latest fashions will be available to more women, but I will also be able to provide employment for women. At the moment the only two choices for so many women from the lower orders is working as servants, or as...' She stopped talking and sipped her tea. Luther and his mother did the same, the other alternative for women hanging unspoken in the air.

'I believe you will be upsetting the aristocracy after all,' his mother said with a smile. 'You'll be taking away their servants by offering them other employment.'

'I think it will be a long time before my enterprise is so large that I am hiring all the servants in England.'

His mother laughed. 'Well, I think you're a thoroughly modern, thoroughly enterprising young woman and I commend you for it.' She raised her teacup as if in a toast. 'Isn't she admirable, Luther?'

'Indeed, Mother.' He had no idea whether her enterprise would succeed or not, but she *was* admirable, too admirable. Then an uncharitable thought occurred to him.

'Will you be looking for investors in this enterprise?' Luther wondered if that was her angle.

'Not at all. I will have enough money for a sewing machine and some fabric, and have already made contact with a few of the new department stores, who are prepared to give my ready-to-wear gowns a trial.'

'Oh, Luther, what a good idea,' his mother said, placing her tea on the side table.

Luther did not believe he had expressed any idea, good or otherwise.

'I should invest in this enterprise,' his mother said, almost causing Luther to splutter his tea.

'You? Mother? When have you ever seen the need to invest money?'

'Never before, but this is such a good idea. All women love fashion, no matter what class they come from. I'm sure this enterprise will be a great success. If I invest, then you won't have to slowly build up. You can start off with several of these sewing machine things, and a team of seamstresses. It will be marvellous and just what I'm looking for.'

She smiled at Miss Daglish then turned to him. 'Oh, don't look at me like that, Luther. I haven't gone mad, but I've been wondering what I would do with my time once my final son is married off. Now I've found the answer. Instead of slipping into the background and becoming the unwanted Dowager Duchess, I'll become an investor, a thoroughly modern, enterprising woman, just like Miss Daglish.'

'You would never be unwanted, Mother,' Luther said, still staring at his mother, who seemed to be transforming before his eyes.

'I will. You know I will. My job will have been completed and I'll have nothing to fill my days. That's the fate of women like me. And it's not one I want. I want to be like Miss Daglish and take control of my life.' She turned from him, and smiled at Miss Daglish, who was looking between son and mother, as if unsure what she had started.

'You will always be wanted by your family,' Luther said, shocked that his mother could think otherwise.

She all but ignored him, her attention focused on Miss Daglish. 'So, what do you think? Would you like an investor?'

She looked at Luther, then at his mother. Then sat up straighter and lifted her chin. 'I think a woman investing in a business that is run by a woman, that employs women and pays them a good salary, and sells to women who couldn't otherwise afford such luxuries, is an absolutely wonderful idea. I would love to have you as my investor.'

His mother clapped her hands together in excitement. Luther had never thought that she might want to do anything other than the role that had been assigned to her, one of wife, mother and duchess. It seemed he was wrong.

Miss Daglish moved from the chair to join his mother on the settee. 'We could hire premises that could house the machines and start making the dresses on a mass scale immediately,' Miss Daglish said, the two women leaning towards each other. 'And we could perhaps train up young women from the workhouses to use the machines, giving them an opportunity for financial independence that they otherwise would not have.'

'And maybe we could take trips to Paris to see the latest fashions?' his mother added, her eyes wide in expectation.

'A capital idea.' The two women seemed oblivious to his presence and were now focused entirely on their plans to conquer the fashion world. 'Although we would want to release our new lines of clothing just after they appear for the Season,' Miss Daglish said.

'Quite right, dear. We wouldn't want to upset the aristocracy too much.'

'No, I didn't mean that. I meant the aristocracy do set the trends. The clothes need to be seen on duchesses, countesses and other Society ladies first. Once other women see what they are wearing that Season, then they will follow and want to buy our dresses.'

'Oh, marvellous. We can get my sons' wives to wear the clothes we plan to sell. They could be unofficially part of our business.'

She looked over at Luther, still smiling fit to burst. 'Another good reason why you need to find a wife, Luther. She can help advertise our business.' Her smile became decidedly sly. 'Lady Olivia always looks so stylish, don't you think?'

Miss Daglish's smile faltered slightly, before returning, as large as before, but not seemingly as genuine.

Luther merely nodded his agreement.

'If you'll excuse me, Your Graces, I really should return to Lady Olivia,' Miss Daglish said, standing up.

'Yes, of course,' his mother responded. 'But you must join us for dinner so we can discuss our new enterprise further.'

She smiled, curtseyed to him and his mother and left the room.

'That young lady really is quite something, isn't she?' his mother said the moment the door closed behind Miss Daglish. 'Rather impressive.'

'Indeed she is,' Luther replied, taking his seat, and keeping his voice as emotionless as possible. His mother did not need to know just how impressed he was with Miss Daglish. Not only was she stunning to look at, but with ambitions as well, ones that did not include a man.

This was not what he had expected of her. With her looks she could have any man she wanted, although perhaps not as a husband. If she became a wealthy man's mistress she would be able to live in comfort and style. While women such as her mother were officially condemned by society, they mixed with the top echelons, and even the Prince of Wales's inner circle included such women. But it seemed that was not to be Miss Daglish's fate. She would be a seamstress and a businesswoman. That was almost as surprising as his mother's sudden announcement that she wished to become a business investor.

'She's so much like her mother, Arabella, in both looks and personality.'

Luther stared at his mother. She was full of surprises today.

'Arabella Daglish was very impressive. She was beautiful, gracious, intelligent. If circumstances were different, she would have made quite the Society hostess.'

'You knew Arabella Daglish?' Luther could hardly get the words out he was so surprised. How could his mother, who lived such a sheltered life, have ever crossed paths with such a woman?

'You're looking at me like I'm insane again, Luther,' she said, reaching over and patting him on the knee. 'Your father and I met her with the Earl on several occasions, at the opera, the theatre, restaurants, places like that. The Earl always claimed that Arabella Daglish was a distant niece, and we always pretended to believe him. I rather liked the woman, even though I wasn't supposed to. I could see why the Earl was smitten with her, and believe me, he was smitten. I heard that he was absolutely grief-stricken when she died.'

Her smile quivered slightly. 'I doubt your father ever felt like that over any of his nieces.'

'Oh, mother, I am so sorry—'

'It's of no matter,' she said with a sweep of her hand, as if brushing away those painful memories. 'But it can't be easy for Lady Dallington, having the daughter of your husband's mistress in your own home, and to be constantly reminded that he was in love with another woman. It was a shame he couldn't have married Arabella Daglish instead, but of course he couldn't.'

'No,' Luther said, still trying to digest this information that his mother actually knew Miss Daglish's mother and had just openly acknowledged that her husband had mistresses.

'But he was an earl and had to marry a woman of his class from a respectable family,' she continued as if having put all sorrow behind her. 'Silly really, but that is the way of the world.' She took another sip of her tea.

'While Lady Dallington is obviously chagrined at having to make a home for her husband's—' he paused, not wanting to use any crude words to describe Miss Daglish '—ward, the two half-sisters seem to be the best of friends.'

His mother beamed at him. 'That just shows how lovely Lady Olivia is. She's graciousness itself and will make a remarkable wife for any man sensible enough to see just what she has to offer.'

Luther was saved from having to listen to yet another list of Lady Olivia's finer qualities by the door opening once again and Dr Campbell entering.

'Duncan,' Luther said, standing up to greet the man. 'Won't you join us for a cup of tea?'

'I won't, thank you,' he said in his Scottish accent. 'Lady Olivia's lady's maid served me tea up in her bed chamber.'

'That was very considerate of Lady Olivia,' his mother said. 'Wasn't it, Luther?'

'Indeed,' he said, hoping it wouldn't start his mother off again on itemising Lady Olivia's virtues. 'So, what is your opinion of the patient?'

Dr Campbell smiled. 'A most delightful young lady.'

Luther frowned at him. Not the doctor as well. Was the entire world determined that he would see Lady Olivia in a good light? 'I meant, when is she likely to be recovered?'

The doctor stopped smiling and looked somewhat shamefaced, as well he should. It was not his place to pass an opinion on any of Luther's guests. 'At this stage, it's hard to say. I've recommended that she remain in bed for a few more days. I'll call again tomorrow to see what progress she is making.'

'Thank you. I appreciate your attentiveness.'

'Right, then, until tomorrow,' the doctor said and departed.

'It seems Lady Olivia has charmed the doctor,' his mother said with a little laugh. 'Now all she has to do is charm you.'

Luther sent his mother a polite smile. He too wished that Lady Olivia would soon emerge from her bed chamber, if for no other reason than to stop himself from constantly thinking of Miss Daglish.

Chapter Eight

Georgina could not blame the Duke. Well, not entirely. Her emotions were once again in flux, but this time the primary cause was Lady Rosemont. Georgina could hardly believe that such an esteemed woman was going to be her investor. It was almost too good to be true.

Her dream had just moved another step closer to reality. She should be excited, overjoyed, dancing down the hallway back to Olivia's bed chamber. And yet that excitement was tempered by one concern. One very big concern. If she went into business with Lady Rosemont there was the danger that she would continue to see the Duke.

She paused, her hand holding the doorknob, pulled herself up straighter and drew in a strengthening breath. No matter what happened she would bear it. If Olivia married the Duke, she would keep her feelings to herself and celebrate their happiness. If her path crossed the Duke's through her business dealings with the Duchess, again, she would reveal none of her true feelings and pretend he meant nothing to her.

With determination she turned the handle and entered the room.

Olivia was sitting up in bed, as if eagerly awaiting Georgina's return.

'What did the doctor have to say?' she asked, which caused Olivia to smile.

'Oh, he's pleased with my progress but believes I should rest for a few more days. He's coming to see me again tomorrow.'

That was very good news for so many reasons. Only a few more days and everything would be as it should be.

She placed her hand on Olivia's forehead, which was now cool to the touch. 'Your fever has gone and you are looking much better. Perhaps you will be able to get out of bed tomorrow.'

Georgina wanted her sister well again, but also had her own selfish reasons for wanting her to be up and about. Lady Dallington had worried that Georgina would take advantage of Olivia's illness to seduce the Duke. That, of course, was ridiculous. But spending time with the Duke was too painful. It was torture being with a man you were becoming increasingly attracted to, knowing that to even have such feelings was disloyal.

Once Olivia was well and she and the Duke were spending time in each other's company, Georgina hoped her unbefitting feelings would die a natural death. She would be able to watch her sister being courted by the man she would hopefully marry, and Georgina would be happy for her.

She would be. Of course she would. It was what she wanted. Wasn't it?

That nasty burning sensation rose up her throat once

more and she swallowed to squash it down. She was not that person. She could not be jealous of Olivia. She wanted with all her heart for her beloved sister to find love and happiness with a good man. To not do so would make her an even worse person than Lady Dallington believed her to be.

'I'm sure the Duke will be pleased to hear that you can soon spend time together before your mother returns.'

Olivia frowned slightly at the mention of her mother, causing Georgina to bite her lip so she wouldn't laugh.

Molly knocked on the door and entered. 'I've come for the tea service, my lady,' she said, drawing Georgina's attention to the two cups sitting on the table.

'Did the doctor have a cup of tea while he was here?' Georgina turned back to Olivia. 'And did Molly fetch it?'

'Mmm…' Olivia responded, lying back on the pillows.

'You were alone with the doctor?'

'Oh, stop fretting, Georgina. You're starting to sound like Mother. He's a doctor. He was here to check my breathing and take my temperature. And looking like this,' she swept her hands over her face, 'I doubt if any man is going to want to ravish me.'

'But the Duke? What would he think about you being alone with another man?'

Olivia sat up straighter. 'You really are starting to sound like Mother. I'm sure the Duke would trust Duncan implicitly.'

'Duncan?'

'Dr Campbell. His full name is Dr Duncan Campbell.'

'Well, don't let it happen again. If you must take tea while the doctor is here, call for a servant, don't send

Molly out of the room. Or better still, I'll remain with you next time.'

'Oh, Georgina, don't be so silly. As much as I love having you here you don't have to stay with me constantly. But if it makes you feel any better, I promise that the next time the doctor is here I won't let Molly out of my sight.'

'Good.' She turned to Molly. 'And I believe it is best not to mention this to the other servants. We wouldn't want any gossip getting back to the Duke.'

'Yes, ma'am,' Molly said with a quick curtsey before carrying the tray out of the room.

Olivia gave a small laugh when the door closed. 'Telling the servants not to gossip is a bit like telling the tide not to come in or the sun not to rise tomorrow.'

'This is no joking matter. The Duke has to know that you are a young lady of impeccable character.'

'I *am* a young lady of impeccable character, unfortunately.'

'Olivia.'

Olivia laughed again. 'I never thought I'd shock you. Your eyes have gone all bulgy. And what I said was just a jest.'

'I should hope so, too.' Georgina knew that Olivia was right. She *was* sounding like Lady Dallington. If her own emotions weren't in such an agitated state, she would probably also find Olivia's behaviour funny. Instead, Olivia's flippancy only increased her agitated state.

'So how was afternoon tea with the Duchess? Was the Duke there?'

'Yes, he was. And afternoon tea was very pleasant.' She picked up the book to continue reading, then remembered her good news and smiled at Olivia. 'In fact, it was more than very pleasant. Something rather wonderful happened.'

'What is it?' Olivia beamed a delighted smile at her. 'You've got good news, haven't you? Was it something the Duke said?'

'No, I'm sorry. Apart from asking after your health, we didn't discuss you, but I'm sure you were constantly in the Duke's thoughts.' Georgina had no idea what the Duke thought but she hoped she spoke the truth.

'Well, what did he say?' she asked, any disappointment not showing in her countenance.

'The Duchess asked me what my plans were for the future. I told her about my idea to set up a ready-to-wear clothing business and she was most excited by it. She's offered to invest money so I can start immediately with several sewing machines and a team of seamstresses.'

'Oh, I see,' Olivia said, as if she didn't really see at all. Then she smiled. 'That's wonderful news. You're going to be an independent woman of means. And I'm going to be friends with a successful businesswoman.'

'And the Duchess had a good idea. I told her about the aristocracy setting the fashion trends, and she said her daughters-in-law could be part of our business.' Georgina paused so her words would have the most impact. 'And she said that would include the future Duchess of Southbridge. Then she went on to say to the Duke how elegant you always looked and how you would be the perfect model for the dresses on which our line of clothing will be based.'

Georgina waited for Olivia to squeal with delight that the Duchess was approving of her, but she merely smiled.

'Or perhaps I could wear the dresses you make.'

'Don't be silly. My dresses will be worn by middle-class women, not the aristocracy.' Georgina was starting to worry. Was Olivia losing interest in becoming the next duchess? If that was the case, she really did need to get out of bed as quickly as possible and spend more time with the Duke.

'The Duchess is, of course, quite correct,' Georgina continued, hoping there was no lecturing tone in her voice. 'If, or should I say when you marry the Duke you will make such an attractive couple that everyone will want to follow your lead when it comes to fashion. And the Duke really is a very handsome man, you must admit. It's unlikely that you'll meet a more attractive man.'

Olivia merely smiled.

'And you have to admit he's charming.'

Olivia nodded.

'And he appears to be a good man in so many ways.'

Another nod.

'I think he will make a wonderful husband.'

'So do I.'

Georgina had her wish, didn't she? That was what she wanted, for Olivia to see the Duke in such a favourable light. And yet, the clenching pain in her stomach did not feel as if she was entirely pleased.

Forcing herself to continue smiling, she picked up *Pride and Prejudice*. 'Right, let's see what Mr Darcy is up to now.'

Olivia snuggled down into the bed, giving all her attention to the story, even though they both knew from constant re-reading exactly what Mr Darcy would do next.

In the early evening, a footman arrived to inform

Georgina that Lady Rosemont had asked if she would join them for dinner.

Georgina looked to Olivia, who appeared decidedly healthy. As much as she was pleased that Olivia was improving, it would suit her purposes now if she looked as if she could not be left.

'Go, go,' Olivia said. 'You two businesswomen must have much to discuss. And you'll have plenty of interesting news to tell me when you return.'

Was that a good idea? Georgina was unsure. Hopefully, the more she saw of him the less effect he would have on her. After a time, looking into those smouldering brown eyes would cease to cause an eruption of emotion deep within her. She would soon cease to have a burning craving to touch his olive skin, to discover what it was like to have those strong arms encasing her. But right now she did not want to put that theory to the test.

'I think it best if I remain here this evening.'

'Don't be silly. If the Duchess wants to discuss her investment, then it would be foolhardy, and not to mention rude, not to attend the dinner. And I have a wonderful business idea.' Olivia sat up straighter in bed, looking very pleased with herself. 'You should wear my green gown this evening. Then you can use it to show the Duchess how you will go about turning it into a ready-to-wear line.'

Georgina started to object, but Olivia held up her hands in a stop gesture.

'I believe that would make good business sense. If you're trying to convince the Duchess to invest in your fashion business you should look fashionable, and you can't do that in those drab clothes Mother makes you wear.'

Georgina could see some sense in what Olivia was saying. Her emerald-green gown was exactly the sort of dress that would be perfect for reproduction. Instead of hand-woven silk, it could be made with a light cotton. Instead of hand-made lace, it could be adorned with machine-made lace. Instead of the hand embroidery that ran down the skirt and onto the train, it could have machine-made applique. They could achieve the same elegant look for a fraction of the cost.

'All right. Thank you, Olivia. You really are so kind.'

'Nonsense. I just want your business to succeed. I'll call Molly and she can help you dress.'

Georgina kissed Olivia lightly on the forehead and departed to ready herself for dinner.

Along with helping her into the gown, Molly also styled her hair, telling her that Lady Olivia had insisted. From a business perspective Georgina could not see the point in having her hair back-combed, plaited and twisted ornately on the top of her head, but had to admit it was nice. Her mother had always insisted that a woman must look stylish at all times, although what she really meant was, a woman had to look good for a man. Even when her mother had been ill, she had made a supreme effort to dress immaculately and to look and act as if she were in the peak of good health whenever the Earl was visiting.

As much as Georgina loved fashion, she had always vowed that she would never dress to please a man, only to please herself. It had been almost liberating when she joined the Dallington household and had been made to wear dour clothing and have her hair pulled back in a severe bun. She knew that Lady Dallington did it because of her resentment towards Georgina and her mother, but it had never seemed like a punishment. But it was rather nice to feel silk on her skin once again, and lovely to free her hair from that tight, rigid bun she always wore.

Once Molly was finished, she walked down the stairs to join the Duke and Duchess in the drawing room, her nerves tingling in anticipation as to how they would react to her new appearance, and in particular what the Duke would say and do.

She entered the drawing room. The Duke stood while the Duchess smiled at her from the chaise longue.

'You look magnificent, my dear,' the Duchess said.

'Olivia suggested I wear this gown this evening as an example of the styles that could be used in my business.'

'I see,' the Duchess said, standing and approaching Georgina. Not looking at the Duke, Georgina rushed on, describing how it could be made much more cheaply and mass produced, and hoping that the Duke did not think she had dressed to impress him.

As the Duchess murmured her agreement and inspected the gown, Georgina looked over at the Duke, standing by the sideboard, a brandy carafe suspended over his glass. His dark eyes met hers. Fire ignited within her as she registered the impassioned look on his face. There was no denying what she saw. Hungry desire. For her.

Slowly his eyes stroked over her, causing every inch of her body to ache with need. A need for him to do more than look at her, for him to touch, explore, caress, to act on that desire.

Frightened by the strength of her reaction, she both wanted to flee, and to cross the room to him, to let him know that he could have what he wanted. That if he acted on the hunger flashing in his eyes, she would put up no resistance.

Breaking the spell, he turned and poured himself a brandy. Georgina closed her eyes briefly and exhaled her held breath in a shaky gasp, then said a silent prayer that she had not revealed too much of what she had been feeling.

'I believe this lace is hand-made,' the Duchess said, breaking through the turbulence of her thoughts. 'Do you think it can be machine-made?'

'Oh, yes.' Georgina was pleased her voice was steady, even if her mind was not. 'It won't be quite as intricate, but it will certainly be lovely to look at, and, while all the embroidery and beadwork is also done by hand, it could be made separately and added later by machine.'

'Oh, that's so ingenious, isn't it, Luther?' The Duchess turned to her son. 'Come and look at this embroidery. It's so pretty, and Miss Daglish says we can put it on our line of dresses as well.'

Georgina wanted to scream out. *No, do not let him come any closer.*

'I'm afraid I have no opinion on embroidery, Mother. I'll leave that discussion to you two businesswomen.'

The Duchess laughed and winked at Georgina. 'Men know nothing about fashion and all the trouble women go to so we can catch their eye. But in a dress like this a woman is sure to catch any man's attention.' She turned to her son. 'I think you can at least agree with me on that, Luther?'

Heat moved up Georgina's neck and face and she was pleased the Duchess had gone back to inspecting the embroidery on the train and did not see the way the

Duke looked at her, in a manner that said she had most definitely caught his eye.

Luther could hardly think straight, but one thing he now knew for certain. He would not be marrying Lady Olivia.

He had hoped his attraction for Miss Daglish would fade, but his reaction to seeing her tonight made it abundantly clear that there was little chance of that happening. And it would be inappropriate in the extreme to marry one woman while lusting after her half-sister. And lusting he was. He could hardly look at her without imagining what it would be like to tear that green gown off her, to feast himself on her luscious, feminine curves and satisfy his hunger deep inside her.

He threw back another brandy, the liquid smouldering down his throat, and looked away. His reaction was as extreme as it was unexpected. No woman had affected him like this before. His desire was so strong, so immediate and powerful, as if he was losing his sense of who he was. And what made it worse was that she could never be his. She was wholly unsuitable as a duchess. Nor would she be suitable as his lover.

Despite being the illegitimate daughter of a former courtesan, and despite the passion he had seen flaring in her eyes, everything else about her suggested she was an innocent.

He wanted her. By God, he wanted her. But he could never have her. He had never seduced an innocent and he was not about to start now. His attraction for Miss Daglish would have to remain unsated.

He would just have to endure the next few days of torture, of seeing her, wanting her, but knowing he could never have her. Then she would leave with her half-sister, and he would never see her again.

Instead, he would set his sights on another, one who would make a suitable duchess and did not have a half-sister who drove him mad with desire.

That would mean enduring another Season, but at least, thankfully, Miss Daglish would not be attending.

As much as he despised the way Lady Dallington treated her, it suited his selfish purposes that she was to prevent Miss Daglish from attending the Season. Enduring another round of balls and parties was going to be hard enough. He did not need the added complication of being pathetically attracted to a woman who was wholly unsuitable.

He looked in the direction of Miss Daglish and his mother, who were now examining the train of her gown. There was the problem of his mother's sudden decision that she wanted to venture into the world of business, but hopefully that would not involve him and would not mean spending any time with Miss Daglish.

All he had to do was get through the rest of this visit without revealing anything of what he was thinking or feeling. That was a task which would be made easier if his mother didn't keep inspecting Miss Daglish's clothing or trying to elicit Luther's impressions on her appearance.

His impression of her appearance was as uncomplicated as it was inappropriate. She looked beautiful, but it mattered not whether she was wearing an expensive gown or her plain brown dresses. But how he would like to see her was wearing nothing at all. Then she would look truly glorious, with that long, thick auburn hair flowing down her body, curving round her full, naked breasts.

She caught his eye again. He should look away but he couldn't. Was he imagining it, or did that look in her eye suggest she knew what he was thinking and did not object? Or was that just the wild fantasy of a man who should know better?

The footman entered and announced that dinner was served. Luther downed the last of his brandy and fought to bring his lustful thoughts under control.

They moved through to the dining room, and after some polite enquiries about Lady Olivia's health they began discussing the family gossip. Miss Daglish's smile was genuine as his mother told her about his brothers, Ethan and Jake, their wives, and Ethan's new daughter, his mother's first grandchild, of whom she was immensely proud.

Every time she mentioned their marriages she sent Luther a pointed look, to which Luther responded in his usual manner, by pretending he was oblivious to her intent.

'I'm so pleased you and Lady Olivia will be attending the Rosemont ball,' his mother continued, still sending Luther that meaningful look. 'My youngest son, Ethan, proposed to his wife two Seasons ago at one of our balls. It was so romantic and people still talk about it. The following year my middle son, Jake, courted his wife at the Rosemont ball.' Her look became even more meaningful, if that was possible. 'Hopefully, this year something equally romantic will happen. Perhaps the announcement of an engagement.'

Luther chose not to answer and tried to keep his face as expressionless as possible. He would have to inform his mother soon that there would be no engagement or a wedding, but now was neither the time nor the place to do that.

'And hopefully you'll also meet your future husband at the Rosemont ball,' his mother said, causing Miss Daglish to actually splutter on her wine.

'I'm not seeking a husband, Your Grace.'

'You might not be seeking a husband but I'm sure there will be plenty of eligible young men interested in making your acquaintance. Don't you agree, Luther?'

'Indeed,' was the only word that Luther could get out. The last thing he wanted to be discussing was Miss Daglish becoming acquainted with any other men.

'At the Rosemont ball I'll introduce you to some of the more suitable gentlemen. I'm quite the matchmaker, you know.'

'Thank you, Your Grace, but really, I'm not interested in marriage, as I wish to dedicate myself to becoming a successful businesswoman.'

'Oh, but the two are not mutually exclusive. I'm sure plenty of men would not object to having a wife who is also a businesswoman. After all, it's nearly the twentieth century and things are different for women now. Don't you agree, Luther?'

'I'm sure whatever you say is correct, Mother.'

'I'm not going to let you get off that easily,' she said with a laugh in her voice. 'Would you object to a wife who also ran her own business or are you so old-fashioned that you believe women aren't capable of such things?'

It was not something Luther had ever considered and was a situation he was never likely to face. The only business most debutantes were involved in was the very serious business of landing a husband with a title, preferably one that moved them further up the social hierarchy. But his mother was waiting, so he knew he had to say something. 'I believe a woman, including a married one, should have the freedom to do whatever she wants. If that includes running a business, then why would I object?'

'See, Miss Daglish. I'm sure Luther is not alone in that opinion.' She smiled to herself. 'You and I can become leading lights for other women to follow. You, a married woman with her own successful business, and me, a dowager duchess who is also a successful investor.'

'Perhaps Miss Daglish does not wish to marry,' Luther said.

'Don't be ridiculous. You know as much about such things as you do about fashion.'

'I'm afraid His Grace is correct,' Miss Daglish said quietly. 'I have no plans to marry.'

The Duchess looked from Miss Daglish to Luther, then back again. 'You two, you're as bad as each other. Why you young people are so reluctant to marry, I'll never know. Ethan and Jake also claimed they did not wish to marry and look how happy they are now that they're wed.'

'This lobster is rather delicious,' Luther said, desperately trying to change the subject.

'Yes, it is,' Miss Daglish said, sending him a small smile. 'Quite succulent. What is this delicious sauce it's served with?'

'Hollandaise, I believe.'

'Mmm, delicious.'

They both looked at the Duchess, who shook her head, but smiled, knowing what they were up to.

'I hope Lady Olivia doesn't share your reluctance to marry,' his mother said to Miss Daglish, returning immediately to her favourite topic. 'Because I'm sure a young woman as lovely as she is will be inundated with proposals. She might even be betrothed before the Season begins.' She raised her eyebrows and turned her attention to Luther.

'When do you hope to start your business, Miss Daglish?' he asked, hoping against hope to get his mother to talk of something, anything, else.

'As soon as I can. It is only a matter of a few months before I come into my trust money.'

'So you'll be starting up during the Season?'

'Yes. While other young ladies are dancing the night away, I will be working hard to get my business established. I suppose we'll all be striving for the same thing, security and a future, but I will be doing so on my own terms.'

There was a challenging look in her eye, as if she somehow blamed him for the role assigned to debutantes.

'Some would say you were lucky.' Including himself. He would rather be doing just about anything other than dancing the night away at yet another tedious ball.

They continued to hold each other's gaze. The challenge in her eyes softened. Her lips parted slightly as a quiet sigh escaped. She really was the most beautiful woman he had ever laid eyes on, beautiful, elegant, intelligent and enterprising. The world certainly was a cruel place that it would bring such a woman into his life, with no chance that she could ever be his.

She blinked, as if breaking an invisible thread that was tying them together, and turned to face his mother. 'Lady Rosemont, I was thinking about what you said regarding trips to Paris to see the latest fashions. Which fashion houses do you think we should visit?'

'I'm not sure. Who do you suggest?'

'Oh, we must see everything at the House of Worth. Most of Olivia's gowns are designed by that house, including this one. They really are the epitome of high fashion and I'm sure we'll be able to get some wonderful ideas from seeing their latest designs.'

While the two women continued to discuss fashion, Luther repeatedly reminded himself that this torture would only last a few more days. Then she would be gone. Out of his life and hopefully out of his mind. Until then, he merely had to keep his desires under control until he was free of the demons that were possessing him.

Georgina had endured countless strained meals at Dallington House. She rarely got through a dinner with Lady Dallington without being on the receiving end of some barbed comment or reprimand.

If Lady Dallington had been allowed to have her way, Georgina would have taken her meals with the servants, but she rarely got her own way, so had to content herself with sending many subtle and not so subtle insults Georgina's way.

Tonight's meal was nothing like that. It should have been enjoyable. Lady Rosemont was a delight. The Duke was amiable company, and the affection between mother and son was plain to see. Even Georgina's statement that she had no interest in marriage had been taken in good spirit.

Despite that, Georgina's nerves were stretched to breaking point, and it was all her own fault. She was far too aware of the Duke's presence. Even when in conversation with Lady Rosemont she was always conscious of him, so close to her she could reach out and touch him.

When the meal was over, Lady Rosemont had asked her if she would play for them again, but Georgina had made her excuses. She had claimed that she was anxious to check that all was well with Olivia. This was true, but, to her enduring shame, it was not the main reason she wanted to escape. She needed time to catch her breath, to give herself a stern talking-to so she could get herself under control. After all, she still had several more days to survive before they returned to the Dallington Estate. During that time, she could do nothing, say nothing, that would reveal how she was feeling about the Duke.

'I'm sure Lady Olivia wouldn't mind if you played one piece for us,' Lady Rosemont urged. 'Your playing is simply enchanting, isn't it, Luther?'

'It is, but if Miss Daglish wishes to retire, I believe it would be remiss of us to make her entertain us.'

'Oh, I suppose you're right. But it would be wonderful if you could play for us again before you leave.'

'I'd be delighted.' Georgina bobbed curtseys at the Duke and Duchess and said her goodnights.

When the door closed behind her she breathed a sigh of relief and her tense body relaxed slightly. As she headed up the stairs and along the corridor to Olivia's room, she hoped and prayed she had done nothing during the meal that had exposed even a hint of what she had been feeling.

She paused at Olivia's door, took a long, slow breath, put on her brightest smile and entered.

Olivia was lying back on her pillows, completely relaxed and reading. When she saw Georgina she sat up immediately, her eyes wide.

'Georgina, you look absolutely stunning. I believe that gown looks even better on you than it does on me.'

'It was very kind of you to let me wear it.'

'Nonsense. I should give it to you. It suits your complexion perfectly. The Duke must have fallen instantly in love with you.'

'Olivia, that's a terrible thing to say,' Georgina gasped out, her heart pounding, her cheeks flushing.

'It was just a jest,' Olivia said, but her admiring gaze suggested she was completely earnest. 'But I'm sure any man seeing you looking like that must have wanted to fall at your feet and beg you to marry him, and I believe the Duke is a man, or haven't you noticed?' She laughed and sent Georgina a cheeky wink.

'Don't be so silly,' Georgina snapped with more disapproval than she had intended. 'But you were right.'

Olivia raised her eyebrows in query.

'About Lady Rosemont. She was most impressed,' Georgina rushed on, trying to cover her embarrassment and trying even harder not to think of the way the Duke had looked at her when she had entered the drawing room. 'Especially when I explained how we could make many copies of a similar dress for a much cheaper price.'

'Excellent. Even if I don't marry the Duke, this visit will not have been a waste of time.'

Georgina rushed to the bedside and took Olivia's hand. 'Don't say that. You'll be better soon and you can spend the remaining days with the Duke before your mother returns, which will give you a good chance to get to know each other.'

'Hmm, yes, I suppose. But I think I'll get some sleep now.'

'Of course. I'll just change out of this gown and join you.'

'No, you sleep in your own bed tonight. You're looking a bit tired and I'm sure you need a good night's sleep.'

'I'm fine and you might need something again during the night.' Georgina remembered meeting the Duke in the kitchen on the first night of Olivia's illness and once again her cheeks burned.

'No, I will be perfectly all right. Sleep in your own bed, and please, take your meals with the family. Then you can report back to me all about the Duke, what he likes, what he thinks, and I'll be prepared to impress him when I finally get better.'

'No, I'd much rather take my meals here.'

Olivia gave her a long, appraising look. 'Did something unpleasant happen at dinner?'

'No, not at all. The Duchess was very kind and the Duke was charming. I would just rather spend my time with you. That's all.' It was the truth, but not all the truth, and she hoped Olivia would not question her further.

'Well, you need to get out some of the time. I have to stay cooped up, but that doesn't mean you have to.' Olivia tapped her chin in thought. 'I know. You should take the opportunity each time the doctor arrives to get out and exercise. Explore the gardens, maybe take the Duke up on his offer to avail yourself of the horses. I know how much you love to ride.'

'All right. Yes, I'll do that.'

'Promise?'

'Yes, I promise.' Georgina would promise anything if it could get her out of spending more uncomfortable hours in the Duke's company.

'Good, then I'll say goodnight.'

Georgina checked to ensure Olivia had everything she needed, said goodnight and departed, ashamed that her still blushing cheeks might be revealing the true reasons why she did not wish to take her meals with the family.

Chapter Nine

For the rest of the week, Georgina settled into a pattern which centred on spending time with Olivia and avoiding the Duke. She took her meals with Olivia, only leaving when the doctor arrived so she could get some exercise by going for a long walk around the estate.

When she had first informed the Duchess that she would be taking her meals in Olivia's room, Lady Rosemont had expressed her disappointment, then had complimented Georgina for showing such dedication to Olivia.

Once again, Georgina had been forced to swallow her guilt. It was true she was staying in Olivia's room over concern for her sister, but the other reason was something which caused her great shame and distress and one she was pleased she was able to keep to herself.

After each walk, she would regale Olivia with descriptions of the estate's captivating beauty, its manicured topiary garden, natural woodlands and lakes, and the charming bridges that spanned the streams. As she often said, Olivia was going to love living in such a magnificent environment. A statement that always caused Olivia to roll her eyes, and made Georgina worry that her time in bed was causing her to lose interest in the Duke.

When she had mentioned that Olivia would also soon be able to take lovely walks in the gardens, and in the Duke's company, Olivia had not responded with quite the enthusiasm she had expected from a young lady anxious to be courted by a handsome man.

'Marriage to the Duke is what you want, isn't it?' she had asked. 'He really is rather lovely and I'm sure will make a wonderful husband, and he is a duke, after all.'

'Yes, I know,' was all Olivia had said.

'Have you changed your mind? If you don't want to marry then you don't have to, you know. Don't let your mother pressure you into doing something you don't want to do.'

Olivia had merely smiled and patted Georgina's hand. 'Don't worry, I won't, and no, I haven't changed my mind. I do want to marry.'

That had gone some way to reassuring Georgina, but she would have liked a little more enthusiasm.

Olivia was improving with each passing day, although she continued to maintain she was still too weak to rise from her bed. If Georgina didn't know better, she would almost suspect that Olivia was also trying to avoid seeing the Duke again.

After seven days, a telegram arrived from Lady Dallington informing them that she would be returning to Rosemont Estate in two days, news which caused both their moods to plummet.

It had been lovely to be free of Lady Dallington's constant criticism and Georgina knew that she would get the blame for Olivia's slow recovery. Olivia's mood had also become melancholy and Georgina hoped it would not cause a relapse.

'I suppose we had better make the most of these last few days,' Olivia said over breakfast after they'd digested the news from the telegram.

'And hopefully today will be the day when the doctor will say you are completely better, and you can spend those last two precious days with the Duke.'

'Yes. I'm sure he will tell me I can get up today. But you should take the opportunity to go for a ride. You can be certain once Mother arrives you won't get another chance. After all, she's not going to want you showing me up by proving you're the better horsewoman. Remember how she chastised you for playing the piano.'

Olivia was right and it would be good to get out and enjoy the fresh air, to savour one last moment of total freedom before Lady Dallington's return.

'Go for a nice long ride when the doctor arrives,' Olivia continued. 'Then, by the time you get back I'll probably be out of bed, dressed and ready to woo the Duke with my charm and grace.'

'A ride through the countryside would be lovely,' Georgina said, still a little unsure about leaving Olivia for so long.

'That's settled, then.'

When the doctor arrived, Olivia all but shooed her out of the room. She might have been somewhat offended if she hadn't been looking forward to riding in the fresh air.

The crisp winter's day was perfect and Georgina suspected Rosemont Estate had never looked better. The Duke had said it was at its best in the other seasons, but there was something magical about the countryside at this time of year. Frost still clung to the grass, making it crackle underfoot, the trees appeared almost black, silhouetted against the pale blue sky, and Georgina doubted that air could ever smell fresher.

Olivia was right. A long ride in the countryside on such a perfect day was just what she needed to fortify herself before Lady Dallington's return.

Despite the fact that her daughter did not enjoy riding, Lady Dallington had a new costume made every year for Olivia, but Georgina did not have one at all. Instead she always rode in her ordinary day dress. But it was of no concern to Georgina what she wore. All that mattered was getting back on a horse and experiencing the glorious feeling of complete freedom.

She strode round to the large stone stables at the back of the house and asked the stable hand to prepare her mount. As the young man went about his tasks she patted several horses, who poked their heads out from their wooden stalls, giving small whinnies and showing their curiosity about the newcomer.

The familiar scent of horse, hay and leather added to her anticipation of the freedom ahead.

Georgina's mother had insisted she take riding lessons, as part of her training for what would be expected from a wealthy man's mistress. While Georgina had known from an early age that such a fate would never be hers, she had loved the riding lessons. It was one of the few times that a young lady could be truly free of the constraints of society.

When she joined the Dallington household her father had bought a mount just for her, and riding had provided her with an escape from the household and Lady Dallington in particular. The only disappointment was she couldn't share this enjoyable pastime with Olivia, who had never got over her early fear of horses.

The stable boy led out her horse into the courtyard and helped her up into the lady's side-saddle. Georgina often wished that she could use a man's saddle and not be restricted to being balanced on the side of the horse. That was yet another annoying constraint that a woman had to endure, and one she was in no position to challenge. Yet.

She rode out of the stables, the horse's hooves clicking on the cobblestones and down the gravel path. Once she was on the grassland, she spurred the horse on and rode across the hills, relishing the feel of the wind on her face. Every worry floated away. Thoughts of the Duke evaporated. Her concern about Olivia's waning enthusiasm for marriage was swept away.

For now, she would just enjoy the moment and let everything else go—her feelings for the Duke, her guilt towards Olivia, her shame that she might be more like her mother than she would ever have wished to admit. All that disappeared, and she just felt the exhilaration of riding fast through the countryside.

Once she and the horse had had sufficient exercise, she brought the mare to trot and they moved alongside a slowly flowing stream, and she allowed the gentle babble of water moving over rocks to further soothe her soul.

As they rounded a bend, that euphoric feeling burst as quickly as a soap bubble. The Duke was standing beside the stream, his black horse beside him, and staring into space as if oblivious to all that surrounded him.

Should she pretend she hadn't seen him and turn back? He looked towards her. Their eyes met. She had lost her chance. To turn back now without speaking would be the height of rudeness. But they would be alone, far from the house. This was exactly what Lady Dallington had warned her never to do. Under no circumstances was she to be alone with the Duke.

Lady Dallington always assumed that Georgina was desperate to become a kept woman, like her mother. She had seen her mother and now Georgina as sirens, hell bent on luring men away from their wives. It was an insult to everything that Georgina believed in. And worse than that, Lady Dallington actually thought that Georgina would try and seduce the man Olivia was expected to marry.

To hell with Lady Dallington. Georgina gently tapped the horse's flank with her heel and they walked along the stream to the Duke. That woman knew nothing about who Georgina really was and what she wanted from life. She was not like her mother, never would be, and would never, under any circumstances, seduce any man away from her beloved sister.

She pulled the horse to a halt beside him. He reached up his hand to help her, but she dismounted in one quick movement. It felt good to do so, as if she was letting him know she did not need his or any other man's help.

Her horse joined his in gently nibbling on the long grass, but she kept hold of the reins, as if unwilling to let go of her security line.

'Miss Daglish, you've discovered my favourite spot.' He smiled. It was such a glorious smile. One that swept away his dark, brooding countenance and lit up his face. It was impossible not to smile back.

'I can see why.' She had hardly taken in the surroundings, having focused entirely on the man, but now she could see he was standing under a weeping willow, naked of its foliage, but waiting to burst forth with spring growth. It was a delightful, tranquil spot, and she could only imagine how it would present a glorious changing appearance with each season. 'You're lucky to own such an estate.'

That welcoming smile faded. 'Indeed. Although such ownership does come with responsibilities and burdens.'

Georgina considered this. She knew what her mother would say to such a statement. She would commiserate with the man, compliment him on doing his duty, and even suggest that she could help ease his burden. But Georgina was not her mother. She did not pander to men. It was not her job to make them feel better.

'Everything comes with responsibilities and burdens,' she said instead.

'Do you too have burdens and responsibilities, Miss Daglish?'

'All women do. It is just that we have to always maintain an untroubled exterior, so men never think we are under any strain or pressure.'

He raised his eyebrows as if he had no idea to what she was referring. It was time for Georgina to educate this man in the ways of the world. That was something her mother would never have done. Her mother had been trained always to put the man first, never to voice an opinion that contradicted his, and to never burden him with any of her own trials and tribulations. But Georgina was not her mother.

'Surely you have seen the pressure that debutantes are under to find a suitable husband. It is immense, much more than any man could ever understand. Their entire future is dependent on a man showing them favour. If they remain unmarried they not only disappoint their family, but also acquire the stigma of Society as an old maid, and they risk having no financial support, which, as you know, for a woman can have dire consequences. And they have to endure this pressure whilst smiling all the time, looking pretty and acting as if they have not a care in the world.'

'Luckily most young woman achieve their goal and do marry.'

She couldn't help but scoff at his response.

'You disapprove of marriage, Miss Daglish?'

'I disapprove of anything that reduces a grown woman to little more than a child. A woman can be more intelligent than her husband and yet he always makes the decisions. When she marries all her property becomes her husband's, and she doesn't even own her own children.'

He looked down at the ground and took in a deep breath. She was sure he must now thoroughly disapprove of her, see her as a blue stocking. Well, so be it. She had no need to impress the Duke and whether he liked her or not was of no importance. In fact, if he did disapprove and dislike her she would at least have pleased Lady Dallington.

'Perhaps then it is important for a young lady to be cautious and ensure she marries a man who will be worthy of her intelligence and treat her well.'

She swallowed a sigh. 'Or she could choose to follow another course.'

'As you plan to, Miss Daglish, with your...' he waved his hand as if trying to remember '...dress-making enterprise.'

'Yes. And as long as I never marry, the enterprise will be entirely mine.'

She lifted her head defiantly, waiting for him to contradict her. He held her gaze. She would not lower her eyes as was expected of her. Who cared if he was a duke? She had spoken her mind and done nothing to be ashamed of.

'Is it just marriage you object to, or do you disapprove of men in general?'

She blinked, and looked away, unsure how to answer. Did she object to all men? She loved her father, and was grateful to him for taking her into his home when her mother died, and yet when her mother was alive she had resented the way she changed the moment the Earl arrived. Even when she was ill, she would pretend that she was full of the joys of life and excited to see him. Georgina had resented the way her mother's friends' lives were structured around making the men who supported them happy, and, when there wasn't a man, moving heaven and earth to find one. But did she blame men for this situation?

Her gaze returned to his. She was uncertain how to answer regarding all men, but she did know that he was one man she most certainly did not disapprove of. How could she disapprove of a man who could make her melt with one gaze, whose dark good looks sometimes held a sombre intensity that intrigued her, at other times a lightness that made her heart soar?

But he had not asked for her opinion of him, thank goodness, but of men in general.

She coughed lightly to clear her throat. 'I disapprove of neither men nor marriage. I just dislike the way that marriage is the only option for most women and they are put under such pressure to find a husband.'

'And what of men? Some of us are also under pressure to marry.'

She couldn't help but roll her eyes at such an absurdity. 'And those men often have the pick of the young women available. And when they do marry, their only duty is to sire a child.' Colour exploded on her cheeks. This conversation was becoming far too intimate. 'That doesn't sound like such a burden to me,' she continued, trying to ignore the heat consuming her face and body.

'That would depend on with whom one was doing the siring,' he said with a laugh, causing the heat on her cheeks to burn hotter.

Despite her embarrassment, she would not let him win this argument. 'And yet the same could be said for the wife. But they are often stuck with their husband, while a man, if he is not content with his wife, can escape and spend time with another woman. As so many men do.'

He sent her a long, appraising look. Damn. Was he thinking that she was propositioning him? She could not let him think that she was such a woman.

'And those women often have no choice either,' she rushed on. 'Their economic survival also often depends on a man.'

'I can see you have given this a great deal of thought, Miss Daglish. Is that because of the circumstances in which you find yourself?'

Her heart raced. He did think she was intending to follow her mother and become some man's mistress. She took on a defiant attitude, tilting up her chin and placing her hands on her hips, while ignoring her body's reaction to the thought of becoming *this* man's mistress.

'What circumstances?' she asked, her voice constricted.

'You are the daughter of an earl, and yet you have no status within the family and are not recognised as such. Your half-sister will have a coming-out, whereas you will not. Lady Olivia is destined to marry a man of equal or better status, and yet, I'm sorry to say, it is unlikely you will marry a man with a title.'

Everything he said was true, and yet it was something no one had ever stated to her in such blunt terms.

'I could see that as a lucky escape,' she said, lifting her chin even higher.

He raised his eyebrows and a slow smile curled at the edge of his lips, one that suggested he did not entirely believe her.

'And despite my lowly status I am grateful for what I have.'

'Grateful for what? To whom?'

'Well, my father for taking me in. Not all men would be so responsible. To Olivia, of course, who has always treated me like a sister. And Lady Dallington.'

His brow furrowed and his dark eyebrows drew together. 'From what I have observed, Lady Dallington treats you with disdain and as someone who has to be kept reined in.'

He was aware that Lady Dallington did not trust her in his company. This surprised her.

'You are right. Lady Dallington never wanted me in the house and every day she makes that clear. But I try not to let that perturb me. She is wrong about my character, of that I can assure you, and there is nothing about me that requires my being kept reined in.'

I am not my mother. I will be no man's mistress. Even yours.

She may not have stated it outright, but the meaning of her words was clear. She would not be following in her mother's footsteps.

Luther refused to be disappointed. To be so would be unforgivable. And yet, if his reaction to her was any indication, if she did decide to follow the same path as her mother had she would have her pick of men who wanted to make her his mistress.

He fought not to stroke his gaze over her body one more time. It was a luscious, curvaceous body made for giving and receiving pleasure. Never had his reaction to a woman been so intense and so immediate. He hardly knew her, and yet every time he looked at her he could not help but picture how she must look naked, spread out before him, waiting for him, eager for him.

He coughed so he would not groan and attempted to push that image out of his fevered mind. Perhaps if he continued to question her about her plans, that would drive out the wild, rampant impulses surging within him. There was nothing like talking business to cool a man's ardour.

'Tell me more about your planned enterprise,' he asked.

And please make it as dull as possible.

She looked at him and smiled. Bad start. He did not need his attention drawn to those full red lips. He did not need to be reminded how the bow of the top lip seemed to be permanently pursed, as if waiting to be kissed. Nor did his mind need to go off onto unwanted tangents of all the things he could imagine her doing with those lips.

'I'm so excited about your mother's offer to help.' She smiled at him once more and he couldn't help but smile back. 'It is hard, if not impossible, for women to get financing for any business enterprise. Without her input it will take many, many years for my business to get established. Your mother really is a life saver.'

This was not the boring business conversation he had hoped for. He did not need those big brown eyes to shine with enthusiasm, did not need to see colour tingeing her cheeks, or to think about other ways he could cause her to flush.

'Now I'll be able to buy several sewing machines immediately, hire a team of seamstresses and premises. I really can't thank you and your mother enough.'

Luther had done nothing. His mother had been left her own money in his father's will and had inherited property from her own family. What she chose to do with that money was her own business, but it was nice to have Miss Daglish's gratitude.

'And I assume you intend to make a tidy profit from this business.' That was a suitably boring question, one that would hopefully distract his mind from images of taking Miss Daglish right here, beside the stream, and to hell with the consequences.

'Oh, yes, of course. Your mother should make a healthy return on her investment.'

He nodded, as if this was a serious consideration, although he suspected making a profit was the last thing his mother cared about. She just liked the excitement of becoming a businesswoman. But he had to appear serious, had to act as if this conversation was of vital importance.

'And for me, more importantly, creating a successful business means I'll be an independent woman who will never be dependent on a man. That is something I am prepared to work extremely hard to achieve.'

He raised his eyebrows, not convinced by her protests. She might not want to follow in her mother's footsteps, but that did not mean she didn't want to find a respectable man from her own class and become his wife, a man who did not care about her background. His jaw clenched tightly at the thought of that man, a man he had never met, but a man Luther despised all the same.

Logic told him he had no right to care who she eventually married, but when had logic ever taken control over lust? And there was no denying that what he experienced every time he looked at Miss Daglish was rampant lust, the power of which was unlike anything he had ever before experienced. Even discussing her business plans had not stopped his mind from wandering onto lascivious imaginings.

'I wish you every success, Miss Daglish. Although it has been my experience that women are not suited to the cut and thrust of the business world.'

'Well, you haven't met a woman like me before, have you?'

She was staring at him, her eyes challenging him to disagree. But she was right. He had never met anyone like her before. While he'd met many attractive young ladies, none seemed to shine with an inner glow the way she did. None created such a strange reaction deep within him, as if he needed to be with her, that without her he was missing a vital part of himself.

'I've never met anyone like you before,' he said quietly, almost to himself. He reached up and brushed a stray lock of hair behind her ear. 'You are unique.'

Her challenging look slowly disappeared, but she did not look away. His hand gently traced a line down the soft skin of her cheek, loving the silky feel of it under his touch. Her lips parted, drawing his gaze, and he watched, mesmerised, desperate to taste those claret-red lips. Slowly, carefully, his hand slid around the back of her head, cupping it and tilting it upwards. She made no attempt to move away. Instead, she edged slightly towards him. Her breath coming in faster gasps, her breasts rose and fell rapidly as if tempting him to give in to his surging needs.

He shouldn't do it, but how could he deny himself? The power of his desire for her was too strong to resist. He drew closer, his lips a few inches from hers, so close he could feel the caress of her soft breath. One kiss. That was all he would take. One kiss and that would surely break the power this woman had over him.

His lips skimmed hers. They were just as soft and pliant as he had dreamed. Slowly his arm moved round her slim waist. He had intended to pull her towards him, so he could feel that luscious body against his own, but he had no need. She moved into him, melding her body against his. This was more than he could bear, more than he could resist.

Releasing the groan that was pent up inside him, he pulled her in tighter and his lips crashed down on hers. Like a man possessed he kissed her, hard and demanding. When her lips parted to invite him in, he knew he could not stop now. His tongue ran along the full bottom lip before entering her mouth, savouring her feminine taste.

Her lips parting wider, she kissed him back with a fervour that matched his own. Feeling like a man who had been lost in the desert, he drank her in, desperate for the relief only she could give him.

Releasing her lips, he kissed a line down her soft neck. She tilted back her head, exposing the creamy white skin to him, her breath coming in fast, moaning gasps.

'You are so beautiful. I want you so much,' Luther murmured. 'I want you as my own.'

'No.' She jumped back from him.

His arms dropped to his sides. He took a quick step backwards. 'I'm sorry... I didn't... I shouldn't...'

He doubted she had heard his feeble, stuttering attempt at an apology. The moment she was free from him she rushed towards her horse, mounted and raced away. Leaving him standing alone, feeling like the immense cad he knew himself to be.

Chapter Ten

Tears stung at Georgina's eyes as she raced back towards the stables. What she had done was beyond unforgivable. She was not like her mother. She was much worse. Her mother had reputably had numerous men in her life before the Earl, many of whom had been married, but she would never have stooped so low as to try and seduce the man who was destined to marry her closest friend, her sister, the person in the world who had shown her the most kindness.

She spurred her horse on faster as if trying to ride away from her shame. Lady Dallington had been right about her all along. She had always been scornful of the older woman's low opinion of her. She had hated being judged for her mother's behaviour, especially as she thought herself to be so different from her mother, but now she had proven every low opinion Lady Dallington held to be correct. She should never have been left alone with the Duke. She could not be trusted.

She arrived at the stables and immediately dismounted, before the stable boy could help her, and led the horse into the stalls. The young lad gave her a strange look, then lowered his eyes. She must look a fright. She *was* a fright.

Horse's hooves racing over the cobblestoned courtyard drew her scattered attention. The Duke. In her haste she had been unaware that he had followed her. Like herself, he immediately jumped off the horse and led it into the stall.

'You may leave us,' he ordered the stable boy, while staring at Georgina. 'I'll tend to the horses myself.'

The stable boy doffed his flat cap, sent them both a confused look and left. What he must be thinking Georgina could not imagine, but hoped her shame was not written large on her face.

She brushed past him, trying not to look at him, trying not to remember what had just happened between them.

'Wait.' He grabbed her arm, preventing her from fleeing, which was exactly what she had intended on doing. Not because she feared the Duke, but because she feared herself. She had already proven she was not to be trusted, that she must not be alone with him, and she had no desire to test herself further.

'We need to talk about what just happened,' he said, his handsome face treacherously close to hers.

Georgina shook her head. What could she say? I'm sorry I kissed you. I'm sorry I'm no better than my mother. I'm sorry I betrayed Olivia, my only friend, the kindest, most loving young woman I have ever met. And I'm even more sorry that, despite everything, I want to kiss you again. 'We don't need to talk about it. It would be best if we can just forget all about it.'

'We both know that is not going to happen.'

Georgina shook her head, then nodded. He was right.

How could she forget something that had made every inch of her body come alive, which had caused her to ache with desire, to be consumed with a powerful longing for a man she had no right to?

He drew in a deep breath and looked over her head at the stable's stone wall. 'I should not have kissed you. I am profoundly sorry that I upset you.'

'You didn't upset me.'

He looked back down at her. His harsh gaze softened, causing an equal softening deep within Georgina. His eyes moved from hers, down to her lips, then back to her eyes. She wanted to be firm, to let him know that their kiss had been a lapse that would not be repeated, but that hungry look in his eyes was slowly stripping away her resistance.

He released her arm and gently stroked his finger along her cheek with a feather-light touch. 'You've been crying. I believe that is proof enough that my kiss upset you.'

'No. I'm crying because I should not have kissed you back,' she whispered. 'It was so shameful of me.'

'You have done nothing to be ashamed of.' His finger continued to lightly caress her cheek. As if she no longer had a will of her own, she tilted her head, loving his touch on her skin. His finger moved slowly down her cheek, then across her bottom lip. She swallowed. Her lips parted, blood pounding to the sensitive spot where his finger stroked her.

'You are not the one who should be ashamed,' he murmured, his eyes still on her lips.

I am, because I wanted you to kiss me. I still want you to kiss me.

'We shouldn't, we mustn't…' she whispered, barely able to think as desire throbbed through her entire body.

'No, we mustn't.' He repeated her words and lowered his hand, but his eyes did not leave her lips.

'Olivia is my sister. I love her more than anyone in the world,' she said, desperately trying to remind herself why this should not be happening. 'We mustn't.'

Despite her strong words, she hoped with all her heart that he would ignore them. That he would take her in his arms and kiss her again. Do more than just kiss her. Her body ached for him to caress her, to relieve the desperate, throbbing desire that was consuming her.

He raised his head and stood up straight, looking off to a distant point. Disappointment ripped through her. He wasn't going to kiss her.

She was tempted to beg him to take her once more in his arms, but he was no longer even looking at her. She might have no self-control, no sense of what was right or wrong, but he did. She took a step towards him, then checked herself.

Before she could do or say anything that would further reveal just what sort of woman she really was, she turned and ran out of the stables, her boots clicking on the cobblestones as she raced over the courtyard towards the house.

When she reached the entranceway, she paused and attempted to compose herself before she was seen by any of the servants. She passed a footman in the hallway. He gave her a quick sideways glance before his face regained its impassive expression.

Could he tell what she had done? Was her shame so obvious? It would not do for her to go to Olivia's room in this state. She had to take some time to still her mind and think of what she would say to her sister, her closest friend.

Her betrayal was going to break her sister's heart, and for a moment Georgina wondered whether it would be kinder not to tell her. But how could she face Olivia again with this terrible secret between them? She had to tell her. And Olivia *had* to know that the Duke had kissed her. Whether Olivia still wanted to marry him or not would be up to her, but she had to know the truth about him, and about her so-called friend.

Georgina entered her bed chamber and threw herself onto her bed. She had to confess all to Olivia. But not yet.

Not while she was still yearning for the Duke, not while she still had the taste of him on her lips, the feel of him imprinted on her body. Until that passed she would stay in her room, alone with her guilt, shame and remorse.

Luther continued to stare at the stable door through which Miss Daglish had passed long after she had gone, trying to come to terms with what he had just done.

He did not seduce innocents, wasn't that what he had said to himself only a few days earlier? Yet that was what he had almost done. He was the worst of all possible men. He had wanted her, so he had tried to take her. He had become the sort of man he despised. He had kissed a woman he had no intention of marrying, a woman he could never marry.

Nor had he any intention of taking Miss Daglish as his mistress. Did he? He had once believed he was not the sort of man who would have both a wife and a mistress, but now he was beginning to wonder just what sort of man he really was.

None of this was clear in his head. But how could he possibly think when he could still taste her, could still feel his arms encircling her, and when her feminine scent still lingered on his clothing?

He had chased her back to the stables because he had wanted to talk to her and try to make things right, but that had been impossible. She hadn't wanted to talk to him, and he had been unable to form the words he needed to say to her. His mind had been clouded by the touch of her lips on his, the feel of her soft breasts against his chest, the exquisite agony of her thighs pressed up against him.

Instead of taking command of himself as a man should have done, instead of attempting to right a terrible wrong, he had lost the ability to think and reason. All he could do was feel and want.

His hands clenched into fists. It was so wrong, and yet, even knowing how wrong it was, he still wanted her.

She had said they should just forget what had happened. Somehow he was going to have to do that, to forget the touch of her skin, the taste of her lips, and the feel of her body. If he didn't, surely he would go mad.

He removed the saddles from both horses, brushed them down and threw blankets over their backs, all the while trying to rid himself of those tormenting memories.

He filled their water buckets from the pump in the courtyard and tossed hay into their stables to ensure they both had plenty to eat. When he left the stables he saw the stable boy waiting at the edge of the courtyard, eager to get back to his work.

He nodded to him in passing, then walked back to the house.

At least Miss Daglish and Lady Olivia would be leaving in two days. When Lady Dallington arrived, he would have to inform her that she was not about to become the mother of a duchess. He would do so in a manner that did not cast aspersions on Lady Olivia's character, nor raise any suggestion that Miss Daglish had in any way influenced his decision.

If Lady Dallington thought Miss Daglish had ruined her half-sister's chances of making it to the very pinnacle of society, the punishment would be as severe as it was unjust. Miss Daglish was not at fault. The fault lay with one person only. Him.

He raced up the stone stairs and into the house. He merely had to endure two more days and Miss Daglish would be out of his life for ever. When Lady Dallington was made aware that there would be no courtship, she would no doubt take her daughter home immediately. Lady Olivia was pretty, sweet and of an amiable disposition. She would have no trouble finding another husband once the Season began, a husband of much better character than he had proven himself to be.

Once he had changed out of his riding clothes he remained in his room, hiding away like a coward, trying to make sense of all that had happened, even though sense and logic had played no part in all that he had done.

At dinner time he had to emerge from his lair and join his mother in the dining room. When a footman informed him that both Lady Olivia and Miss Daglish would once again be taking their meals in their rooms Luther breathed a sigh of relief. He would have a small reprieve before having to face the consequences of his actions.

Over dinner his mother chatted about her business plans. Luther hardly heard a word, but she was so caught up in the excitement she appeared oblivious to his silence.

Her involvement with Miss Daglish hopefully would not pose a problem for Luther. He doubted that Miss Daglish would ever want to see him again, so any business meetings would hopefully be conducted away from his estate, and if she did visit there would be no reason why he would have to be present. As much as he would like to avoid even hearing Miss Daglish's name ever again, he would not deny his mother her obvious excitement of being involved in this business venture. Nor would he prevent Miss Daglish from having an investor in a business that she obviously felt passionately about. His mother and Miss Daglish were innocent. He was the only guilty one, and it would compound his sins if the guilty took any actions that would punish the innocent just to save himself further pain.

'Luther, is everything all right?' his mother asked, finally coming to an end of her list of reasons why this new business was bound to be a success.

He forced himself to smile. 'Of course it is. I apologise for my reserve tonight. I know little of fashion, but everything you say makes perfect sense.'

Not that I heard a word.

'Hopefully Lady Olivia will be able to join us tomorrow. The servants say she looks much better.'

Luther cringed, unsure how he would break the news

to his mother that he still hadn't found his duchess. 'Lady Olivia is a delightful young woman, but…'

The expression on his mother's face told him he did not need to say any more.

'Oh, dear. I'm so sorry, Luther. Do you not think that if you spent some more time with her, then maybe…?' She left the question unfinished.

'No, Mother, I do not believe so.'

'Well, hopefully once the Season begins you will find your duchess.'

Luther stifled a groan. He had been so hoping that Lady Olivia would be the one, and he would not have to endure yet another Season. Now he would have to go through the entire ordeal again. He just hoped he would not spend the Season comparing all the young women he met to Georgina. It was so unfair to the debutantes. How could any of them ever match her? He would like to think it was unfair to him as well, but that would be indulgent self-pity. Attending another Season, enduring the ennui of seemingly endless balls, parties and soirees, might feel like sufferance, but he deserved a much greater punishment, one that would equal the magnitude of his transgression.

Chapter Eleven

It took a sleepless night, with endless tossing and turning, for Georgina to finally formulate the words she was going to say to her sister. Her conscience was never going to be eased until she made a full confession, and Olivia deserved nothing less than complete honesty.

In making her confession, she would ensure that Olivia knew the fault lay entirely with Georgina. Olivia might hate her for what she was about to tell her, but that was something she would have to accept with fortitude.

Whatever Olivia decided when she heard of their kiss, Georgina would live with it. She would let Olivia know the kiss meant nothing to either of them. If she still wanted to marry the Duke, Georgina would do nothing to dissuade her. She would also inform her of her intention never to see the Duke again. Once she had heard this shameful confession, if Olivia wished to have no further contact with Georgina, then it would be no less a punishment than she deserved.

With both determination and dread, she approached Olivia's bed chamber and tried to prepare herself for what might be the hardest conversation she would ever have.

Quite possibly, this would be the end of their friendship. She had betrayed the person in the world who meant everything to her. Georgina could still hardly believe that she had done such a thing, but now she needed to face the consequences of her actions.

Pausing outside the door, she braced herself with several deep breaths. She knocked. There was no answer. If Olivia was sleeping, she did not want to wake her, so she quietly opened the door a fraction and peeped in.

The bed was empty.

Georgina opened the door fully, stepped inside and stared at the neatly made bed. Was this a good sign? Had Olivia fully recovered? She hoped so. Maybe even now she was down in the breakfast room chatting happily with the Duke. Georgina bit the edge of her lip to stop herself from once again crying. They were tears of self-pity, and she would not allow them to fall.

This painful conversation would have to wait. Georgina had no stomach for food and had no intention of joining Olivia and the family in the breakfast room. Until she had made her confession she could not face Olivia, and her resolve to never see the Duke again had to start now.

How she was going to achieve that while still in his house Georgina was unsure, but at the very least she would make sure she was never alone in his company.

But she was anxious to know the state of Olivia's health, so she sought out her lady's maid and found her napping in a chair in the upper servants' parlour.

She was reluctant to wake her. Servants worked long hours, and attending to an unwell mistress meant Molly's workload had been increased over the last few days. But Georgina needed answers, so she gently shook the lady's maid's shoulder.

'Miss Daglish,' she said, rousing herself, quickly standing up and bobbing a curtsey. 'I was—'

'It's all right, Molly. I just need to know, is Lady Olivia completely recovered now?'

Molly gave her a curious look, no doubt wondering why Georgina had not asked Olivia herself.

'I've just been to her bed chamber and she's not there,' Georgina explained.

Molly's expression became wary. 'She's left.'

That could not be right. Georgina must have misunderstood the answer, or Molly did not understand what she had been asked. 'What do you mean?'

Molly gripped her skirts, twisting the fabric tightly in her hands, her brow furrowed as Georgina waited for her to explain.

'Did you not see the note?' she finally whispered.

'What note?' This was becoming more and more bizarre.

'I believe Lady Olivia left you a note on her bedside table before she left.'

'What do you mean, left? Where would she go?'

'I'm sorry, I don't know any more. Perhaps you need to…'

Before Molly could finish Georgina rushed out of the upper servants' parlour and all but ran back to Olivia's bed chamber. There it was, an envelope propped up on the table beside the bed bearing Georgina's name. She was unsure how she could have missed it, but then she had been looking for her sister, not a note, and she had been preoccupied with her own concerns.

She ripped it open and quickly scanned the contents. Then read them again, more slowly, trying to make sense of the words.

> *Duncan and I are to wed. I know Mother will not approve, and that is why we have taken this action and decided to run off together to get married before her return. Don't worry and don't try and find me. I know what I'm doing.*

Who the hell is Duncan? was the first thought that went through Georgina's mind. Was Olivia's sickness making her delirious? was her second thought. Had she conjured up some Scotsman who had rescued her from her sick bed? She sank down on the bed, the note crumpled in her hand.

Georgina wished that Olivia *were* delirious—it would be better than what she knew to be the truth. Duncan, of course, was Dr Campbell. Olivia, the daughter of an earl, a woman who could have married a duke, had thrown it all away for a man of little means and even less status.

This was a disaster and it was all Georgina's fault. One of the servants must have informed Olivia of what had happened in the stables and she had reacted in this impetuous manner.

Georgina was going to have to stop this marriage, and quickly. She had to find Olivia before Lady Dallington's arrival and bring her back to Rosemont Estate. Once she heard that the kiss had meant nothing, Georgina was sure she would forget about marrying a doctor.

But how was she to find Olivia, and how was she to do so without the Duke finding out?

Crumpling the note tighter in her hands, she knew the answer. She couldn't do it without the Duke's help. Once he was informed that Olivia had run off with the doctor, Georgina was sure he was unlikely to want to marry Olivia, but that did not mean she had ruined her chances of making a good marriage to someone else. As long as she was found and brought back to Rosemont Estate before Lady Dallington or anyone else found out, they might be able to keep this impulsive act a secret. But she was going to need the Duke's help.

To that end she rushed downstairs. He was not in the breakfast room, but a footman informed her he was in his study and escorted her along the hallway. The man walked at the expected pace of a footman, and Georgina had to restrain herself from yelling at him, *For goodness' sake, hurry up*! Finally, he opened the door and announced her.

Georgina suspected that the Duke's objections to seeing her again, especially alone, would be as strong as her own, so she pushed past the footman before he could deny her entry.

She ignored his questioning look and thrust the letter under his nose, without preamble or explanation. 'Here, read this.'

'That will be all, thank you, Charles,' he said to the footman, taking the letter from her hand. Drumming her fingers on the desk, she waited while he read. He exhaled loudly as he handed the letter back to her. 'And what do you expect me to do about this?'

'I have to go after them, but I need your help. We have to catch them and bring Olivia back before her mother arrives and before anyone finds out that she has done something so ruinous to her reputation.' Georgina's words tumbled out in a rush. 'Lady Dallington will never forgive her. The Earl will never forgive her. If news of this gets out she will never make a suitable marriage. And if we are too late and she does marry the doctor...' Georgina paused and drew in a breath. 'We must find them before Olivia does something she will regret for the rest of her life.'

'Dr Campbell is an honourable man. I do not believe your sister will come to any harm from him.'

'I need to hear that from her myself. I can hardly believe she has actually done this, run off with a man she has known for such a short time... How can she possibly do something so reckless?'

He raised his eyebrows and she was certain of what he was thinking. Hadn't Georgina done something equally reckless and regretful, after knowing a man but a short time? But this was different. This was Olivia, a young woman with expectations of making a good marriage. Nor was it merely a kiss that both parties immediately regretted. It was marriage. Once she was married there would be no turning back. They needed to find them and stop this before anyone, including Olivia's parents, found out.

'Please,' she said, extending her hands towards the Duke. 'We must find them. Do you know where they have gone? Will you help me?'

'Dr Campbell would not have left town without letting his housekeeper know where he could be reached in the case of an emergency. As I said, he is an honourable man and would always do his duty to his patients.'

'Right. Good. That's where we'll go first.'

'It might be advisable to ask the lady's maid to pack you a bag, and I'll advise my valet to pack mine. If they have done as the letter suggests they will have left town and we might have to follow them.'

'No.' Georgina grasped his arm. 'Tell no one. Not even your servants, especially not your servants. You know how gossip spreads and news of this must not get out. If you can light a fire and bake scones, I'm sure you can pack your own bag. I'll do the same. You'll have to drive the carriage as well. No one, and I mean no one, must know of this.'

Georgina knew she was giving orders to a duke and had no right to do so, but the importance of saving Olivia's reputation overrode any such protocol.

The Duke nodded. 'But what of you? If you travel with a man unchaperoned your reputation too will be tarnished.'

'I do not care. Now, let's get going.' Georgina did not want to explain to him that after what had happened she deserved a tarnished reputation, and that such an outcome would be a very small price to pay for saving Olivia from disaster.

'As you wish. The carriage will be waiting for you at the front of the house once you are packed.'

Without answering, Georgina raced up the stairs and pushed some clothing into her carpet bag, then raced back down the stairs. It wasn't long before the Duke arrived in a small gig pulled by one horse. They drove down the path to the village, and all the while Georgina prayed that they were not too late.

Luther had meant what he said. Duncan Campbell was an honourable man and would make an ideal husband for any woman. Perhaps it would not make Lady Dallington happy. She would much rather have her daughter married to a duke, even one as remiss as him, rather than a respectable country doctor as upstanding as Duncan Campbell. But Miss Daglish was worried, so he would help her, despite his better judgement.

He pulled the gig to a halt in front of the doctor's residence. Miss Daglish chewed on her lip, and he could tell what she was thinking. The two-storey brick cottage in the middle of a small village, quaint though it may be, was a far cry from the grand house and countless servants Lady Olivia was used to.

'It will all be all right,' he said, although what 'all right' looked like he had no idea.

He helped her down from the carriage and they rushed up the pathway. Mrs Armstrong, the doctor's housekeeper, answered the door.

'Why, Your Grace,' she said with a curtsey. 'I'm afraid the doctor isn't home at present, but if you'd like to—'

'Where has he gone?' Miss Daglish cut in, causing the housekeeper to frown briefly.

'He's gone to Edinburgh. That's where his parents live and he is expected to be away for a few days.'

'Do you have an address?' Miss Daglish asked before the housekeeper had barely finished.

'Yes, one minute. If you'd like to come in, I'll find it for you. Perhaps you'd like a cup of tea while you wait.'

Luther placed his hand on Miss Daglish's arm to stop her from once again giving the housekeeper a curt reply. 'I'm sorry, Mrs Armstrong, but I'm afraid we are in a bit of a hurry and need to contact the doctor immediately.'

'Oh, yes, of course, Your Grace.' She rushed off down the hallway and quickly came back with an envelope bearing the return address of Mr and Mrs Campbell in Edinburgh.

He thanked Mrs Armstrong and they got back in the gig and headed towards the train station, hoping they would not be too late to make the train that would connect them to the one from London to Edinburgh.

With little time to spare, he took the horse and gig to a local stables, bought their tickets, then, taking Miss Daglish's arm, ran along the platform, the porter racing behind with their luggage. Just as the whistle blew they found their first-class compartment, and settled back onto the leather bench with matching sighs of relief.

Finally, Luther had time to think about what he had just done. It had all happened so fast he had not even informed his mother that he was leaving. The moment he had an opportunity, he would send her a telegram to put her mind at ease.

He looked over at Miss Daglish. Her pretty face was still pinched with worry, her hands clasped tightly together in her lap. She too needed to have her mind set at ease.

'Lady Olivia will come to no harm,' he said, wishing he could reach out and comfort her, but knowing that would be inappropriate.

She released a small, shaky sigh. 'You don't know that for certain. You're only saying it to reassure me.'

'I don't know for certain what will happen, but I know the doctor. He would never do anything to harm Lady Olivia, nor do anything to sully her reputation.'

Unlike me, the doctor would not take liberties with a young woman.

'I can't help but think this is all my fault.'

'It is not your fault. Lady Dallington will no doubt find a way to blame you for Lady Olivia's behaviour, but you do not need to blame yourself. Lady Olivia made her own choices.'

Instead of reassuring her, these words caused her

hands to clench tighter, her brow to furrow deeper. 'But what if she did this to punish me?' She looked up at him, those brown eyes beseeching. 'What if one of the servants told her about...about what happened between us, and that's why she ran off with the doctor?'

'I'm sure that is not true.' At least he hoped it wasn't true. If it was, then he was even more to blame for Lady Olivia's behaviour than Miss Daglish was.

'I can think of no other reason why she would act so impetuously, and with a man she hardly knows.' Colour burst onto her cheeks and the unspoken words hung in the carriage between them. Hadn't Miss Daglish acted impetuously with a man she hardly knew?

'As I said, Dr Campbell is a good man.' *A much better man than I will ever be.* 'Even if we are too late, even if they have married, Lady Olivia will be married to a man who will care for her. Isn't that what you want for your half-sister?'

She shrugged.

'And perhaps she has fallen in love.'

She sent him an incredulous look, as if falling in love in such a short time was an impossibility.

'Whatever her reasons, you cannot blame yourself for what happened.'

'I can, and I do. This is all my fault. We should never have... What I did was unforgivable.'

'No one can ever blame you. It is I who should have exercised more control.'

And I will need to continue to exercise control, something that would be easier if you weren't so damn tempting.

Once again she was dressed in a plain brown dress with no ornamentation, and once again she looked more beautiful than any woman he had ever seen. He had attended countless Society events where women were dressed in expensive gowns, dripping with priceless jewels and their hair styled and bedecked with ribbons and feathers. But none looked as elegant as Miss Daglish did today.

The simple dress could not detract from those tempting curves he had felt when he held her in his arms. Full breasts, small waist and the sensual curve of her hips and buttocks seemed designed to undermine a man's determination. His eyes moved to the creamy skin of her neck, exposed by the tight bun at the back of her head. His lips seemingly remembered what it was like to kiss that soft skin. As if unable to stop, his gaze moved to her luscious lips, and the temptation to take her in his arms and feel them again against his own lips filled him like a physical presence.

He suppressed a groan and looked up at those brown eyes, which were focused on him as if she was reading his mind. His gaze flicked to the passing scenery, but he hardly registered the green fields outside the window. All he could think was that he was alone with this woman, would be alone with her until they reached Edinburgh, and already he was having inappropriate thoughts about her. This woman was not for him, and if he had even a modicum of decency he would control his lust. To succumb would not only be unforgivable but would also be a further betrayal of everything he believed himself to be. He considered himself honourable, a man who put his duties and responsibilities as a duke before his own base needs. Now was the chance to prove that he was that man.

He had to think of something, anything, to take his mind away from her. Think of the prices he would get for this season's spring lambs, the repairs that needed to be done to the tenants' homes, the pensions that he would have to arrange for the farmhands who were of an age to retire from their labours. He should think of all that needed to be discussed with his estate manager when he returned from this quest. That should distract him from the feminine scent that was filling the carriage and sending his senses reeling. Because a distraction was what he desperately needed if he was to survive this journey.

Chapter Twelve

Even the train timetable seemed to be against him. Arriving at the station for their connection, Luther discovered the next train to Edinburgh would not be leaving until the following morning. They would have to find accommodation for the night. Together, alone.

He bought their tickets, then sent a telegram to his mother telling him that he, Lady Olivia and Miss Daglish had been called away, that she was not to worry, and he would explain all on his return.

Then he started to worry himself, and his sense of guilt intensified. Throughout the journey, Luther had found it all but impossible not to apologise repeatedly to Miss Daglish. He had told her that none of this was her fault, and yet he too felt as if he was responsible for all that had happened. Not that he blamed himself for Lady Olivia running off with the doctor, or saw it as a catastrophe, the way Miss Daglish did. The doctor was a good man. Wasn't that the most important thing for a woman? Unlike him, Lady Olivia was not honour-bound to marry someone who would bring prestige to the family. She could marry for love.

But he did feel guilty, and never more so than now. Logically, he knew it was not his fault that they were going to have to stay together unaccompanied overnight. He did not control the railway timetable and had not manipulated this situation. But still he felt as if he was somehow responsible for their predicament. Again it was illogical, but after the way he had been thinking about Miss Daglish on the train it was almost as if he had willed it so they would spend even more time alone in each other's company.

He hailed a hansom cab from the station and asked the driver to take them to reputable accommodation.

'It will perhaps be best if I say that you are my cousin. That would explain why I am travelling with an unchaperoned young woman,' he said to Miss Daglish, once they were alone inside the small carriage.

She nodded but made no comment. It was the only thing he could say. No one would believe that a woman dressed so plainly was his sister. Nor would anyone believe they were man and wife, not that he would ever think of passing them off in such a manner, as appealing as that might be.

'To that end, it would be best if you stop calling me Your Grace and call me Luther, and I'll have to call you Georgina.'

'As you wish... Luther.'

His name had never sounded so seductive. It seemed to roll off her tongue like a caress, or was it merely that his fevered brain had immediately conjured up an image of her whispering his name as he held her close?

They arrived at the inn, and he booked two rooms. Fortunately, the friendly couple who owned the inn showed no reaction when he referred to Miss Daglish as his cousin, even though to Luther it sounded like an obvious lie.

The innkeeper arranged for luncheon to be served in the private dining room, and they sat at the table to eat a meal of chicken pie.

Miss Daglish merely picked at her food, and Luther found he too had little appetite.

'Don't worry. By tomorrow we will be in Edinburgh.'

She continued to move her food around her plate. 'This has all gone so horribly wrong.'

'Not necessarily. Hopefully we will still be in time to stop the marriage.' Although, as Lady Olivia and Duncan Campbell were both adults, Luther could not really see how they could do that, or why they should.

She sighed, and the furrows in her forehead grew deeper. 'She was supposed to marry you, and I suspect, if everything else hadn't happened, you two might now be a courting couple.'

'Hmm, perhaps. But everything did happen.'

Colour tinged her cheeks and she once again looked down at her uneaten meal. 'I've ruined everything.'

Before he had time to think, he reached out and placed his hand over hers. 'No, you have not.'

Her warm hand remained under his for a tantalising few seconds before she slowly withdrew it. 'But if you had not met me…if we had not…' she looked around the room and lowered her voice '…kissed, perhaps none of this would have happened.'

Luther wanted to deny everything she said, to tell her it had nothing to do with her. While she was not to blame, there was no denying it *was* all because of her. The moment he had seen Miss Daglish—Georgina—he had hardly even noticed Lady Olivia. Even if they had not kissed, he was sure his focus would have been on her, and not on the woman who would have made a suitable Duchess of Southbridge. But it was hardly her fault that she was so enchanting that she had seemingly bewitched him. Nor was it her fault that she was wholly unsuitable as a duchess.

'I am a duke. One of my duties is to marry and sire the future Duke of Southbridge,' he said, as much to himself as to Georgina. 'As much as you may scorn this situation, it is a reality, and yes, Lady Olivia might have made an ideal duchess. You're right that we should not have kissed. Or, should I say, I should not have kissed you? I should have remembered my duty.' Luther knew he sounded somewhat pompous, but what he said was the truth.

'Might have? Does that mean you will not be forgiving her this transgression?'

Luther almost laughed. How could she possibly think he would want to marry Lady Olivia? 'No, I will not be considering her as a future duchess, but it has nothing to do with any so-called transgression on Lady Olivia's part.'

She raised her eyebrows as if she did not believe him, then frowned. 'That is why we have to keep this a secret. No man of your class will want to marry Olivia if they hear about this. Men can transgress as much as they like, but a woman, never.'

'I said, that is not the reason I would not consider marriage to Lady Olivia.'

She waited, frowning and shaking her head slightly in question.

'I knew, even before we kissed, that I would not be

marrying Lady Olivia, but our kiss confirmed it,' he said, as if merely stating an unemotional fact.

Her hand covered her mouth, in shock, or because she was trying to take back that kiss.

Slowly she lowered her hand. 'But you owe me nothing. I told you I expect nothing from you and will not hold you accountable for what happened.' She looked down and drew in a long breath. 'When I went into Olivia's bed chamber this morning I intended to tell her all that had happened between us, and to assure her that the blame was all mine. I had also planned to tell her that if you did marry I would ensure that I never saw you again, so she would know that there would never be anything between us.' She looked back up at him, gauging his reaction.

Luther fought to keep his face impassive. How could he tell her he was obsessed with her, a woman he could never marry? That was the main reason why he would not consider marrying Lady Olivia. While he had no expectations of marrying for love, he could hardly marry one woman when he was constantly thinking of and fantasising about her half-sister.

'But none of that matters now,' he said instead.

'No, I suppose not, but we still need to save Olivia so she can make another suitable marriage.'

'And what if she is in love with Duncan Campbell?' Luther could hardly believe he had just said that, that he was the one talking of love.

'And what if she's not? What if she is doing this because she is angry with me, or so upset she doesn't know her own mind?'

'I suppose we will not know that until we get to Edinburgh tomorrow and find them.'

She nodded slowly.

'In the meantime, if you're not going to eat your meal, perhaps we should stretch our legs with a walk around the township.'

Once again she nodded compliantly.

They left the inn and he offered her his arm. She hesitated.

'You are my cousin, remember?'

For another second or so she hesitated, then took his arm and they walked along the busy footpath.

Every moment that passed Georgina's anxiety increased. She should not be wandering through this town on the arm of the Duke. She should be saving her friend from making a dreadful mistake and ruining her life.

And her anxiety was not helped by once again being alone with the Duke. Completely alone. They would be spending the entire trip to Edinburgh alone. They would be alone together at the inn tonight. It was almost more than she could endure. But at least the Duke, or Luther, as she must now remember to call him, was giving no suggestion that he wanted to kiss her again. He had been the perfect gentleman. But the same could not be said about how she was feeling, being so close to him. So close she could smell his cologne, that tantalising masculine scent of bay and leather, a scent that had filled her senses when he had held her tightly. All she could think about was kissing him again.

She swallowed a small moan but could do nothing to stop a shiver from running through her body at the memory of his lips hard against hers, his body pressed tightly to her own, his arms encircling her.

'Are you cold, Georgina?' he asked, halting and looking back along the footpath. 'Perhaps we should return to the inn.'

'No, no, I'm not cold at all.' The last thing Georgina wanted was for them to retire to somewhere private. They were much safer in a public place. She was much safer from the thoughts and desires that were possessing her. In public her self-control would not be tested.

'Are you sure?' he asked, with a frown of concern.

'Perfectly.' She turned and looked into the nearest shop, so she would not have to stare up into those brown eyes, or worse, look at those enticing lips. 'Oh, they are pretty, aren't they?' She hardly saw the hats, ribbons and rolls of lace displayed in the milliner's window.

Without asking, he opened the shop door, the small bell tinkling a welcome. Georgina had no real interest in looking at hats, but at least it would provide a distraction from her tormenting thoughts.

She entered the shop and the assistant rushed out to greet them. Georgina knew it was not she who had elicited such excited attention. Luther's expensive suit and his demeanour marked him out as a man of substance, one who not only had money to spend, but who would also bestow an honour on the shop owner by purchasing her products.

Georgina smiled at the assistant, who curtseyed low to both of them. Even dressed as she was, the shop owner obviously thought she was someone who merited being treated with a high level of respect, at least as long as she was in the company of a duke.

'May I be of assistance?' the shop owner said, looking at Luther. 'I have just created a new line of hats that I'm sure would look lovely on the young lady.'

Luther smiled at her, and the milliner looked as if she

had been honoured with a great gift. 'I'm afraid I know nothing about hats, but I'm sure…my cousin would be delighted if you could show her your merchandise.'

The milliner flicked a quick look at Georgina. She had picked up on the pause before *cousin* and had made assumptions about their real relationship.

'I've recently finished creating this.' She pointed to a large hat bedecked with ostrich feathers. 'It's exactly what all the fashionable young women in London are now wearing.'

Georgina inspected the hat. The workmanship was meticulous, but the style was a season behind what Olivia and other aristocratic women would be wearing this coming summer. 'Do you make them yourself?' Georgina asked, inspecting the neat rows of stitching that were almost invisible.

'Yes, miss.' The milliner smiled, rightly proud of her work.

'It really is excellent craftsmanship. The local ladies are lucky to have someone of such talent in their town.'

'Thank you, miss, and please try it on,' the milliner said, beaming a smile at both Georgina and the Duke.

Georgina was reluctant to do so—after all, she did not wear such ornate headwear, but before she could object the milliner had placed it on her head.

'Oh, it looks marvellous, miss. It suits you perfectly. Doesn't it, sir?'

'Yes. You must have it, Georgina,' the Duke said, removing a leather wallet from the inside pocket of his jacket and taking out several coins.

'No!' Georgina almost shouted, removing the hat from her head and thrusting it back at the shocked milliner. No man had ever bought Georgina a gift and no man ever would. Her mother had been showered with jewellery, clothing and other trinkets by the Earl. They were supposed to be presents but that was not how Georgina saw it. He was buying her, paying her for the services she provided. While her mother never saw this as demeaning, Georgina did. In exchange, her mother was expected to be exactly what the Earl wanted her to be at all times, no matter how she felt or what mood she was in. She always had to be the agreeable mistress, even when she was unwell, as she had been for the last months of her life.

The Duke handed the coins to the milliner, whose expression changed from shocked to pleased. 'Thank you, sir.'

Georgina scowled at the Duke, hardly able to believe that he had ignored her wishes and purchased a hat she neither wanted nor would ever be able to wear.

While the milliner wrapped the hat in tissue and placed it in a hat box, Georgina left the shop. Fury coursing through her veins, she paced up and down the pavement. The milliner had made the assumption that she was the Duke's mistress, and in purchasing that hat he had confirmed the woman's suspicions. She looked like a kept woman, who could be purchased with a hat. How dared he put her in that humiliating position?

The bell above the door tinkled as he exited the shop, and Georgina turned on him, determined to give him the full force of her wrath.

'I did not want that hat. I don't want you to buy me anything, ever. Is that clear?'

'Perfectly,' he said, his voice calm as if he was not even registering her anger.

'What do you think that woman thought I was?'

'I have no idea, but I do know that if we hadn't made a purchase, she would have been disappointed. The woman needs to make a living.'

She glared at him, wanting him to feel her rage, but he merely smiled at her.

'It's only a hat, Miss... Georgina.'

'That's not the point.'

He raised his eyebrows. 'What is the point?'

She lowered her voice. 'The milliner knows I am not your cousin. She thinks I am your mistress.'

'And you care what the milliner thinks of you?'

'Well, no.' She looked towards the shop, her anger starting to ebb. 'But I do not want you to buy things for me.'

'It's just a hat, and I had no intention of offending you.'

Georgina's anger continued to bubble. She doubted he could ever understand that to her it would never be *just a hat*.

'If you're worried about what the milliner is thinking, then perhaps we should conduct this argument elsewhere.'

She looked back at the shop. The milliner was looking out of the window. When she caught Georgina's eye, she quickly started adjusting the display of ribbons and lace.

'Shall we?' he said, offering her his arm.

She did not forgive him, but he was right, they should not be arguing in the middle of a busy footpath. With reluctance, she took his arm and they continued to stroll through the streets and she fought to make polite conversation about the sights that they passed. He gave every appearance of being completely relaxed, further proving that a man like him would never appreciate what life was like for a woman like her.

Eventually their walk brought them back to the inn. They were greeted by the innkeeper's wife, who informed them that dinner would soon be served.

The Duke held out the hat box towards her. 'Mrs Cooper, I have brought you a gift.'

Mrs Cooper's eyes grew wide at the sight of the hat box. 'Why, Your Grace, that is… I mean, you're so… I don't know what to say.' She took the hat box from his outstretched hands, and lifted the lid, her face excited as if she was opening a treasure chest.

'My, oh, my,' she said, twirling the hat round and examining it from each angle. 'It is the most beautiful hat I have ever seen. Thank you, thank you, so much.' She smiled up at the Duke, tears in her eyes.

'I'm sure it will suit you admirably,' he said. 'Won't it, Georgina?'

Georgina nodded and smiled at Mrs Cooper, feeling somewhat abashed by her outburst in the street.

'That was so kind of you,' she said as Mrs Cooper hurried off to continue her work, holding the hat box out in front of her in delight.

'I had to do something with it. The only other option was to wear it myself, and I'm sure it will look better on Mrs Cooper than it will on me.'

Georgina couldn't help but smile as a ridiculous image of him wearing a large hat decorated with ribbons and ostrich feathers entered her mind.

He looked towards the door through which Mrs Cooper had departed. 'I can only hope that Mrs Cooper doesn't think I now expect her to become my mistress.'

Georgina placed her hand over her mouth to stop a

giggle from escaping. This was a side of the Duke she had not seen before, and she rather liked it. Olivia had described him as brooding and wondered whether he ever smiled. Well, he was smiling now. Smiling and joking and she would be able to tell her friend that when he did so he looked glorious.

Her friend. How had she possibly forgotten about Olivia? That was why they were here, to save Olivia. Not to joke about hats.

'I think I'll freshen up before dinner,' she said, beating a hasty retreat. Why did everything she did and said when she was in the Duke's company make her feel so guilty? The answer to that was obvious. Because being with the Duke caused so many emotions to well up in her, emotions she was not entitled to, ones that had so far created too many complications for herself and for Olivia.

When she entered her room, she collapsed into the chair beside the fireplace, drained of energy from the trying day. She just had this evening and tomorrow to get through and then she would be free of the Duke and free of these riotous emotions. She had always prided herself on her ability to control her emotions. Lady Dallington tested her almost to the limit, but she never lost her temper, and did her utmost not to let that woman discompose her. And yet, with the Duke her emotions were in a constant state of flux, as if every emotion a human could feel was fighting within her for dominance.

One more evening, and one more day, she reminded herself, standing up and moving to the washstand, where a bowl of water had been left for her. She could maintain her composure for that brief period of time. She knew she could. Then it would all be over.

The Duke would no doubt be expecting her to change for dinner, but, as she had packed so few dresses, the same plain brown dress would have to do. Not that it really mattered and not that she cared what he thought or how she looked. In fact, the brown dress could act as a statement of how little she did care of what he thought of her.

She joined him in the private dining room, where Mrs Cooper was fussing over him. Something she continued to do throughout the meal, bringing them tankards of ale they had not ordered, along with extra servings of dessert, and a cheese board that would do any grand house justice.

'She might not agree to become your mistress,' Georgina said to him quietly, 'but you have certainly made a conquest today.'

His quick wink caused Georgina's heart to skip a beat. 'It's nice to see that some women do appreciate me,' he said.

'Oh, it's not that I don't appreciate you…it was just that the hat… I didn't want you thinking…'

He held his hands up to still her words. 'I was teasing, Georgina.'

Her heart once again did that strange skipping. This time at the sound of her name. It was lovely to have him call her by her given name, even if it was just to convince people that they were cousins.

'I'm sorry,' she said, not entirely sure what she was apologising for. 'My mother received a lot of gifts from my father, so unfortunately I saw the gift as…' Heat rushed to her face. 'I know that was not what you meant by it.'

'No, sometimes a hat is nothing more than just a hat,

and a gift comes with no expectations. But I apologise for upsetting you and being so thoughtless.'

'You have nothing to apologise for.' She reached over to take his hand, then realised what she was doing and quickly retracted it.

'We seem to spend a lot of time apologising to each other.'

She smiled. 'Yes, we do. If nothing else, we're both terribly polite.'

He laughed. 'That's something, I suppose. We may make mistakes, we may do unforgivable things, but at least we're polite about it and we always apologise afterwards.'

Georgina knew she shouldn't—after all, nothing they had done was funny—but she couldn't help but join in with his laughter. 'And at least we're as terrible as each other.'

'Agreed,' he said, raising the tankard Mrs Cooper had kindly left.

She raised her own untouched tankard and they clanged them together in a toast.

'But I think if we don't retire soon we're going to have another regret tomorrow, as we have an early train to catch.'

Georgina lowered her tankard and that familiar guilt gripped her. While they had been enjoying a convivial meal, she had once again forgotten all about Olivia. Again and again, she kept proving to herself what a disloyal friend and sister she was.

'I'll wish you goodnight, then.' She stood up abruptly and walked out of the room, before she could once again forget herself, her purpose, and fall under the Duke's irresistible spell.

Chapter Thirteen

The next morning Georgina woke bright and early, eager to start the day and anxious to get to Edinburgh. She was confident that by the end of this day she would have saved her sister from making the biggest mistake of her life. They would return immediately to Rosemont Estate, hopefully before Lady Dallington's arrival. Olivia's mother would be none the wiser and Olivia's reputation would be safe. There was no chance now that Olivia would be marrying the Duke, and for that Georgina had to admit she was secretly relieved. Despite her determination to put what had happened between them behind her, despite her desire to put Olivia's happiness first, if she had married the Duke it would have been a constant torture seeing them together. That would not happen now, but it did not mean Olivia could not marry some other suitable man who could give her the life she deserved. As long as her reputation remained unblemished, there was no reason why Olivia could not have a splendid Season and capture the heart of a good man who would make her a happy, contented wife.

All they had to do was catch Olivia before she married Dr Campbell.

She met the Duke down in the reception area, where he was chatting with Mrs Cooper, who had become quite coquettish. Georgina had to smile. The Duke really did have a winning way, and a kindness that was surprising in a man with such an elevated position in society.

He paid the bill and escorted Georgina out to the waiting hansom cab that would take them to the station. As they settled themselves on the benches, Georgina made a surprising discovery. She no longer felt constantly anxious in the Duke's company. Perhaps it was because their time together was drawing to a close, or perhaps it was because last night they had laughed together and enjoyed each other's company. It was as if they were now a couple, united in a quest.

'I haven't thanked you for all that you have done,' she said as the cab took them through the quiet morning streets.

He frowned as if unsure what she was talking about.

'It was kind of you to accompany me on this trip, to take the time out to chase my sister across the country, especially as I know you don't really think a marriage to Dr Campbell will harm Olivia.'

'There's no need to thank me.' He paused. 'While I do think you are worrying for nothing, it does you credit to be so concerned for your sister's well-being and safety.'

That was not how Georgina saw it. She had betrayed her sister, driven her into the arms of an unworthy man, so all she was trying to do was right an enormous wrong. Before she could say that, he continued.

'And it has been a pleasure to spend this time in your company, so you do not have to thank me.'

She stared at him, unable to speak, unsure how to respond. 'It's been a pleasure for me as well,' she finally said, her voice little more than a whisper.

It was a curious feeling, but one she knew she should not put too much importance on. They were from different backgrounds and had different paths mapped out for them, paths that would never cross again.

When they reached Edinburgh and found Olivia, whatever the consequences of Olivia's behaviour, it would be the last time Georgina would spend time with the Duke.

Her buoyant mood deflated at the thought of never seeing him again. That too was something Georgina was having to get used to, the way her moods could fluctuate wildly when she was with the Duke. To regain her equilibrium, she reminded herself it was all for the best that their time together was coming to an end. Wasn't that what she wanted? Wasn't she desperate to free herself of all this emotional turmoil over a man who could never mean anything to her?

But she would miss him, there was no point denying that. He was unlike any man she had ever met. Not just because he was handsome, although he was certainly that. It was not because he was charming, although he had undeniably charmed her. There was something else about him that drew her to him. It was as if on some level they had a connection. That was something she had never experienced before. Not with her mother. Certainly not with her father. Not even with Olivia.

And, she suspected, she would never feel such a connection again. That was something she was going to have to accept. Women like her and men like him did not move in the same social circles. The only way a

woman like her could have a man like him in her life
was if she became his mistress. Even if he wanted that,
it was something she would never do. Not with him.
Not with any man.

They arrived at the station and he reached out his
hand to help her out of the cab. Their eyes met and he
smiled at her once again. It was that smile that made
her seemingly melt. Could she? She pushed that thought
away before it was fully formed. No, she never could.
She was not her mother. She would be no man's mistress, not even the Duke's.

They waited on the platform until the train from Edinburgh came puffing round the bend. Unlike yesterday's frantic rush, they had plenty of time to find their
first-class compartment and were soon settled on the
plush leather benches. They passed the journey making
idle chit-chat, like old friends, or, as they were pretending to be, cousins who had known each other all their
lives. Their journey took them through green countryside, large and small towns and countless villages.
Sometimes other passengers joined them in their compartment, and they would converse with these strang-
ers, as if they were just any other couple taking a trip
up north. At other times they were alone, alone to enjoy
each other's company.

But that changed when they reached the outskirts of
Edinburgh. Then the real reason for this journey drove
out all other thoughts. Georgina was not taking this
journey in order to watch the picturesque countryside
pass by outside the train, or to exchange gossip with
the Duke about his family and his estate. She was here
to save her sister.

With much belching of steam and smoke, the train

came to a halt inside Edinburgh's bustling Waverley Station. Georgina looked out of the window at the crowds of passengers rushing hither and thither, at the porters racing by dragging trolleys laden with bags, cases and trunks. Even from inside the compartment, the sound of whistles, shouting from the station staff, and chatter from the passengers assaulted her ears.

The Duke helped her step onto the platform and took her arm as people rushed by them. Georgina looked around the grand building, which was a temple to this modern form of travel, and couldn't help but marvel at its magnificence. But the Duke was less awed, quickly retrieved their bags and hurried her out to the waiting line of hansom cabs, where drivers hustled for the passing patrons' attention.

'I could find a hotel first, so you have a chance to freshen up from the journey,' he said as he helped her into a cab.

'No, I want to try and find Olivia as quickly as possible. Can we please go straight to Dr Campbell's parents' home?'

He gave the driver the address and they set out, driving through narrow, winding cobbled streets. The city was just as enchanting as the station had been. Shrouded in mist from lightly falling rain, brown stone buildings towered above them, while the castle dominated the skyline and appeared to cast a protective eye on the citizens below.

They drove away from the town centre to the more modern area of respectable middle-class terraced houses.

If it weren't for the seriousness of their visit, or their need to quickly find Olivia, Georgina was sure she would enjoy exploring this city with its romantic, almost mystical aura.

But they were on a serious mission, and Georgina needed to remember that at all times. The cab stopped in front of a stone terraced house, identical to all the others in the street, except for its brightly painted red door.

They walked up the steps, pulled the bell and waited.

'It will be all right,' the Duke assured her once again.

Georgina hoped he was right, but knew her agitated state would not settle until she had confirmation that Olivia was safe and her life was not ruined.

A maid opened the door, her smile showing her dimples, and gave a quick bob.

The Duke handed her his visiting card, which the maid scanned, then looked at him aghast. It was apparent that dukes did not usually pay visits to this household.

'Would you please inform Mr and Mrs Campbell that Luther Rosemont, the Duke of Southbridge, and Miss Georgina Daglish wish to visit?'

'Yes, of course, Your Grace,' the maid said, stepping back but still staring in awe at the Duke, while rubbing her finger along the embossed crest on the top of his calling card.

'Please wait here and I'll inform the master,' she said, suddenly remembering herself and rushing off, leaving them in the hallway.

'I just hope we're not too late,' Georgina muttered to herself, pacing backwards and forwards to try and exercise away her anxiety.

The door opened. Georgina stopped pacing and turned in expectation. It wasn't the maid, but Dr Campbell. Instead of his looking ashamed or shocked, as

Georgina would have expected, his expression was quizzical.

'Your Grace?' he asked, his voice a question.

'I'm accompanying Miss Daglish and we are hoping to find Lady Olivia. Is she here?'

He smiled. 'You mean my wife, and yes, she is.'

'Oh, no,' Georgina gasped, taking the Duke's arm in support.

The door opened again and Olivia emerged, wearing a beaming smile. 'I didn't believe it when the maid told me, but you really are here. Georgina, Your Grace, I know I told you not to follow me, but I'm so happy you're here. Please join us in the parlour. We're just sharing a wee dram with my new in-laws.' She giggled and placed her arm through Dr Campbell's. He smiled down at her as if she had said the most amusing thing it was possible to say.

They were married. She was too late. 'When did you marry?' Georgina asked, her voice strangled.

'First thing this morning.'

If they had only married this morning, that hopefully meant the marriage had not been consummated. There might still be time to have the marriage quietly annulled and save Olivia's future.

'Olivia, may we have a quiet word? In private.'

'Oh, yes, if you insist, but not until you've toasted my marriage. I am now Mrs Dr Campbell,' Olivia said, laughing as if she had made a particularly funny joke.

'I believe you will remain Lady Olivia, no matter what your change in status,' the Duke said, and Georgina frowned at him. It hardly mattered, and now was not the time to get distracted by such things as titles.

'No, I don't want that. Mrs Campbell will suit me just fine.'

'Please, Olivia, can we talk?' Georgina said, her voice pleading.

'Oh, if you insist. Will it be all right if we go into the kitchen?' she asked Dr Campbell.

'Of course it will, my love. This house is as much your home now as it is mine,' Dr Campbell said, smiling at his bride.

Before anyone could say anything else, Georgina took Olivia's arm and led her down the corridor.

The door shut behind them and the two men were left alone in the corridor. Luther was unsure what he was supposed to say or do. This situation had nothing to do with him. Both Duncan and Lady Olivia were free to make their own choices in life and did not need his approval, but he did not like to see Miss Daglish upset, and she quite clearly was. Hopefully, her talk with Lady Olivia would assuage all her worries.

'I suppose you've come to reprimand me,' Duncan finally said. 'But you're wasting your time and your breath. I love Olivia. She is my wife now and no matter what you say or do it will make no difference.'

Luther was about to interrupt, to tell him that it was not his place to approve or disapprove, but Duncan held up his hand to halt his words.

'If you no longer want me to be your doctor or to care for your family and tenants, then so be it. If you wish I'll arrange for another doctor to take over my practice and I will find another elsewhere. All that matters is that Olivia and I are together.' He stared at Luther as if to signal that he would not be bullied, not even by a duke.

'I have no intention of reprimanding you, and you must certainly decide for yourself where you wish to practise. I'm merely here because Miss Daglish was worried about her...' he paused, then decided there was no point in any more pretence '...worried about her half-sister.'

Duncan nodded; obviously Lady Olivia had informed him of her relationship to Miss Daglish.

'I see.'

The two men remained standing in the hallway, as if no longer sure what to say to each other now that there was to be no reprimand.

'Your wife mentioned something about a wee dram,' Luther said to break the silence.

Duncan laughed. 'That she did. Olivia is already becoming a Scotswoman and she's only been in the country just over a day.' He indicated a nearby door.

'How did you marry so quickly?' Luther asked as he opened the door to the parlour.

'I sent ahead for a special licence. That was Olivia's idea. She said her mother was due to return to Rosemont Estate and she wanted to get married immediately before her mother could stop it. That's why we came up to Edinburgh. I'm still a citizen of this city so could get an immediate licence. Anyway, come and meet my parents and have that promised drink.'

They entered the parlour. Mr and Mrs Campbell rose from their wing-back chairs beside the fire, matching expressions of concern etched on their faces.

'May I present Luther Rosemont, the Duke of Southbridge?'

Mrs Campbell curtseyed while Mr Campbell bowed.

'I believe we all have a marriage to toast,' Luther said.

'Aye, that we do,' Mr Campbell said, his face relaxing. He moved to the sideboard and poured Luther a generous glass of Scotch and they all raised their glasses.

'To the happy couple,' Mr Campbell said. 'May they grow old together with happiness and riches.'

'And have a house full of bonny wee bairns,' Mrs Campbell added.

They all drank, and a warmth flooded through Luther, one not caused by the fire in the small room, or by the liquor now coursing through his veins. This was a happy scene. Duncan Campbell and Lady Olivia were obviously in love. His parents had welcomed their new daughter-in-law into their home with warmth and affection. As a daughter, the prestige of the family did not rest on Lady Olivia's shoulders. Her eldest brother would have to marry out of duty, but Lady Olivia had the luxury of marrying for love, and she quite obviously had done so. He just hoped that Miss Daglish could also see what was so obvious to him.

Georgina had so much she wanted to say that she hardly knew how to begin. Instead, she paced beside the coal range, which was still sending out its warmth into the small kitchen. Olivia sat at the wooden table, looking like a contented cat who had just consumed a bowl of cream.

'Did you do this to punish me?' Georgina finally said, her constricted throat making her voice almost a whisper. She moved towards the table. 'If you did, then I am deeply sorry. More sorry than you could ever know.'

Olivia shook her head slowly, her brows drawn together. 'What on earth are you talking about?'

Georgina took a seat and reached out across the table

to Olivia. 'Did you hear about what happened between me and the Duke? Did Molly say something? Is that why you ran off with the doctor? Because you were angry?'

Olivia's lips moved slowly into a smile. 'You? The Duke? This sounds like it's going to be an interesting tale. Please, do tell.'

Georgina sat up straighter and withdrew her hand. 'If you didn't know about us, then why did you run off? Why have you gone through with this sham of a marriage?' She leant forward once more and lowered her voice. 'It hasn't been consummated yet, has it?' She hoped and prayed that Olivia would say no.

'You are the nosy one, aren't you?' Olivia said with a laugh. 'No, Duncan insisted we wait until our wedding night. Unfortunately, he's rather moral, which so far seems to be his only failing.'

'Thank goodness. It's not too late. You can still get out of this marriage.'

'Why would I want to do that?'

Georgina looked around the sparsely furnished kitchen. At the scrubbed wooden dresser with its stack of pots and pans, the blackened coal range and the small table surrounded by a simple set of straight-backed wooden chairs. It was tidy and cheerful, but far from the luxurious surroundings of Olivia's home. 'This is not what you were born for.'

Olivia shrugged. 'I know what I was born for. To marry a man of my mother's choosing. A man who would elevate her position in society, just as she did for her family when she married my father.' She gave a resigned sigh. 'Father never loved my mother. We all know that. He loved your mother. And I think that is why he always loved you best of all his children, because you were the daughter born out of love, not out of duty.'

Georgina stared at her sister, struck dumb by the words coming out of her mouth.

'I always wanted to marry, to have my own home and children,' Olivia continued. 'But I don't want a man to marry me simply because I am from the right family with the right breeding. And I certainly don't want a man who has another woman in his life, one he really wants to be with, the way Father did. I want to be married to a man I love and who loves me. And now I am and I don't care what anyone else thinks.' She crossed her arms in defiance, but her belligerence was undermined when that contented smile once again crept onto her lips.

'You never said anything about this before. I didn't realise you knew who my mother was. And how could you possibly think the Earl loved me more than you?'

'Until you joined the household, I hardly saw my father. He was always away, on business, Mother used to say. Those so-called business trips stopped when you arrived. It was then that I realised that he had been visiting his other family.'

'Is that why you're doing this?' It was all starting to make sense. 'Have you married an inappropriate man to get revenge on your father for having a…' once again she lowered her voice '…a mistress?'

Olivia laughed and shook her head. 'Perhaps my father is to blame, but only because he unintentionally taught me that I never want to be the woman a man marries because of what their families and Society expect. I want to be the woman a man marries because he wants her and loves her.'

'But you might have fallen in love with the Duke and he with you. You didn't even give it a chance.' Georgina placed her hands on her stomach to try and ease the pain suddenly assaulting her.

'No, I couldn't, because I fell in love with Duncan.'

'But you've only known him for a few weeks. How can you possibly know that you are in love with him?'

Olivia laughed, as if Georgina's questions were a merry jest.

'Oh, Georgina.' Olivia reached forward and took her hands. 'I feel as if I've known Duncan all my life. The moment I first saw him I knew he was the man I wanted to marry. It was the strangest thing.'

An image of the Duke entered Georgina's mind, of how he had looked when she saw him on that first day as she emerged from the carriage. It wasn't so much a picture as a memory of a feeling, of something significant happening that she knew was going to change her life.

'That's nonsense,' she said, as much to push away that lingering memory as in reaction to what Olivia was saying.

'No, believe me, it is not.' Olivia sighed. 'I'm sorry that I worried you, but we had to act quickly before Mother returned. Now I'm married she won't be able to do anything about it. Oh, please be happy for me, Georgina.'

Georgina stared at her smiling sister, unsure what to think.

Olivia squeezed her hand. 'I'm in love with a man who loves me. I'm happy. That's all I've ever wanted.'

She certainly looked happy. The happiest Georgina had ever seen her.

'I know I've gone against everyone's expectations, but I don't care. I've done what I want, and have chosen the life *I* want, not the one that others had mapped out for me.'

Georgina knew she was defeated and was now unsure what battle she was actually fighting. Wasn't that exactly what she wanted for herself? To follow her own path?

'If you are happy, Olivia, then yes, I am happy for you.'

'Good.' Olivia released her hand and narrowed her eyes in question, still smiling. 'Now, what were you saying about you and the Duke? What did you think Molly had told me, something that had caused me to run off with Duncan?'

Georgina braced herself for what she was about to say. It was not going to be an easy conversation but one she had to have. 'I'm afraid I have a confession to make. I did something terrible and I need to beg for your forgiveness.'

Olivia blinked in confusion. 'I doubt you could ever do anything so terrible that it would require begging or need my forgiveness.'

Georgina drew in a long, slow breath to try and give herself courage. 'I behaved inappropriately with the Duke.'

Olivia's eyes grew wide, then she covered her mouth to stifle a giggle. 'Oh, Georgina, don't look so ashamed. What happened? Did you fall into his arms? Did he sweep you off your feet?' She lowered her voice. 'Did he ravish you?'

'This isn't funny, Olivia, and you don't understand what I'm telling you and why. It happened before I knew you had fallen in love with Dr Campbell. You were supposed to be courting the Duke, hopefully marrying him.' Georgina gulped in some air, suddenly feeling breathless. 'I knew all that and yet I still allowed him to…no, that's unfair. I can't blame the Duke. I encouraged him. I wanted him to kiss me.'

Olivia bit her bottom lip, and to Georgina's mortification she seemed to be stifling another laugh. Then she leant forward and took hold of Georgina's hands. 'I'm sorry. I can see you're upset, and I shouldn't be making light of what happened. But you have done nothing that needs my forgiveness, so stop worrying. I more than anyone know what it's like to lose your head and your heart to the wrong man. I was supposed to fall in love with a duke, not a country doctor, but the heart does what it wants to, regardless of what other people and your head tell you.'

Georgina blinked away her tears. 'You are so gracious. I don't deserve a friend as good as you.'

'Yes, you do. Now, when are the Duke and you to wed? I assume he proposed after he kissed you.'

'What? No. It wasn't like that. It wasn't like you and Dr Campbell. We're not in love and we certainly don't want to marry. It was just something we did without thinking. It shouldn't have happened and it meant nothing. If I hadn't felt that I had betrayed you I would have forgotten about it immediately.'

Olivia raised her eyebrows. 'Are you sure? After all, I'm the impetuous one, not you.'

Georgina shook her head, as if shaking off the very idea that the kiss could have meant anything to either her or the Duke.

'Do you not want to marry the Duke?'

'No. Of course not. And even if I wanted to, which I don't, the Duke needs to marry a respectable woman from his own class, not a…well, you know what I am.'

Olivia started to object, but Georgina cut in. 'When I discovered that you had run off with Dr Campbell I thought that I had ruined your chances of making a good marriage. I will not let that one foolish kiss ruin the Duke's chances of making a good marriage as well.'

'A marriage to you *would* be a good marriage.'

'It doesn't matter, as I do not want to marry anyone, ever.'

Olivia frowned at her, as if unconvinced.

'Anyway,' Georgina continued, wanting to move the conversation away from this uncomfortable topic. 'In an attempt to make amends for what I did, I should be the one to tell your mother about your marriage and if necessary to bear the blame for all that has happened.' Although she suspected she would get the blame whether she intended to bear it or not.

Olivia gave a delighted smile. 'You don't have to do that. I sent off a letter the moment we got married to give her the happy news. I must say I would love to see Mother's expression when she reads it. I hope the servants have the smelling salts handy. And as for blame, if my marriage requires any blame, which it most emphatically does not, then Mother is the one who should bear it. If she hadn't arranged for me to go to Rosemont Estate, then I would never have met Duncan. If she hadn't insisted that I travel in that silly summer dress in the middle of winter, and take off my cloak when I arrived, then I might not have taken ill and might not have met Duncan. I mentioned all that in my letter and thanked her profusely for her actions that led to me finding the love of my life.'

Georgina couldn't help but laugh at Olivia's cheekiness. 'Marriage has made you rather bold, I see.'

She gave a small giggle. 'Och, aye, lassie, that it has.'

'And are you sure you can be happy, living the simple life of a country doctor's wife?'

'Oh, yes.' That contented smile returned. 'If wealth and status don't come with love and happiness then they are worth nothing. I have love. That makes me the richest woman in the world.'

Georgina smiled at her sister. 'I don't believe I have ever admired you more than I do now. You are a very impressive woman, Mrs Campbell.'

'Och, away with you, lassie,' she said with another laugh. 'Now, let's go and have that wee dram and drink a toast to love, marriage and happiness.'

Georgina and Olivia linked arms, and, both laughing at Olivia's hopeless Scottish accent, left the kitchen to join the others in the parlour.

Chapter Fourteen

As a wedding present the Duke insisted he pay for a hotel suite so the happy couple could celebrate the first night of their marriage in style.

When they headed off in the carriage from Mr and Mrs Campbell's house they were a jolly party, laughing and talking excitedly. Georgina had never seen Olivia looking so radiant, as if she was glowing from some internal light, and she was beginning to see that the Duke was right about Dr Campbell. He gave every appearance of being an honourable man who loved Olivia as she deserved to be loved.

At the hotel, the Duke arranged for a private supper to be served in his suite, and they all settled down to champagne, cheeses, pâtés and fruits. After they had toasted Olivia and Duncan's marriage little more of the champagne was drunk, as they were all intoxicated by their shared joy.

All four were planning on travelling back to Somerset the next day, and Olivia had invited Georgina to stay with them for as long as she wanted, rather than returning to Dallington Estate and the wrath of Lady

Dallington. It was an invitation Georgina was grateful to accept. In a few months she would be twenty-one and would come into her trust money. Then she would be independent and free to go wherever she wanted. Staying with Dr Campbell and Olivia until then would be delightful, although she had every intention of keeping out of the way of the married couple and giving them as much privacy as possible.

Once the meal was finished, the newlyweds began a somewhat exaggerated and unconvincing display of tiredness.

'It really has been a long, exciting day, and I'm quite exhausted,' Olivia said with another fake yawn, causing Georgina to smile. Olivia most certainly had no future as an actress.

'Yes, you're right, my love,' Dr Campbell said. 'Perhaps we need to retire early—after all, we do have a train to catch tomorrow.' Like a ham actor who would be booed off any stage, he made his own fake yawn.

Olivia smiled at him as if he had said something delightful. 'Quite right, my dear. It wouldn't do to miss our train.'

They both turned to Georgina and the Duke, who were united in smiling knowingly at the couple. 'We'll bid you good night,' Olivia said. 'This has been such a lovely party, but I really am tired.'

'I completely understand,' the Duke and Georgina said together.

'After all, you do have a train to catch,' the Duke said.

'And you wouldn't want to be late,' Georgina added with a stifled laugh.

Dr Campbell stood and pulled out the chair for his

wife, his hand lightly stroking across her arm as he did so.

Olivia kissed Georgina on the cheek, placed her arm through her husband's and her head on his shoulder and departed.

The Duke and Georgina continued looking towards the door after they had left, smiling like benign parents. Olivia was right. It had been a lovely party, and Georgina was sorry it was over.

Still smiling, she turned towards the Duke. He held her gaze as his smile slowly faded. Heat flooded Georgina's body. She was uncomfortably aware that they were now alone together.

She should leave. To stay would be inappropriate. Yet she remained seated, as if held by the strength of his gaze. His eyes moved slowly, from her eyes to her lips. She knew she should not react but was unable to stop her lips from parting slightly. Her breath catching in her throat, her lips strangely suddenly dry, she ran her tongue along her bottom lip, and watched as his eyes followed the movement.

Slowly his eyes moved lower, causing her chest to rise and fall with her increasingly rapid breathing. His gaze like a caress, her breasts swelled towards him. This was wrong. She should leave. And yet she still stayed.

He reached over, across the table, and a small gasp escaped her parted lips. She expected, hoped, he was reaching for her, but he picked up the champagne bottle and refilled her glass.

'Shall we drink one more toast to the happy couple before you retire?'

Hardly capable of thought, she nodded. He held out the champagne flute towards her, almost in challenge.

She took hold of the stem, her fingers lightly touching his. Fire seemingly rippled up her arm to her chest and lodged itself deep in her rapidly beating heart.

His eyes fixed on hers, his fingers lightly stroking the back of her hand, and she closed her eyes, relishing the sensation of his skin on hers.

His hand withdrew and disappointment flooded through her, leaving her weak with need. Her eyes flew open. She was being silly. She should drink her champagne and leave.

'To the happy couple,' she murmured and took a sip of the delightful, bubbly drink.

Finish your drink and leave. Now.

If anyone knew they were alone together, in his hotel suite, her reputation would be in unrepairable tatters. Lowering her glass back to the table, she once again stared into those deep brown eyes, determined to tell him that she must go. Her resolve to leave evaporated as his eyes held hers. Desire wrapped itself around her, imprisoning her. She gazed back at him, almost dizzy with need.

What did it really matter? She had no real reputation to preserve. She was the illegitimate daughter of a former courtesan. Her reputation was sullied the moment she had been born. And a reputation was only important if you wanted to make a respectable marriage, which Georgina did not. She wanted no marriage, respectable or otherwise.

She picked up her glass once more and took another sip of her champagne. Being the daughter of a scandalous woman did have some compensations.

'You are happy for them, aren't you?' he murmured.

'I am,' she replied on a breath.

'But I think you still blame yourself.'

Georgina lowered her eyes, remembering her guilt over kissing him. Olivia had made light of their kiss, but she had still betrayed her closest friend. 'Yes, perhaps, a bit.'

'There is no need. Lady Olivia, or should I say, Mrs Campbell, is in love,' he said quietly, as if they were not alone and needed to keep their voices low. 'It's quite apparent that their love was immediate and deep. You can't be blamed for that. In fact, it is hardly something that deserves blame. It is something that should be celebrated.'

The Duke was right. She might have done wrong but the outcome would have been no different whether she had kissed him or not. So perhaps, just perhaps, she should let go of her guilt at kissing him, and just remember the glorious touch of his lips on hers.

She lightly bit her lower lip, which was now tingling, as if remembering the feel of his lips against hers and the gentle, sensual stroking of his tongue.

'So, what now for you, Miss Daglish? Will you be returning to the Dallington estate?'

'No, thank goodness. Olivia has said I can stay with her and Dr Campbell.'

'We will be neighbours.'

Georgina merely nodded. That thought had also occurred to her. Not so long ago she had vowed never to see the Duke again so he would be free to court Olivia. That impediment had now been removed.

'My mother will be pleased to have her future business partner so near.' He held her eyes in a steady gaze. 'And so will I.'

Georgina's heart seemed to lurch inside her chest, at

his words, at their meaning, but most of all at the way he was looking at her. She had seen that look before, when she had been in his arms and he was about to kiss her. It was a look that held such intensity and desire. A look that was both exciting and frightening. A look that elicited a powerful reaction in her, as if every inch of her was suddenly alive and craving his touch.

'I think I should retire as well,' she said quietly, hardly hearing her own words, her gaze never leaving his dark eyes. 'We have been alone together too long. People might talk.'

He raised his eyebrows and she knew what he was thinking. They had already spent two days alone together. If she cared about such things, would she not have insisted that a servant accompany them? But it was not the threat to her reputation that was causing her heart to pound within her chest, or her breath to come in increasingly rapid gasps. It was her own confused emotions, the power of the yearning consuming her, that was telling her she must flee from this man. If she stayed any longer, she suspected she would be no more capable of holding back her growing desire than she was of stopping an incoming tide.

'If you're worried about the staff at the hotel, I'm sure they'll just think we are two cousins sharing a convivial meal together,' he murmured. 'Just as they did at the inn last night.'

She forced a small laugh, desperate to make light of the situation and not expose what she was really thinking, really feeling. 'I think Mrs Cooper had her suspicions that we were not related, but after you charmed her with that gift of a hat she forgave you everything.'

A slow smile crept over his lips. 'The power of a hat—who would think?'

'Well, it was a rather lovely hat. I'm sure Mrs Cooper looks stunning in it.' She smiled at him, still trying to act as if they were merely having a polite conversation, and the unspoken conversation taking place between them was not happening.

'I just hope Mr Cooper doesn't question its origins and think his wife has been up to mischief,' he said, smiling that heart-melting smile.

'Perhaps a bit of jealousy will do their relationship the world of good.' She swallowed a gasp, remembering her own jealousy over the Duke and Olivia, an emotion she had no right to feel then, just as she had no right to feel the tempestuous emotions now gripping her.

His smile faded. 'I'm pleased that all your worries for your sister have now been resolved. I take it you are pleased that there has been a happy outcome for Lady Olivia?'

'Yes, you were right. Dr Campbell—Duncan—is clearly a good man and he and Olivia are so obviously in love.'

Her voice faltered, causing heat to rush to her cheeks. She could only hope that he would not think she was getting sentimental about love or wishing for such a thing for herself.

'It looks like we didn't have to race off in pursuit of them after all,' she said, giving a light laugh as if dismissing all that had happened.

'But I have no regrets that we did so.' His gaze once again locked onto her eyes, holding her prisoner.

Georgina's laughter died. She did not know how to respond. Did she have regrets? If she had not met the

Duke she would not have experienced so many conflicting emotions, would not have felt like a leaf being tossed around on a rapidly flowing stream. She would not be experiencing the tempestuous emotions she was feeling now, emotions it would be better to keep under control, and the only way she knew how to do that was to excuse herself from his company.

She closed her eyes, trying to break the invisible chains that drew her towards him every time their eyes met, and fighting to regain control over her mind and her body.

'No, I have no regrets,' she said, aiming to keep her voice light. 'But perhaps, like Olivia and Duncan, I too should retire early.'

Increasing heat exploded on her cheeks. They both knew that Olivia and Duncan had not retired early because they were worried about catching the train, and that it was unlikely that they would be getting much sleep tonight.

The jealousy that Georgina knew she should not feel once again raised its head. Not because she was jealous of Olivia's love of her husband, but because, as a married couple, they were now free to give full rein to their passion for each other. Her heart increased its furious beating and seemingly pounded throughout her body. She ached for the Duke to reach out to her, to feel his hands on her, his lips on hers, but, as much as she desired it, that was something that was forbidden to them.

She placed her hand across her heart to try and still its frantic beating and looked into his dark brown eyes. He was forbidden to her. But why? What harm would it really do if they just forgot about propriety, just this once, and gave in to their passions?

If they did, they would hurt no one, not any more. She would no longer be betraying Olivia. If Georgina surrendered to her desires, her reputation would be completely ruined, but, as she could only ever live on the fringes of Society, at best, what did that really matter? And yet her reputation was one of the few things she did possess, the only thing that proved to the world and to herself that she was not going to follow in the same path as her mother.

She stumbled to her feet, confusion making her light-headed. 'I really should go to bed.' The heat in her face rushed to the rest of her body and she collapsed back into her chair. Why had the word *bed* slipped out? And why did it seem like more than just a word, but a declaration of what she wanted?

He took hold of the back of her chair to pull it out for her. He was so close to her his breath gently teased the back of her neck. He was but a few inches from her. All she had to do was lean back to feel the muscles of his chest hard up against her.

'I was wrong when I said I have no regrets,' he said, leaning down close to her. 'My only regret is that we will soon part and we only kissed once.'

Georgina closed her eyes and swallowed as his hand left the back of her chair and he gently ran his finger across her cheek. 'Do you really need to retire to your own room?' he said, his voice a soft murmur. 'Won't you stay a bit longer?'

Georgina knew she should say something, or should leave, right now, but instead she turned to face him and looked up into his dark eyes, silently pleading for him to kiss her again.

He waited, saying nothing.

Her head tilted back in anticipation. Her lips parted in invitation. Her body was crying out to him, and still he waited.

'Please,' she finally murmured.

That one word barely out, he took hold of her and lifted her to her feet. Then his lips were on hers, hard, insistent and hungry. As if he had been waiting a lifetime to have her back in his arms, he pulled her tightly against him and devoured her with his kisses.

And Georgina kissed him back, no longer thinking, and her body reacted with a fervour she had not known she possessed. All thought, all reason was now lost as she responded to the raw need of his kiss. Her hands encircled his head. Her fingers ran through his thick black hair and she parted her lips, running her tongue along his bottom lip, loving the masculine taste of him.

He deepened the kiss, his tongue entering her mouth, tasting, probing and setting off an eruption of sensations deep within her. This was what she wanted. This was what she needed. This was what she had to have.

Every inch of her body ached for him. As if in the grip of a fever that only he could quench, she rubbed herself against him, desperate for release.

His hands moved from her waist to her buttocks, pulling her in hard against him. A sensual moan escaped her lips, and she arched her back, urging his hands to move from her buttocks to the site of intense need that was clenching deep inside her core.

His lips left hers and kissed the sensitive part of her neck behind her ear. 'Yes,' she murmured, the word a strange, guttural cry.

'You are so beautiful,' he murmured. And she did

feel beautiful. His kisses made her feel beautiful and desirable.

His lips continued to nuzzle the sensitive skin of her neck, while his fingers attempted to undo the buttons of her blouse.

When his hand brushed against her tight nipple, she knew what she had to have. Quickly opening the small buttons, she guided his hand to her breast. His kisses returned to her lips and her excited gasps were stifled as his hand slid inside her chemise and cupped her naked breast, his fingers rubbing the hard, sensitive nub. Georgina could hardly believe such ecstasy was possible. With each caress the intensity grew, pounding through her body, making her forget all else except the exquisite, growing torment of his caresses. She tilted back her head, her body consumed by the mounting ecstasy pulsating through her, as her breath turned to moans of mounting need.

Once again he kissed a slow, tantalising line down her throat, but he didn't stop there. His kisses moved lower. Slowly his lips moved over the mounds of her breasts. When he took her other tight nipple in his mouth she cried out, unsure if her body could endure such exquisite torture.

Her panting breaths turning into loud cries, the tension within her body grew with each caress of his tongue and hand until an explosion erupted deep within her, sending shock waves rippling through her entire body. It was unlike anything Georgina had ever known, had ever thought possible.

Taking hold of his head, she drew him back to her lips, kissing him in grateful thanks for what she had just experienced.

Reaching down, he scooped her up into his arms and carried her through to his bedroom. It was not over. There was more to come and whatever it was Georgina wanted it, wanted every delirious sensual experience this glorious man could give her.

He placed her on the bed, stood at the edge and gazed down at her. 'I want you so much,' he murmured, his voice raw.

'Then have me,' she murmured back, feeling deliciously sensual.

'Remove your hair clips,' he commanded.

She did as he asked and shook her long hair free, then removed the open blouse that was hanging off her shoulders.

He stood at the foot of the bed, and she lay back on the pillows as if offering herself up to him. She loved the way his eyes were stroking over her body, loved that look of hungry desire smouldering in his eyes. But she wanted him to do more than just admire what was laid out before him.

'Remove your skirt,' came his next command.

Almost delirious with desire, she reached behind her, opened the buttons, lowered her skirt and dropped it to the side of the bed. Still gazing up at him, she rolled down her silk stockings and took off her boots, then pulled down her drawers and threw them to the side of the bed. It was such a wanton thing to do but she felt deliciously wanton. He joined her on the bed and pulled her chemise over her head and discarded it.

'Turn around,' he said, his voice rough with emotion.

He kissed her shoulders as he loosened her corset, then kissed a line down her spine, causing her to writhe under his touch.

He pulled the corset off her and tossed it to the floor, then lifted her up and laid her back on the bed. 'This is how I imagined you when I first saw you,' he murmured. 'Naked, beneath me, your long hair curling around your full breasts.'

Her heart pounding so hard she was sure he must be able to hear it, she looked up at him, desperate for him to join her, to feel the weight of his body on hers.

'You know what I want, don't you, Georgina?'

'Yes,' she murmured back. 'I want it too.'

He stood up and tore at his clothes, threw them aside and joined her once more on the bed. She ran her hands along his firm chest, took hold of his strong shoulders and pulled him towards her. Her mother had told her about the act of love, of what would be expected of her and how she was to pleasure a man. Her mother had never said that she would also feel such intense pleasure herself, or that she would experience such an intensity of emotions that she would completely lose herself.

Kissing her once again, he slid his hand slowly up the inside of her leg, towards the sight that was throbbing for him. When his finger slid between her legs and stroked her most intimate part she cried out, her legs parting wider, letting him know what she had to have. She was desperate for him to relieve the surging tension that was once again mounting within her, but more than that, she wanted to be as close to him as it was possible for a man and woman to be.

His fingers lightly stroked her, and she rubbed herself against his hand, pushing harder, faster, urging him on, encouraging him not to be gentle with her.

'Are you sure?' he whispered in her ear.

'Yes, yes,' she gasped. 'I want you.'

Before the words were out he moved between her legs, the tip of him lightly stroking her parting. She waited, her breath held. He paused. Was he reluctant to do what she so desperately wanted?

If he was, she would have to show him how much she needed him. She cupped his tight buttocks, urging him towards her. Slowly, gently, he pushed himself inside her. But she did not want slow, did not want gentle. Wrapping her legs around his waist, she arched her back towards him, opening herself up to him.

'Please,' she said.

He did as she asked and entered her fully. Georgina moaned with satisfaction. This was what she wanted. To feel him deep inside her, to feel him filling her up. Slowly he withdrew then thrust himself back into her, deeper each time. She moaned louder, her cries coming in time with each thrust. She cupped his hard buttocks, loving the feel of the muscles clenching and releasing under her hands as he entered her again and again, harder and faster. She now knew what to expect, knew the intensity of what was soon to come, but when it did the power of it took her by surprise.

Wave after wave crashed over her, engulfing her and causing her to loudly cry out *Luther, Luther,* before collapsing back onto the bed in sated exhaustion.

With one last thrust he withdrew from her, and she felt the result of his own pleasure on the inside of her leg as he released onto the bed.

Georgina gave a small sigh of thanks. She had forgotten all about such consequences, but he had made sure there would be no unwanted pregnancies.

He rolled off her, took her in his arms and kissed her lightly on the lips, then lay back as their breathing and heart rate slowly returned to normal. With each passing moment her mind seemed to clear of the fog that had prevented her from thinking, but despite that she could still hardly make sense of what had happened. How had they ended up lying in each other's arms? And, more importantly, what were they to do now, now that they had transgressed in such a monumental manner?

Chapter Fifteen

Luther lay back on the bed, his arms enveloping Georgina, her head on his shoulder. There were going to be consequences for what had just happened, serious consequences, but for now he just wanted to enjoy the sense of satisfied euphoria engulfing him, and the comfort of holding her close.

As his heartbeat returned to normal and his breathing settled, his brain was once again capable of thinking logically. His life had just altered, for ever. His hand lightly stroking her shoulder, he tried to grasp that idea. His changed circumstances were something he would have to come to terms with, the sooner the better.

'I suppose we shouldn't have done that,' he said, as much to himself as to Georgina. At the very least, that was a monumental understatement.

She gave a small, contented sigh and snuggled in closer to him. It was hard to know if that was an agreement or a dismissal. Whatever it was, they were going to have to talk about what had just happened. He ran his fingers slowly along the soft skin of her arm. Yes, they needed to have a serious discussion about what they were going to do next, but for now he wanted to bask in the warmth and satisfaction of what they had just shared for a few moments more.

He gently kissed the top of her head, lifted himself up onto his elbow and looked down at the beautiful woman lying back on the pillows, her auburn hair falling across her creamy shoulders, and curling round her full breasts. It was hard to believe, but the reality of seeing her naked was even more breathtaking than his imaginings could ever be.

She looked up at him, a small, almost naughty smile quirking the edges of her lips. 'Perhaps we shouldn't have done that,' she said, those lovely brown eyes looking up at him from under thick black lashes. 'But I have no regrets.'

He gently touched her cheek. He had never seen a woman look more stunning than she did right now. Or perhaps she had looked more beautiful when he was deep inside her and she was crying out his name. His eyes slowly traced along her body, taking in her full breasts, the gentle round of her stomach, and those lovely legs that not long ago hads been tightly wrapped around his waist.

'Nor I.' He lifted one of her auburn locks and coiled it gently around his finger. He could add that he was hoping to do so again, soon and often. Making love with her had been unlike anything he had experienced before. It had been more than just the giving and taking of pleasure, although there had certainly been plenty of that. It had been as if they had joined on more than just a physical level. He couldn't explain it but making love to her had brought him closer than he thought it was possible to be to another human being.

He wanted to experience that again, but they needed to talk about what their future would hold. And he had to do it now, before he once more lost the ability to fight against the fog of desire.

He rolled over onto his back and stared up at the ceiling. While he was looking at her, it would be too easy to give in to what he wanted. Far too easy. Her beauty was so distracting, so tempting.

Her lovemaking had been passionate and without restraint, but she had been a virgin. She was no longer. He had taken her virtue from her and that was something she could never get back. Now there was only one way he could make amends for what he had done.

Right now he needed to focus and not let his passions take control of him and once again drive out all rational, sensible thoughts. Before desire enveloped him and stripped him of the ability to think, he had to make this right. Then, and only then, could he once again try and satisfy his insatiable need for her.

'I will of course do the right thing by you and make you my wife. To do otherwise would be unforgivable,' he said, still staring up at the ceiling so he would not be distracted.

Luther could almost hear his father and all the previous Dukes of Southbridge rolling over in their graves. He had just asked the illegitimate daughter of a former courtesan to be the next Duchess of Southbridge, to join that esteemed line of respectable ladies who came from the highest ranks of the nobility.

He had failed in his duty to them and to himself, but what choice did he have? Without thought of his position as a duke, he had disregarded his ancestors and let his passions take him over. This would be a failure in his most basic duty, to make a suitable match to a woman who would add to the prestige of the Rosemont name, or, at the very least, not detract from it.

But actions had consequences. Although she was wholly unsuitable to be a duchess, having Georgina permanently in his life would have its compensations. He rolled onto his shoulder and looked down at her. His gaze stroked along her creamy skin, to those tempting full breasts, to those enticing nipples pointing up at him, waiting for his kisses and caresses.

Once she accepted, he knew the perfect way to celebrate their future together.

His gaze returned to her full lips, desperate to kiss them. They were not smiling as he expected. Instead they were pinched tightly together, her brow furrowed.

'Was that supposed to be a proposal?' she said, stating what he would have thought was obvious.

'Yes. After what just happened between us, of course we must marry. I will make you my wife. You will become a duchess.'

She lifted herself up onto her elbows, those lovely, tantalising breasts moving closer to him, as if presenting themselves for his appreciation, an appreciation which he willingly gave.

'You'll do the right thing?' she asked, her voice surprisingly terse.

His gaze returned to her eyes. 'You have no need to be so worried. We will marry in a quiet ceremony as soon as we return to Somerset. It will inevitably cause a scandal and tongues will no doubt wag, so it will be best if we marry quickly and in secret.'

Society could be merciless to those who transgressed. She would know that more than anyone, and he was prepared to do everything in his power to protect her from its cruelty.

The crease between her brows deepened and those lovely lips that had kissed him with such intensity pinched tighter together.

'Don't worry, once you are a duchess no one will reprove you. No one snubs a duchess, no matter what her background or the circumstances of her marriage. And I will make sure you are always treated as if you were born to the role.'

'How gracious of you.' Her words made it clear she did not think there was anything gracious about what he had said, and she was not convinced by his promises.

Luther sat up, unsure what he had done wrong, but he had upset her. That was the last thing he wanted to do. He was trying to do what was right, but her reaction showed that she did not see it that way.

'I'm sorry if I've offended you, Georgina, but I'm just being realistic. You must realise that our marriage will cause a scandal. I've been attending Society events for ten years and have dismissed countless suitable debutantes. People are bound to speculate on why I turned down all those respectable young ladies from high-ranking families and married...'

'And married an earl's bastard. The daughter of a woman who had once been a courtesan, then became a kept woman.'

He winced at the venom in her voice. 'Unfortunately, that is the reality. I'm just being realistic. You know how people talk and you know what they will say. That is why I believe it best if we marry quietly and quickly. I'm doing this for you as much as for the Rosemont name.'

'You're not trying to insult me? Really? Because to me it certainly sounds like you're being insulting.'

He reached out to take her in his arms, to comfort her, to reassure her that his proposal was not an insult but was the greatest compliment a duke could bestow on a woman. She would be elevated to the highest rank of society. How could she possibly take offence to such an offer?

She swatted his arm away and jumped off the bed.

'Georgina, be realistic. I want to marry you. How can you possibly be insulted by that?'

She said nothing, but retrieved her clothing from the floor, and hastily began dressing.

He watched, speechless, as item by item of added clothing removed the sight of her body from his view.

'I've just offered to make you a duchess. How can you possibly be offended by that?' Did she not realise that for the last ten Seasons women had all but thrown themselves at him, desperate to be the next Duchess of Southbridge? For those women it would be a dream come true, and she was acting as if he was beneath contempt for bestowing this honour upon her.

She did up her blouse, with a fierceness that suggested she was also angry with the small buttons. Given her mood, he thought it imprudent to point out that they were in the wrong holes.

Completely clothed, albeit in some disarray, she turned to face him, her eyes flashing, her hands on her hips. 'You really are insufferable, aren't you? What do you expect me to do? Thank you for making such a sacrifice in marrying me? Promise not to disgrace you ever again the way I just have?'

Luther jumped off the bed to join her. 'That is not

what I said. You have done nothing wrong. It is I who has forgotten his duty and disgraced the Rosemont name.'

The fire in her eyes burned brighter and he wished he could retract those words. 'I don't mean that what we did was a disgrace, far from it…it was wonderful, it was…' Words failed him, as nothing was adequate when it came to expressing what had happened between them. 'But I was duty bound to marry a woman from my own class with an impeccable background. It is what is expected of dukes. It is what I have been trained for my entire life. All I've done is be honest with you about the situation in which we find ourselves. I was warning you about how Society will react when we marry. All I was doing was telling you the truth. I thought you'd appreciate that.'

Surely, she had to see that. After all, she was an intelligent, rational woman who, more than most, knew how the world worked.

She shook her head slowly, her eyes narrowed, her brows drawn together. 'Oh, yes. I do appreciate your honesty. And I'll be honest back. I told you I don't want to marry anyone, ever, and that includes you.'

Luther stared at her, uncertain that he had heard correctly. 'But that was before…' He pointed to the bed.

'That,' she swept her hand to the bed, 'has changed nothing.'

'It has for me.' That too was an honest statement. He'd had other women in his bed, but they had merely provided a pleasant diversion; with Georgina it was as if a world of emotion had been opened up to him. He had never felt so close to a woman as he had when he had been deep inside her, and by God, he wanted to be there again. He did not want to be fighting with her. He wanted her back on the bed, naked, once again asking him to make love to her.

'Yes, it's changed everything for you, hasn't it?' she fired at him. 'Now you're forced into an inappropriate marriage.'

He shook his head, trying to clear his thoughts. 'Did our lovemaking mean nothing to you?'

The tension was released from her body. 'Yes, of course it did. It's just…' She drew in a long breath and exhaled slowly. 'I do not want to be your wife.'

He sank down onto the bed, defeated. 'Then what do you want?'

That could not be the end of the matter. She could not walk out of his life now, as if nothing had happened between them. He would not let that happen. Even if she would not be his wife, that could not be the end of things between them. He had to have her in his life. Had to have her back in his bed. Now.

And he was sure she wanted that as well. Making love was not something that either of them had done lightly. She had been a virgin who had surrendered to her passions. He was a duke who knew his actions would have consequences. Neither could walk away from this as if nothing had happened, as if they meant nothing to each other.

'Do you want to be my mistress instead?' He smiled to himself. 'After all, I suppose you already are.'

He climbed off the bed, ready to lift her up, carry her back to bed and make love to her once again. He smiled at her in expectation, but his expectations could not be more wrong. Anger raged in her eyes, like a thunderous sky during a fierce storm.

'How dare you?' she all but spat at him and headed to the door. He grabbed her arm. She could not leave like this, not until she told him why she was so angry.

'What is wrong with you?' he said, his voice becoming louder and more forceful in his confusion. 'We have already made love. How can you be offended by my suggestion that we continue to do what we have already done?'

She pulled at his arm but he would not let go until she had seen sense. 'I've asked you to be my wife, and you said no. I want you in my life and I believe you also want me in yours, and certainly in your bed. Isn't this the most sensible solution?'

'Sensible for whom?'

'For both of us. You don't want to be my wife, so become my mistress. Then you will be able to continue to live however you want but you will be my lover.'

Her body relaxed. She looked towards the bed, and he could see she was faltering. If he took her in his arms now and kissed her, he was sure she would succumb. He could carry her back to the bed, slowly remove all those layers of clothing she had so hastily covered herself in. He would make love to her again, taking his time to savour every inch of her glorious body, before having the immense satisfaction of once again making her writhe beneath him as she cried out his name in ecstasy.

The temptation to do so was all but overwhelming, but before he did that he wanted her to agree to be either his wife or his mistress. To admit that she wanted him in her life.

'You're wrong,' she said in a faltering voice, as if she too was forcing herself to be strong against the powerful pull of her desires. 'If I became…' She looked away from the bed and stared into his eyes, her face once again tight with anger. 'If I became your mistress, it would benefit only one person. You.'

Luther recoiled as if she had struck him. How could she say that after what they had just shared? How could she possibly think that all he cared about was his own desires? Did she really think that he only wanted her in his life so he could satisfy his lust for her and give nothing back?

'For God's sake, what do you want from me?' He released her arm and stepped back. 'I've asked you to be my wife. You've said no. Now you don't want to be my mistress.'

'I'll tell you what I want. I want you to go off and find yourself a suitable, respectable debutante to be your duchess, and some compliant woman who wants you to keep her as your mistress. Because neither of them will be me.'

She grabbed the door handle, then turned towards him, her eyes flashing. 'I had thought you were different, but I was wrong—you're just like every other man from your class.'

Luther took a step backwards. How could she say that? He was not some rake who seduced and abandoned virgins without a thought for anything but his own pleasure. He had asked her to become his duchess, for God's sake. That was certainly more than his father would do or most other men of his standing in this situation.

'But I asked you to be my—'

'You are right that this should never have happened,' she said, cutting him off. 'It was a mistake for both of us and it would be better if we forgot all about it.'

He stared at her. Was she saying it meant nothing to her? He knew that was not true. She might be lying with her words, but her body had not lied. She had wanted him as much as he wanted her. So why was she playing this pointless game?

'I will be returning to Somerset with Olivia and Duncan tomorrow,' she continued. 'I would appreciate it if you made an excuse to take a later train so we never have to see each other again.' With that she left the room, leaving him staring at the slammed door in stunned disbelief.

The woman was impossible. What she wanted was unfathomable. She obviously wanted to be his lover. The way she had writhed sensually beneath him, called out his name with such passion, made that obvious. But if they were to continue to be together there were only two ways he knew that could happen—she agreed either to be his wife or his mistress. She wanted neither and he, for the life of him, could think of no third option.

Chapter Sixteen

Rage pounded through Georgina's veins as she flew down the corridor back to her own room. She was furious with Luther but even more furious with herself. She had betrayed her principles when she had first kissed him. That should have taught her a valuable lesson, one she should not have ignored. Instead, she had thrown all her values to the wind and ended up in his bed…she had made love to him, had given herself entirely to him.

How could she be so weak? She had been so determined not to be like her mother, and that was exactly what she had become. She had succumbed so easily. All he had to do was kiss her once more and she forgot everything she believed in.

Thank goodness he had made that insulting proposal or she might never have come to her senses. She might have remained in his bed all night, made love to him again. Her pacing halted. She looked in the direction of his suite.

No, she would not think of what might have happened if she had remained in his room.

Desperate to take some action and distract her

thoughts, she grabbed her clothes and threw them into her carpet bag. If she could leave right now, she would. She would put as much distance between herself and that insufferable man as she possibly could.

Once there was distance between them, she would forget all about the touch of his hands on her body, of him kissing her, caressing her, of him holding her tight against him, of naked skin against naked skin as he entered her.

The carpet bag dropped to the ground, as that now familiar tingling rippled through her. Why did he have to be such a spectacular lover? Why did he have to make her feel things she had not known possible? Nothing could have prepared her for what they had shared. It wasn't just the heights of ecstasy he had taken her to, but also the feeling that she was exactly where she was meant to be. It was as if they were joined both physically and emotionally, as if they had become one.

Then he had made that proposal, reminding her that they were not one, and never would be. He was a duke and she was someone far beneath him and always would be, even if he married her.

She picked up the carpet bag and punched at the clothes to make them fit into the small space. He had made it clear that having her as his duchess would be a degradation, and he was making an enormous sacrifice for her. And he could not have made it any clearer that he did not really want her as his wife. He was merely making things right. As if their lovemaking had been a shameful mistake that he needed to make amends for.

Such an insult made it obvious that there was nothing between them, apart from a physical attraction. She was right when he said he was no different from any other man. He had offered to marry her, which was, she had to admit, more than any of the men who visited her mother's friends ever did. Even more than her father had done for her mother. But that really made him no better than them, not when he saw such an arrangement as demeaning for him. Not when he believed she demeaned him.

And worse than that, he could not see how offensive his proposal was.

Rage once again surged up within her and she went back to pacing. And then he insulted her even further by suggesting she become his mistress. The audacity of the man. She winced, remembering how she had reacted. Not with immediate anger, not with disgust as she should have, but for a moment she had been tempted. Thoughts of making love to him again had caused her body to ache with desire. Images of him setting her up in a house somewhere discreet, where he could visit her often, became a tempting possibility. For one passing, traitorous moment it was something she wanted so desperately it was like a physical need.

How could she have thought such a thing, even for a second? She would not be a kept woman. She would be no man's possession.

What she had said to him was right. It would be best for both of them if they pretended tonight had never happened. They should put it behind them, forget all about each other and return to their own, separate lives.

That was the best thing to do, the *only* thing to do.

She just had to forget their lovemaking and focus on those demeaning proposals. She had to remember that he was no different from every man she had met in the company of her mother's friends, and those proposals proved it.

She took comfort in the rage once again bubbling inside her. Rage did not confuse her. Rage did not cause her to ask questions. Rage reminded her that there was nothing between her and the Duke and there never would be.

She had to remember he was just like all other men. For a brief moment she had thought him different, but she had been wrong.

How could she be so naïve? Hadn't life with her mother taught her that all men were the same? Now the Duke had proven that to be the case.

How dared he think he was better than her because he was a duke from a noble family? How dared he believe that marrying her would be a taint on that noble name? She had seen how dukes, earls, viscounts and barons acted when they were with her mother's friends. There was nothing superior or noble about such men. Her mother's friends had kept no secrets and would regale each other with tales of what these men were really like. Georgina was often in the room, and they considered it part of her education to hear these stories, so she would know what was one day expected of her. She had learnt very early that there was nothing superior about these men.

Well, tonight she had proven that she was superior to him by saying no. She would not be owned, not by him, not by any man.

She collapsed down onto the edge of the bed, her head in her hands. Her victory would be so much sweeter if she didn't still want him so much. It would be easier to bear the thought of never seeing him again, if she did not know what it was like to have his lips on hers, his hands caressing her body, of having him deep inside her as she reached that sensual pinnacle.

She closed her eyes, her cheeks burning. She was such a silly fool.

She should never have succumbed to her passions. One thing the Duke was right about—making love to him had changed everything. She had shown him how desperate she was for his touch, how much she desired him. And he had shown her what lovemaking could be like. How the intensity of their union was unlike anything she had thought possible. How it had been more than just physical...a deep emotional connection.

And she could experience that again.

All she had to do was agree to become his wife or his mistress. All she had to do was become his embarrassment of a wife, or his kept woman. All she had to do was become just like her mother.

But neither was an option she would take. She wanted her freedom. She did not want to belong to any man. She would not be available to provide pleasure to a man whenever, wherever he wanted it, as her mother had done.

She drew in a sudden breath as a tingling erupted deep within her, a tingling that was a memory of their lovemaking. The intensity, the ecstasy...they had taken her by surprise and nothing was how her mother had told her it would be. She had given instructions on how to give pleasure to a man, what different men wanted and expected from their mistress, but she had never told her that it could be so exquisite for a woman. Luther had expected nothing of her, demanding none of the tricks and techniques her mother had said men wanted from their mistresses. Instead, he had been so loving and had focused entirely on her.

She stood up and paced the room, trying to walk off the traitorous sensations possessing her. Why did her treacherous body keep trying to change her mind? Why wasn't her rational mind taking control? She did not want Luther Rosemont in her life.

Tomorrow she would leave and she would never see him again. She looked down at her bag and scoffed at her own ridiculous behaviour. Everything was packed, but she still had to remain at this hotel for one more night.

She ripped open the clasps of the carpet bag and dumped all the contents onto the floor, rummaged through and found her nightdress. Once changed, she climbed into bed, knowing that in her agitated state sleep was unlikely to come easily.

Minutes and hours ticked by, with thoughts and arguments still whirling round in her mind, and every insulting thing the Duke had said to her being repeated again and again, followed by the memory of their lovemaking, which she forced away by once more recounting his arrogant, demeaning proposals.

When she could take no more she climbed out of bed and crossed to the desk. She would never see him again, but she wanted him to know exactly why she had turned him down. She wanted to make it clear to him how deeply he had offended her, and how being a duke did not give him the right to treat others in such a demeaning manner.

He saw making love to her as a mistake, a wrong he felt compelled to correct. Now she would let him know why making love to him had been as much a mistake for her as it was for him.

To that end she pulled out a sheet of the hotel stationery and penned a letter, stating her arguments clearly and precisely, and letting him know why she wanted no more to do with him.

That done, she returned to her bed, pulled up the covers and tried to sleep.

Luther did as she had requested. After a sleepless night, the next morning he scribbled a note to Duncan informing him that he had been detained in Edinburgh by business and would not be returning to Somerset with them as arranged.

That done, he ordered breakfast to be served in his room, not wanting to risk running into Georgina. It was as if he was being punished, but then, he had to admit he deserved to be punished. He should never have given in to his desires, even if at the time they had been so powerful he had been incapable of resisting.

His attempt to make things right with her did not excuse his behaviour, but he had tried. And in doing so he had betrayed everything his father had drummed into him, repeatedly, while he had been growing up. His father would have been furious at him for asking a woman with Georgina's background to become his wife. He knew exactly what his father would say. Dukes did not marry women like her. Dukes took women like Georgina as their mistress—in fact, they were expected to do so. They most emphatically did not marry them.

'*You are a duke. You have your duties to perform. Never forget that.*'

His father's voice kept coming back to him, again and again.

If she knew how much he was giving up for her, how in asking her to marry him he was turning his back on his esteemed ancestors and all that was expected of him, surely she would not have been so dismissive.

It would be laughable if he felt like laughing. So many suitable young women had vied for his attention over the last ten Seasons. They had made it clear that being courted by him would be the greatest of honours, and they would give anything to be the next Duchess of Southbridge. And yet, when he finally made a proposal, to a woman who was completely unsuitable, she had spurned him.

Last night he had lain awake and gone over and over what had happened between them and he still could not understand her.

He had thought she wanted him as much as he wanted her. The way she had reacted when they made love certainly suggested that. There had been such unbridled passion, such desire, as if what they were sharing was uniting them as one.

But he was quite obviously wrong. When he had proposed he had not just been doing the right thing, it had been because he wanted her in his life. If he couldn't have her as his wife, then he would have her as his mistress. But she wanted neither.

Despite the passion that had been unleashed when they made love, despite the way she had given herself to him so completely, she simply did not want him. That was what he was finding so hard to grasp, but it was something he was going to have to accept.

Once he had finished his breakfast he dressed and

consulted his fob watch to ensure sufficient time had passed for Georgina, Lady Olivia and her husband to have departed for the station. He was unsure what he would do with this unexpected break in Edinburgh, but, as the next train would not be until that evening, he might as well explore a city that he had not visited for a long time.

He passed through the busy foyer, bustling with the excited chatter of people arriving and leaving and staff ferrying luggage backwards and forwards. The receptionist approached him before he left and handed him a letter. The hotel stationery and the feminine handwriting could mean only one thing. It was from Georgina.

He smiled at everyone and no one in particular. She had come to her senses. Thank goodness for that. One way or another he would soon have her back in his life and back in his bed, either as his wife or his mistress. Both arrangements would cause him some problems, but it would be worth it. She was worth it. She would be his.

He was tempted to tear open the letter to get to the contents, but, as the letter was one he was sure to want to treasure, he carefully eased open the flap. His smile died as he read her words. He read them again, then crushed up the paper into a tight ball and shoved it deep into the pocket of his jacket.

The letter was an affront to his dignity as a duke and as a man. It was unforgivable.

As the daughter of a woman who was a man's mistress, one who was still friends with many courtesans, I know what it is like for a woman who is the possession of a man. I know how such men treat women and what they expect from them. Many of those men also came from the so-called best families in England, but there was often nothing noble about how they treated their kept women.

Was that how she saw him? Was that how she saw their lovemaking? Like a one-sided financial transaction where she was supposed to give while all he did was take? He reached into his pocket and crushed the ball of paper tight in his hands.

My mother taught me many lessons, but the most important one she taught me was unintentional, and that was to never be a man's possession. I am an independent woman and I intend to remain that way.

He did not want her as his possession. He wanted her as his wife, and if she didn't want that then they could remain as lovers, whichever she chose. He never wanted to own her, nor would he do anything to thwart her independence.

I cannot be bought, not with hats and not with offers of being made a duchess. We cannot undo what happened, but it would be best if we put it in the past, returned to our own lives and did not see each other again.

That damn hat again. He wished he'd never bought that stupid hat. And as for suggesting he was asking her to become his duchess in payment for their lovemaking, that would be laughable if it wasn't so offensive. The position of Duchess of Southbridge had never been for sale, and it was an affront to him and his ancestors to suggest otherwise.

Last night she had shown herself to be unreasonable and irrational, but now she was being downright rude. He had made love to her. He had then wanted to do the right thing, and she had turned it into something sordid.

Well, thank goodness she had said no to both his offers. She had told him she wanted nothing from him and never wanted to see him again. Well, good riddance to her.

If she thought that he, a duke from a family that stretched back to Tudor times, was not good enough for her, then he would not give her another thought.

He returned to his room. He had no desire to do anything as inane as sightseeing. Instead, he pulled his clothes out of the wardrobe and pushed them into his suitcase. The letter seemed to be burning a hole in his side, so he took it out, ripped it into small pieces so no one could read it, and threw it in the wastepaper basket.

He glared down at the torn shreds. He had asked her to marry him, and this was how she repaid him. With that outrageous letter.

He was tempted to chase after her. To accost her at the train station and tell her how wrong she was, but dukes did not chase after anyone. Dukes did not confront women at railway stations and argue with them like fishwives. Nor did dukes care if they were rejected by a woman who was socially their inferior, a woman who should be honoured to be made a duchess.

Dukes did not care about such things. Not one fig.

He threw another shirt into his case then sat down on the bed.

Who was he fooling? Of course he cared. Georgina was unlike any woman he had ever met and had affected him in a way that he did not think possible. He cared deeply. If he didn't care, he wouldn't be so angry or feel so betrayed by her cruel words.

But that would pass. It had to. She did not want him in her life. As she'd said in that now shredded letter, it would be best if they forgot what had happened and went back to their own lives as if they had never met.

If she could do that, then so could he. He sat up straighter on the bed. He would do whatever it took to put this entire incident behind him and pretend that he had never met her. He would forget about her, just as she had requested.

If she thought he was going to go chasing after her to Duncan Campbell's house, begging her to come back to him, then she didn't know how dukes behaved. They did not demean themselves. They did not beg.

He stood up and shut his case with a defiant click. Despite what she said in her letter, no one could reproach him for his behaviour. He had done what was expected of an honourable man in the circumstances. Even if his father would have called him an imbecile and reminded him you never, ever proposed to such women, he had still done what was right.

But Georgina was not *such women*. She was right when she said she was not like her mother. She was not a courtesan, nor was she a woman looking for some harmless, meaningless fun, as all his previous lovers had been. She had been a virgin and he had taken her virtue. Despite his anger, he would never be able to forgive himself for doing so.

His father's voice entered his head. Telling him that such things did not matter. While women like Lady Olivia were expected to remain pure until they married, no such requirements were made of women like Georgina. His father would probably have actively encouraged him to seduce her, to sow his wild oats, before he took a respectable woman as his wife. But that was something Luther had never approved of. He had even once bravely told his father that he saw such behaviour as disrespectful to women, which had caused the older man to laugh, slap him on the back and tell him that would change once he grew up.

His father had been wrong. He had not changed. That was why he had asked her to become his wife. Could she not see what a sacrifice he had made for her? Unlike the men she alluded to in her letter, he had not seduced and abandoned her. *He* had tried to do the honourable thing. *She* was the one who had rejected *him*.

He collapsed onto the bed. Perhaps this was all for the best. They were from different worlds. It would have caused a scandal if she had become his duchess. Her refusal had saved him and the Rosemont name from that.

Taking her as his mistress would also be wrong. His mind knew that, even if his body did not want to accept it. All he had been thinking when he made that suggestion was how much he wanted her.

If he had taken her as his mistress, he would still have had to find a duchess, and he would have proved his father right. His father had always said, you marry a respectable woman, and have another woman with whom you can take pleasure.

He had always told himself that he would be a better duke than his father. That he would be a loyal and faithful husband and a good father. He had always said he would not risk fathering illegitimate children to a string of mistresses, the way his father probably had.

Yes, her rejection had saved him from that.

Luther pushed the call button to summon a porter to take his suitcase. He could not stay in this hotel a moment longer. Nor would he walk the streets of Edinburgh like some lost soul. He would take the next train out of the city, anything that got him closer to home and back to his life before it was turned upside down by Miss Georgina Daglish.

He would just have to see this as a test. His father had always said that the Dukes of Southbridge showed their true metal when they were being tested. Although he was usually referring to their heroism at famous battles, not their ability to contain their lust for an enchanting woman. But his test would be to stay away from Georgina Daglish and concentrate on his duty of finding a suitable duchess.

If he couldn't pass this test, which paled in comparison to the ones the other dukes had endured, he was hardly worthy of the title.

Picking up his hat and gloves, he headed out, determined to put all thoughts of Miss Daglish from his mind. He would never again dwell on her curvaceous body, would not think of those red lips, pursed ready for his kisses, nor would he remember what it was like to make love to her.

As he waited in front of the hotel while the doorman hailed a hansom cab, he knew that in reality there was little chance of achieving that goal, but by God he would try.

Chapter Seventeen

Luther was determined to get on with his life. It was just a shame the life he was determined to get on with was so dull and was about to get even duller. The Season would soon begin, with its endless round of excruciating balls, boring dinner parties, dull soirées, picnics and nights at the theatre. And while he was enduring this tedium he would be inspecting the new batch of debutantes on offer, in the seemingly endless pursuit of trying to find a wife who would bring a suitable level of prestige to the title of Duchess of Southbridge.

Every time he thought of the Season to come energy drained from him. But he would have to summon up that stoicism that the Dukes of Southbridge were known for, and hopefully by the end of the Season he would have found his duchess and this ordeal would be over.

But that duchess would not be Lady Olivia, nor would it be Georgina Daglish.

His mother had informed him that when his telegram arrived she had harboured a faint hope that Lady Olivia would come back from Edinburgh as a married woman, but to Luther, not Dr Campbell. She had been disappointed but not overly surprised.

She had also questioned him, repeatedly, on his morose state since his return from Scotland. Luther had denied, repeatedly, that he was the slightest bit morose. When his mother pointed out his untouched food and the dark circles under his eyes, he made a determined effort to prove her wrong by eating hearty meals he did not want and blaming the lack of sleep on concern about the estate.

She remained unconvinced, and had even made the ludicrous suggestion that he appeared to be suffering from the classic symptoms of a broken heart, a claim that Luther could only scoff at.

To prove that his heart was completely intact, he suggested to his mother one morning over a breakfast he was forcing himself to eat that they should invite Lady Olivia and Dr Campbell to dinner one evening. His hope was, when his mother saw how comfortable he was in Lady Olivia's company and how he still regarded Duncan as a friend, it would disabuse her of this ridiculous notion that he was in any way suffering from broken-heartedness or any other absurd malady.

'That's a wonderful idea,' she responded. 'And we must ask Miss Daglish as well.'

Luther's chest tightened at the mention of her name, and he placed his knife and fork on his plate, no longer able to stomach his eggs and bacon.

'That's hardly necessary.' He covered up the constricted sound of his voice by taking a sip of his coffee.

'Perhaps not, but it would be nice. She's staying with Lady Olivia and Dr Duncan, you know?'

That was something Luther knew very well. 'Is she?'

he said, taking another mouthful of coffee and hoping he appeared suitably uninterested.

'Yes. And thank goodness for that. Had she returned to Dallington Estate I'm sure Lady Dallington would have blamed her for Lady Olivia marrying the doctor instead of you. As if that poor girl was in any way responsible.'

'Hmm,' was all Luther could bring himself to reply.

'We must include her in the invitation, so she doesn't think that we too blame her. Plus, she's such an interesting young woman, as well as pretty, intelligent, gracious, and just lovely company. Almost the perfect Duchess of Southbridge, one could say.' His mother gave a little laugh as if such a thing would be ridiculous.

Luther took another drink of his coffee, unable to meet his mother's eye, only to discover his cup was empty. 'I believe it would make more sense to just invite Lady Olivia and Dr Duncan—after all, they are an important part of our community.' He kept his voice level and as unemotional as possible so his mother would see this was a completely reasonable suggestion. 'Unlike Miss Daglish,' he coughed lightly, 'who will soon be leaving and is not part of this community.'

Luther reached over and picked up his newspaper, as if to say that was the last word on the matter.

'Yes, you are right. But have you forgotten that Miss Daglish and I are soon to become business partners? We still have much to discuss and dinner will be the perfect time to do so.'

'I don't invite any of my business partners to dinner. If I have business matters to discuss I do so in the appropriate venue, at their place of business.'

'Well, Miss Daglish doesn't have a place of business

yet, but you're right. Finding business premises is something else we will have to discuss.'

Luther flicked his newspaper in annoyance, aware that he was losing this battle.

'I'll send out an invitation this afternoon for Friday evening,' she said, rising from the table. 'I must say, I'm rather looking forward to seeing Miss Daglish again. Perhaps you and I could hand deliver the invitation this afternoon and pay a visit to the newlyweds and their delightful guest.'

'I'm afraid I'm far too busy,' Luther said with more fervour than he intended, causing his mother's eyebrows to rise in surprise. 'I've been neglecting the estate somewhat lately,' he continued in a more constrained tone, 'what with the visit from Lady Olivia and that fruitless chase to Edinburgh, and with the Season starting soon my attention will be diverted once again. I need to spend this time constructively to ensure everything is in order, not making pointless social visits.'

His mother said nothing, but continued to stare at him, that quizzical look still on her face. 'Very well, Luther. I'll deliver it myself. But you won't make an excuse to be absent from the dinner, will you? After all, I can't imagine any duty that would require you to be that ill-mannered.'

Luther merely nodded and continued staring at the paper, digesting nothing of the latest news. He was going to have to endure one dinner in Miss Daglish's company. He could do that. He was a duke, after all, and the Dukes of Southbridge were known for their mettle under pressure.

He would face it with the necessary fortitude, stoicism and rectitude.

It wasn't as if he was expected to joust with the Plantagenets on the field of battle, or face down the might of the French infantry at Waterloo. It was just one meal with one young woman who was supposed to mean nothing to him. And yet, right now, the thought of dressing in heavy armour and preparing for war seemed infinitely preferable.

The trip from Edinburgh to Somerset had demanded every ounce of acting skill that Georgina possessed. It was vital that Olivia knew nothing of what had happened between her and the Duke. It was not that she cared about her reputation, but Olivia was so happy, and Georgina did not want anything to detract from that happiness.

Both Duncan and Olivia had expressed their surprise and disappointment that the Duke would not be travelling back with them, but they were so consumed with each other that it did not occupy their thoughts for long. On the train journey home, they included her in their polite conversation, but it was obvious they wanted to be alone. The constant eye contact, the touching of hands and arms, the way they sat so close on the train's leather seats and leant in towards each other made that clear.

When they returned to their cottage, she tried to give them as much privacy as possible. That meant taking long walks around the village and countryside, walks that were never relaxing, as she was constantly on her guard to ensure she would not cross paths with the Duke.

After she had been at the house for little over two weeks, Olivia stopped her before she left for yet another walk, and said she wanted to see her in the parlour. Her sister's tone was serious, which was unlike her, so Georgina followed her into the small room at the front of the cottage, hoping she was not about to hear bad news. Olivia and Duncan seemed so ecstatically happy together, there could not be problems in the marriage already. Perhaps she had heard from Lady Dallington again. She had already sent Olivia a series of terse letters, informing her she no longer considered her to be her daughter, and she would be getting no dowry, something Olivia had laughed off at the time. Perhaps this was worse than yet another horrid letter. Perhaps Lady Dallington was planning a visit. Whatever it was, Georgina would do everything in her power to help Olivia endure it.

'Right, I need to know what is going on,' Olivia said, the moment they were seated on the sofa beside the fire.

Georgina turned her palms upwards in question.

'You've been miserable since we left Edinburgh. It is obviously something to do with the Duke. I want to know what it is.'

At the mention of his name a dull pain hit Georgina in the stomach, and she hoped it had not registered on her face. 'I'm sorry I've appeared miserable; I can assure you I am not, but I will endeavour to be more cheerful.'

Olivia actually rolled her eyes, much to Georgina's surprise.

'I'm not judging or criticising you,' she said. 'I'm just concerned. This is not like you. Please, Georgina, tell me what has happened. I'd like to help.'

Georgina sighed. It was impossible to hide anything from her sister. 'That is kind of you, but honestly, there is nothing you can do.'

'I can listen.'

Georgina bit the edge of her lip as she considered

what Olivia had said. It did feel as if she was carrying a heavy burden and perhaps sharing it would lighten her load. 'Oh, Olivia, you said you wouldn't judge me. Do you really mean that?'

'Yes, with all my heart.' Olivia took Georgina's hands. 'All I want is to help you.'

'All right.' Georgina drew in a deep breath, unsure she could really say out loud what had happened between her and the Duke. 'When we were in Edinburgh...'

She paused, drew in another deep breath to give herself courage. Olivia said nothing, only waited.

'When we were in Edinburgh, the Duke and I were intimate.'

She braced herself and waited for Olivia's shock. She merely nodded.

'I know it shouldn't have happened,' she rushed on. 'But... I don't know...it just did. And then the Duke made the most insulting proposal I suspect a man has ever made to a woman.'

Anger once again bubbled up inside her at the memory.

'What did he say?'

'He made it clear that he would be lowering his standards by marrying me, but under the circumstances he had no choice but to do so. Then he expected me to be grateful that he was going to lift me up to the lofty position of duchess.'

'Were those the words he used?'

'Not exactly, but it most definitely was the intent.'

'And what did you say?'

'I said no!' Georgina's voice rose as if it were now Olivia she was angry with for not grasping the obvious. 'I'm sorry. I said no,' she repeated in a more con-trolled tone.

Olivia nodded and once again waited, her expectant expression making it clear she knew there was more.

'Then he insulted me further.' Her breath caught in her throat and she was hardly able to choke out the words. 'He said if I wasn't going to become his wife, I could become his mistress.'

'And what did you say to that?'

Georgina stared at Olivia, hardly able to believe she needed to ask.

'You said no,' Olivia answered for her.

'Of course I said no, and he was lucky I didn't slap his face.'

'Oh, Georgina, I wish I could make this all right. I wish I could make you happy again.'

Georgina forced herself to smile. 'I *will* be happy again. Of that I am sure. My trust money will be avail-able to me soon. I will start my business and that will make me happy. It won't be long before this is all just an unpleasant incident that I can put in the past.'

Olivia's eyes grew wide. 'Unpleasant? Did the Duke…was the Duke…did he…?'

'Oh, no.' Georgina clasped her sister's hand in re-assurance. 'No, the lovemaking was certainly not un-pleasant.' Heat tinged her cheeks. 'It was wonderful,' she said quietly. 'I didn't know it was possible to feel like that, to experience such things. It was as if I was part of the most glorious fireworks display, and I was feeling the tingle of every spark and every explosion of light deep within me. If that makes any sense.'

Olivia sent her a cheeky, knowing smile. 'Oh, yes, it makes perfect sense.'

'But that doesn't change a thing,' she said with as much determination as she could muster, trying to suppress the memory of the ecstasy that had coursed through her when she had been in his arms. 'The man might be...' she lowered her voice '...he might be an expert in the ways of pleasuring a woman, but he is so arrogant it takes my breath away, and how he could not see how both his proposals were offensive I can hardly believe.'

'Yes, he has certainly acted like a cad. You have every right to despise him.'

'Well, I don't despise him, and no, he's not really a cad.' Georgina was unsure why she was defending him but it was vital that Olivia know exactly what his crimes were. 'He did nothing I wasn't willing to do—I was more than willing. And he did propose, I suppose. And after what, well, you know, what we did, I suppose it is understandable that he might think I would consider becoming his mistress, but it proves he knows nothing about me.'

'Then he's a buffoon who should know better. I can see why you wouldn't want to be associated with such a man.'

'No, he's too intelligent to ever be called a buffoon.'

'Well, he's acted in a manner completely unbecoming to any gentleman, and especially a duke.'

'It's not as if he seduced me!' Georgina exclaimed, not wanting Olivia to think he was a complete rake with no conscience.

'Well, he should have exercised some self-control. That's what a gentleman would have done.'

Georgina frowned. 'And so should I,' she said in little more than a whisper. 'And I suppose the proposal was something which many men in his position would not have done. So I suppose that was, in some way, the behaviour of a gentleman.'

'You do seem to be accepting his faults with an admirable level of graciousness. I'd almost think that you admired the man.'

'I do not,' Georgina shot back, affronted that her sister could think such a thing.

'Then how would you describe him?'

As the most handsome man I have ever met. As a man who can bring my body alive just by looking at me. As a man I can't stop thinking about, day and night.

'You can't believe that he has behaved in an honourable manner?' Olivia asked, her eyebrows drawn together in question.

'No—yes. I don't know. What I would say is that we are both at fault but it was the nature of his proposal that was unforgivable. At the time I treated it with the contempt it deserved, and I will continue to do so.' Georgina puffed herself up with justifiable anger. 'And if I ever see him again, which I certainly hope I don't, for his sake, I will let him know the extent of my contempt for him.'

'Yes, I can see he elicits very strong emotions in you.'

'Of course he does.'

Olivia continued to look at her with a questioning expression, as if not fully understanding the depth of her grievances against the Duke.

But what could she say? Sometimes she hardly understood her emotions herself, they were so turbulent, as if she were a small boat in a storm, constantly being tossed about on a vast ocean.

'Thank you for listening to me, Olivia, and for your

concern,' she said, trying to sound more composed than she felt. 'Now you know the reason I have been out of sorts lately. But fear not. It will pass and soon I will give that man not even the slightest thought.'

'Mmm,' was the only response Olivia gave, but her expression suggested she was as unconvinced as Georgina was herself.

Chapter Eighteen

Talking to Olivia had provided Georgina with some comfort. It was also good to know that she had someone on her side who understood what she was going through.

Olivia had not judged her, nor had she criticised her actions. She truly was the best sister a woman could ever have.

Once again, she spent the day on a long walk to give the couple as much privacy as possible. This time she had actually enjoyed herself, and was able to take in the beauty of the countryside. That was something she previously had not been able to do. Not when thoughts of all that had happened between her and the Duke had repeated themselves, again and again, driving out the ability to concentrate on anything else.

When she joined Olivia and Duncan for dinner that evening she felt more relaxed than she had for some time. Some of the tension that had been gripping her since her return from Scotland had loosened its hold. It was as if she was no longer wrestling with her guilty secret.

She exchanged pleasantries with Olivia and Duncan

and her smile came naturally, rather than being something she had to force.

'We had a visit from the Duchess this afternoon,' Olivia informed them, smiling with delight as the housekeeper served the first course. 'She's invited us for dinner on Friday evening.'

That familiar clenching took hold of her and Georgina drew in a few deep breaths and deliberately relaxed her suddenly tight shoulders. It was inevitable that Olivia and the doctor would socialise with the most pre-eminent family in the region. It did not need to affect Georgina, although any reference to the Duke unfortunately did.

'I think I'll wear my pale pink gown. Whereas you, Georgina, will look best in my dove-grey satin gown with the silver embroidery.'

'What?' Georgina blurted out in a most undignified manner.

'The one with the spring-flower motif that you admired so much. After all, I won't be wearing it this Season, so you should.' She smiled at her husband. 'I've already found my Prince Charming, so have no need to dazzle anyone with pretty gowns.'

Duncan smiled back at her, and the two seemed oblivious to Georgina's horrified expression.

'I'm not talking about dresses,' Georgina choked out, trying to get Olivia's attention back from smiling inanely at her husband. 'I'm sure the invitation doesn't include me.'

Still smiling, Olivia turned back to Georgina. 'Yes, it does.' She rose from the table, crossed to the mantelpiece and removed a crisp white card, which she handed to Georgina. The card was embossed with the Southbridge crest and the name Miss Georgina Daglish was listed in elegant feminine handwriting that was presumably the Duchess's, along with the names Lady Olivia and Dr Campbell.

Georgina stared at it then looked up at her smiling sister. 'You will have to make an excuse for me.' She did not want to elaborate, not in Duncan's presence, but Olivia must know that this was impossible. Had she not made it clear this very morning how much she did not want to see the Duke again?

'I think it will be fun,' Olivia said, further shocking Georgina.

'It won't be fun for me,' she said under her breath. 'I don't want to go.' Georgina could not believe she even had to point that out.

'I'm afraid it would be rude not to accept.' Olivia plucked the card from Georgina's fingers, placed it on the table and went back to eating her dinner, as if oblivious to Georgina's objections.

Georgina stared at her, her clenched jaw making it hard to express how little she cared about being rude to Luther Rosemont. In fact, right now she had few reservations about being rude to anyone, including her beloved sister, as long as it meant she would not have to see him again.

'Please, Olivia,' Georgina begged, certain her sister would not commit such a betrayal and expect her to endure the unendurable.

'And you can't be rude to the Duchess,' Olivia continued as if heedless of Georgina's plea. 'Not only was she a gracious hostess when we stayed at Rosemont Estate, even through my illness...' once again she smiled at her husband, who patted her hand. Then she turned back to Georgina '...but also, as the Duke owns all the surrounding land, including most of the houses in the village, and employs almost everyone who lives in the area, he is effectively Duncan's employer. We cannot be rude to Duncan's employer, can we?'

Damn it all, Georgina wanted to say, let's just be rude, just this once, shall we? But Olivia was right. Georgina had no choice. She would do nothing that would put Duncan in an awkward position. He had been so kind, allowing her to stay, even though she was sure he would rather be alone with his new wife.

'Oh, all right,' Georgina said in defeat.

'And you'll wear the dove-grey gown?'

'Yes, if you wish.'

'Excellent. I'm sure we'll all have a wonderful time.'

Had love and marriage made Olivia addle-minded? That constant smile and dreamy expression suggested it. It was hard to believe she had so quickly forgotten all that they had discussed just this morning.

And how on earth could she actually think it would be *a wonderful time* for Georgina to be in the Duke's company? After spending the last two weeks doing everything she could to avoid him, now she was going to be forced to spend an entire evening in his presence. She would be expected to make polite conversation and act as if they meant nothing to each other. She was going to have to pretend they had not shared the most intimate of moments, and that he hadn't insulted her in an unforgivable manner.

Georgina did not know whether she was capable of such artifice, but it seemed she was about to find out.

'I visited Lady Olivia this afternoon,' his mother said over dinner that evening. 'And all three guests will be attending.'

Luther swallowed a sigh of annoyance. 'I still don't see why you extended an invitation to Miss Daglish,' he said, his voice sounding embarrassingly petulant.

'Because you need to apologise for your appalling proposal and make things right.'

Luther's knife and fork clattered to his plate and he stared at his mother. He must have heard wrong.

'Oh, Luther, close your mouth and stop staring at me like that. It is so unbecoming. And yes, I know all about what happened between you and Miss Daglish.'

Luther knew he had to say something and provide an explanation, but a rush of blood to the head made it all but impossible to get his thoughts straight. His mother knew what had happened in Edinburgh. How was that possible? Was his mother some sort of witch, with divine powers? 'You? What?' he finally gasped out.

'Oh, I had a nice long chat to Lady Olivia this afternoon, and she told me all about it.'

'I can explain, Mother.' Luther was unsure how he could explain anything to anyone, and certainly not to his mother, but he needed to stall for time while he thought of something, anything to say. He picked up his fallen knife and fork and lined them up neatly on his plate, giving himself time to regain his composure.

'Oh, you don't have to explain,' she said. 'I perfectly understand what you did. I just don't approve of the way you did it.'

He coughed, picked up his knife and fork and put them back down again. What on earth had Lady Olivia told her? He could not believe that Georgina had gone into detail about their lovemaking to Lady Olivia, who had then passed such details onto his mother. Did women really talk about such things? He had no idea, but he certainly hoped not.

'Miss Daglish was offended by your marriage proposal and quite right too,' his mother said while he was still scrambling for an explanation. 'I would have thought I had taught you to be a bit more sensitive to a young lady's feelings.'

'You consider my proposal insensitive?'

His mother tilted her head and looked at him with raised eyebrows. 'From what Lady Olivia told me, yes, I most certainly do.'

'I'm a duke. I proposed to a young woman outside our class, one with, shall we say, questionable origins. How could that possibly be considered insensitive?'

'Oh, Luther,' she shook her head slowly, 'you know so little of women. Perhaps it's because you only had brothers, or perhaps it's my fault. Yes, I suppose I should blame myself.'

'It hardly matters how I proposed. Miss Daglish turned me down. And I would have thought you would be pleased. After all, she is quite obviously an unsuitable duchess. If there is one thing my father taught me, it is that it is the Duke's duty to...'

'Oh, for goodness' sake, Luther.' She held up her hands to stop his speech. 'Your father, God bless him, could be a complete ass at times. It's a wonder to me that you boys ever paid him any attention whatsoever.'

He stared back at his mother in disbelief. His father had laid out the rules regarding how a duke must conduct himself. They were plain and simple and no one had ever questioned them before, not him and certainly not his mother. 'My father was correct. It is a duke's duty to marry a woman who does not lower the name of Rosemont, who comes from a prestigious family and has an unsullied reputation.'

As he waited for her response he said a quick prayer that she would not ask him why, if he felt like this, he had seen the need to propose to Miss Daglish at all. He most certainly did not want to discuss what had happened in Edinburgh with his mother.

'I'm sorry to say this, but you sound just like your father. And just like him, you're wrong. He used to talk as if all the Dukes of Southbridge had been such upstanding characters and had only married women who were little short of saints. Yes, there were some good ones, but believe me, there were also rascals, reprobates and rapscallions among them. And as for a few of the Duchesses, well, the least said about some of them the better. If anything, Miss Daglish should question whether she wants to be associated with a family that contains men of such low character and women whose behaviour I'm too much of a lady to discuss. But my, oh, my, the stories I could tell you about what they got up to. Sometimes there is very little that is noble about the nobility.'

Wasn't that what Georgina had said as well? That there was nothing noble about many of the titled men, or their behaviour when they visited her mother's friends.

'Well, it hardly matters. She said no.' He picked up his knife and fork again as if to resume eating, even though he had no appetite.

'Which just shows what a sensible woman she is.'

'Exactly.' He was pleased his mother agreed with him and that would be the end of this uncomfortable conversation. Although he'd prefer it if she did not think a woman sensible for rejecting him.

'If she had accepted your appalling proposal all it would have proved was that she wanted your title, not you.'

'What? That makes no sense whatsoever. I am my title. I am the Duke of Southbridge.'

'You're also a man. And women fall in love with men, not titles. At least the sort of woman that I would want as a daughter-in-law do.'

'Love? Dukes do not marry for love.'

'That is another piece of so-called wisdom from your father and is also best ignored. All I can say is dukes are men first and their title second, and all men are capable of falling in love, even dukes. And the only reason anyone should marry is because they are in love.'

She raised her eyebrows again. 'I assume you are in love with Miss Daglish.'

Luther was unsure how to answer. He thought about Georgina constantly. The mere mention of her name sent shock waves ripping through him. The knowledge that she would never be in his life again was a constant physical ache. Was that love?

'My darling boy, despite this uncharacteristically foolish behaviour, I do know that you are an honourable man.'

Luther clenched his jaw tightly as if stopping a confession from escaping. If his mother really did know what had happened in Edinburgh, she would not think her eldest son had an ounce of honour in him.

'I also know that you take your duties as Duke rather more seriously than are necessary, which makes your proposal to Miss Daglish all the more intriguing.' She sent him a small smile. 'I know all sons think their mothers naïve, but I am not so innocent as to not know what would have caused you to turn against what you believe to be your duty as a duke and propose to Miss Daglish.'

'Mother, I…'

She held up her hand once again to stop him, and for that Luther was grateful. How on earth did one explain to one's mother that lust and passion got the better of you and you did the unforgivable?

'As I said, I know your character, Luther. I know that would not have happened if you were not in love with Miss Daglish.'

There was that word again. Love. Was that what he was feeling? To Luther it was more as if some unexplained illness had gripped him, one that made it hard for him to breathe properly, had crushed his appetite and had left him incapable of thinking straight. Was that love? It was more like madness.

'Now, it's time you forgot about all those silly rules about what a duke should or shouldn't do, push aside your foolish pride and for goodness' sake make this right.' With that, she returned to eating her dinner, as if there was nothing more to be said on the matter.

Chapter Nineteen

Luther had initially been loath to admit it, but the more he thought of it, and he could think of little else, he could not deny that his mother was right. Georgina was also right. Everyone was right, except Luther. And now he had to right a wrong. He had insulted Georgina, a woman who did not deserve such appalling treatment from anyone, especially him. No matter how she felt about him, he had to undo the damage he had done in Edinburgh.

She had now been in the village for more than two weeks and he had not seen her, although, he had to admit, during that time he had been trying to avoid her.

Tonight he would have his opportunity to say everything that needed to be said. Somehow, he would contrive to have some time alone with her during the dinner party and he would tell her how sorry he was for all that he had done.

Now all he had to do was think of what he would say. He had to be humble, something, as a duke, he had not been trained for. He had to be sincere. That would not present as much of a problem—after all, he was sincerely sorry.

As his valet helped him into his dinner jacket, words ran through his head, none that seemed adequate to express what he felt. He had to think clearly. What he was about to say was too important. He needed to have a carefully rehearsed speech that clearly stated all that he had done wrong and left no room for misinterpretation. A task that would be made easier if he was not uncharacteristically nervous.

That was another new experience. Dukes had no reason to be nervous. They were always admired, no matter what they did or said. Crassness was forgiven as amusing high spirits. Demented behaviour was seen as mere aristocratic eccentricity. If a duke expressed an opinion that was completely facile others responded as if he spoke with the wisdom of Solomon.

Was that why he was so nervous, because Georgina was one person outside the family who saw him for who he really was, not the title he possessed? Was that why making a humble apology to her was activating nerves that had remained dormant since he was a schoolboy?

Or was it because his mother was right on another matter? Was it because he was in love with Georgina Daglish? Was he nervous because he would soon be in the company of the woman he loved, the woman he thought about constantly, the woman he dreamt about every night?

The valet brushed down his jacket one more time, did a quick inspection and with a small nod declared Luther fit to make his appearance.

He had still not composed his apology, but there was no time for that now. She would soon arrive and he needed to greet his guests.

He had sent his carriage to Dr Campbell's home. Instead of waiting with his mother in the drawing room, he anxiously paced up and down at the entranceway. When his carriage appeared at the end of the long, tree-lined path that led to the house, he pulled at his collar, which appeared tighter than usual, then pulled down his cuffs and adjusted his cuff-links. He should be using this time to compose his apology, but his mind was blank. All he could think was, he would be seeing her soon.

The carriage came to a halt. Duncan climbed down the steps and held out his hand to help his wife, then the two of them walked up the stone steps to the entranceway, while the footman closed the carriage door and climbed back up onto the footboard. Luther continued staring as the horses trotted off, in the direction of the coach house.

He rushed down the steps towards the carriage. 'Where is Miss Daglish?' he blurted out as he rushed past his guests, even though he knew it was hardly good manners.

'I'm afraid Miss Daglish sends her apologies. She will not be joining us tonight,' Duncan said, looking down at him from the top of the steps. 'She claimed she wasn't feeling up to...'

Waiting to hear no more, Luther ran down the path towards the coach house. 'Change of plan,' he told the driver. 'I need to return to Dr Campbell's home.'

'Very good, Your Grace,' the footman said.

Luther jumped inside and the driver turned the horses around and headed back down the path.

As they travelled away from the house Luther was able to take stock of what he had just done. Tonight was supposed to be all about making amends for his behaviour, and he had started the evening by being rude to his guests.

He looked out of the window. Should he shout out his apology or would that be seen as even more bizarre than running off into the night?

His mother had emerged from the house and was standing with Dr Campbell and Lady Olivia at the top of the steps. Instead of being bewildered by his actions, all three were smiling. His mother even gave him a little wave goodbye, as if everything he had done was perfectly acceptable.

The carriage pulled up in front of Dr Campbell's house. Before he could change his mind, before he could question the appropriateness of what he was doing, he jumped out of the carriage, rushed up the pathway and knocked on the door.

He now had something else for which he would need to apologise. A man did not pay a woman a visit when he knew she would be home alone. After what had happened between them that did tend to pale into insignificance, but that still did not mean he wanted to subject her to local gossip.

He looked up and down the street, at the sleepy village. Hopefully no one had seen him, although he doubted the sound of hooves or the turning of carriage wheels would have been missed.

The housekeeper opened the door, curtseyed and ushered him in. Once again, being a duke meant he was above reproach. He could even make an inappropriate visit to a young lady and servants would not question his behaviour.

'I wish to see Miss Daglish,' he informed Mrs Armstrong.

'Yes, Your Grace,' she said with another bobbed curtsey.

She opened the door and announced his presence, as if he had every right to enter, whether Miss Daglish was at home to him or not.

He paused at the doorway. She was sitting beside the fire, the flames lighting up the copper strands in her hair, her complexion bathed in a golden glow. He was tempted to remain standing at the door, enjoying the beautiful sight before him.

She stood up, her expression wary, made a small curtsey and signalled towards a wing-backed chair across from her. She sat back down and he seated himself, then he stood up, walked to the mantelpiece, then sat back down again. Hopefully, she would dismiss his actions as the eccentric behaviour of an aristocrat, and not see them for what they really were…those of a man who had no idea what he was doing or what he was going to say, only knowing that this was the most important moment of his life, and every word he said had to be the correct one.

'Did Dr Campbell not pass on my apology?' she said.

'Apology? You need to apologise for nothing.'

She frowned slightly. 'My apology regarding this evening's dinner.'

'Oh, yes, that. Yes, he did,' he burbled on. She was dressed in a light grey dinner gown, suggesting she had intended to attend the dinner party but had changed her mind. He knew the reason why. She did not want to see him again, and for that he could not blame her.

'Georgina—Miss Daglish—it is I who have come to apologise.'

She said nothing, merely stared straight ahead, her

arms crossed. It was clear she did not think him capable of a sincere apology and was bracing herself for another harrowing encounter with an idiot who knew no better. He too braced himself, determined to prove her assessment of him to be wrong.

'Firstly, I must apologise for visiting you when you are home alone. I had no intention of causing any gossip in the village.'

She raised her eyebrows but still did not look at him. They both knew that if the gossips really knew what had occurred in Edinburgh then such a visit would hardly even register as worthy of comment.

'But most of all I must apologise for my proposal in Edinburgh.'

She turned to face him. Her crossed arms gripped her chest more tightly, but still she said nothing.

'You were right to take offence. The manner in which I proposed was unforgiveable. I should never have suggested that in any way would I be lowering myself by marrying a woman such as yourself.'

Her chin rose, her face guarded.

'I should have said that in every way you are a woman far superior to myself, and far superior to any young woman I have ever met.' He paused, knowing how true those words were. 'Any man who won your hand in marriage would be honoured indeed.'

Her guarded expression did not change.

'And again, I must apologise for suggesting that your background made you unsuitable as a duchess. Nothing could be further from the truth. You are elegant, refined, intelligent, cultured, kind and compassionate, possessing therefore all the qualities that would make you perfect for the role of duchess.'

Her blinking was the first sign that she was starting to thaw and accept his sincerity.

'Not to mention that you are the most beautiful woman I have ever met,' he added, almost to himself. 'Beautiful in appearance and beautiful in spirit.'

He leaned towards her, appealing for her to understand. 'I am so sorry for my boorish behaviour and I most humbly beg your forgiveness. I never meant to insult you but that is what I did.'

She slowly nodded, causing his heart to soar in expectation that maybe, just maybe, she was going to accept his inadequate apology.

'I understand,' she said quietly.

He was tempted to leave it at that, but he knew his apology was not complete. Slowly he drew in a deep breath, and even more slowly exhaled it. 'And I must also beg your forgiveness for my inexcusable suggestion that you become my mistress.'

Once again she raised her chin, her arms folding around her body.

'That was not only offensive but insensitive as well. At the time I was only thinking of myself, of how much I still wanted you in my life. I was not thinking of how such a proposal would affect you, how it would make you feel. I was a selfish and thoughtless fool, and I am so profoundly sorry.'

She unfolded her arms unfolded and placed her hands in her lap. 'You are perhaps being rather hard on yourself.'

'Does that mean there is a hope that you might forgive me?'

'You are forgiven.'

This was more than he could have possibly hoped

for. More than he deserved. But he knew her forgiveness was not all he wanted. Somehow, he was going to have to tell her what was in his heart.

Once again, he fought for the best way to express what he was thinking. It required poetry, lyrical words that made the heart take flight, the spirit float off on a cloud and one's emotions to dance and sing.

'Georgina, I love you,' he said instead, the words sounding almost blunt in their inadequate simplicity.

She gasped, presumably shocked that something so profound, so life-changing, should be expressed in three rather simple words.

'I wish I had the soul of a poet, so I could describe what it means to be in love with you. I will do my best, but please, forgive my clumsy efforts. Georgina, I love you with all my heart. I love you for all the reasons I have already mentioned. For your beauty, for your intelligence, your charm, your strength of character, your kindness, your wit. There are so many reasons why I love you they are too many to list. All I can say is I love everything about you.'

Her hand covered her mouth and he hoped she was not laughing at him. When she lowered it, he could see she was not. She was smiling. A joyous smile that was like the sunshine emerging on a grey day.

'I believe you have nothing to worry about,' she said. 'That certainly sounded poetic to me.'

He smiled back at her, his own heart seeming to lighten and take flight. 'That is what I should have said to you in Edinburgh. I now know that my unforgivable behaviour was because I was denying what I cannot now deny. I have fallen in love with you. I am in love with you.' He looked into her soulful brown eyes, beseeching her to understand him. 'And I would love to marry you, with all my heart, but after all that I have done, all that I have said, I can understand why you would reject me.'

'Was that another proposal?'

She adopted a serious expression, but the small smile she was fighting to hold back gave him hope.

'I would make another proposal if I thought there was any chance of being accepted,' he teased.

The smile did escape, making his heart expand in his chest with happiness.

'Perhaps you should be brave and take a risk,' she replied, her voice equally teasing.

It was all the encouragement he needed. In one quick movement he was out of his chair and down on one knee in front of her. 'Georgina, I love you more than any man has ever loved a woman. If you consented to be my wife you would make me the happiest man alive, and I would dedicate my life to trying to make you as happy as you make me. I know you fear being controlled by a man, of losing your independence, but I would never do such a thing.' He gave a small laugh. 'Knowing you as I do, it would be pointless to even try.'

Her smile grew wider.

'Georgina, will you do me the enormous honour of consenting to marrying me so I can love and honour you as you deserve to be loved and honoured?'

She nodded. 'Yes, yes, yes.'

Hardly able to believe this was really happening, he stood up, took her in his arms and kissed her. He had merely hoped for forgiveness, but now he had what he really wanted, even though, fool that he was, it had taken him far too long to realise what his heart truly desired.

* * *

Georgina melted into his kiss. She had missed this so much and had thought she would never again be in his arms. Now she was, and he had declared his love for her, had proposed in a manner that she did not want to refuse.

His kisses were even more sublime than she remembered. They contained the same passion, but now there was trust. Now there was love. This magnificent, exciting man loved her and wanted to marry her. Not out of duty, not out of some misguided sense of honour, but because he loved her.

She had secretly dreamed of this moment but could still hardly believe she had just received another proposal of marriage, never mind accepted it. Nor could she believe it was possible to move from despair to such complete happiness so quickly.

The reason for her change of mood was both complicated and simple. She too was in love. In love with the most wonderful man in the world. She was in his arms. He was kissing her and they would be spending their lives together. How could she not feel as if the greyness of the world had been washed away and it had been infused with glorious colour?

Her kisses intensified, her hands encircled his head, her fingers weaving through his thick hair, as she gave vent to the fervour that had been building up for more than two weeks. Two long, lonely, desperate weeks. Passion swelled within her chest, knowing that those dark, desolate days and nights were over, because Luther Rosemont loved her and she loved him.

He pulled back from the kiss, his lips still a tempting inch from her own. 'I meant every word I said,' he whispered, his soft breath warm on her cheek.

She nodded, wanting less talk, more kissing.

'I would never try to control you, to own you. I know you want your freedom and that is what you will have.'

'But I'll still be your wife, won't I?' she blurted out in panic.

He tilted back his head and laughed. 'You've said you will, so there will be no going back now.' His face became serious and he looked deep into her eyes. 'But I know how important independence is for you. I know you never want to feel owned by a man. I would hate it if you ever thought I owned you.'

She nodded. 'Yes, I want my freedom, but I would never be truly free if you were not in my life. I love you. I want to be with you. I want to spend the rest of my life with you.'

He continued to stare down at her. Did he need more convincing? If he did, she would give it to him. 'Without you I am not free. When we are together, I can be who I truly am. I can be a woman who loves and who is loved.'

He took her in his arms again and lightly kissed her neck. 'You might not own me,' she whispered, hardly able to speak as her body registered the soft touch of his lips on her sensitive skin. 'But you do own my heart.'

'And you own mine,' he said, still kissing a line down her neck, causing her to sigh with contentment.

'I love you, Luther.' It was so good to say that out loud she just had to repeat it. 'I love you with all my heart.'

'And my heart is yours, and always will be,' he whispered back. 'It has been yours from the moment I first saw you.' He took her hand and placed it in the middle of his chest, where his heart pounded strong and hard.

'I also believe you claimed my heart the first time I saw you, if such a thing is possible,' she murmured.

He nodded slowly. 'I do believe it is possible. For ten years I've been looking for a bride and dismissed prospect after prospect, imagining faults with each. Now I know why. I was waiting for you.' He brushed back the hair on her forehead. 'The moment I saw you step down from the carriage, deep down I knew that I wanted to marry you, even though I tried to deny it. It was as if I had found the woman who would complete me.'

He kissed her again and Georgina sank back into his arms. He was right. This was where she was meant to be, where she had always been meant to be.

He withdrew from her lips, took hold of her hands and lightly kissed her palm. 'But we are being very selfish.'

She shook her head, unsure what he was referring to.

'We need to share our joyous news. The world needs to know that there will soon be a new Duchess of Southbridge.'

She couldn't help but wince slightly. 'Perhaps we should just marry quietly, as you suggested.'

'Our wedding will be whatever you desire, but I still want to share our happiness with the world. If people gossip, then let them. If they are scandalised, then that is their problem, not ours. If they can't see what happiness looks like, if they don't know what it's like to be in love, then I pity them.'

'I pity them too,' Georgina said with a laugh. 'I pity anyone who doesn't know what it is like to feel the way I do right now. Oh, Luther, I didn't know such happiness was possible.'

'Nor I, my love, but before we let the world know

there are some people we need to share our love with. Tonight.'

Luther took her hand, and as if they were floating he led her out to the waiting carriage and they drove through the quiet streets of the sleepy village to Rosemont Estate, which was sending out its welcoming light from every illuminated window.

Holding hands, they walked through to the drawing room, where Olivia, Duncan and the Duchess were taking coffee.

'We have some news for you,' Luther said as they entered the room.

The Duchess, Olivia and Duncan cheered as if the engagement had already been announced.

'I'm so pleased,' the Duchess said, crossing the room and patting her son on the arm before kissing Georgina on the cheek. 'You will make a wonderful duchess.'

Georgina looked at Luther, who appeared as surprised as she felt, then to the Duchess, then to Olivia and Duncan.

'We haven't told you our news,' he said.

'You're getting married,' all three said at once, then laughed as if they had just made the funniest of jokes.

'We knew it had to happen sooner or later,' Olivia said, kissing Georgina's cheek, while Duncan shook Luther's hand. 'We were hoping it would be tonight. The Duchess and I had plans to leave the two of you alone together. Then Georgina ruined everything by feigning a headache.'

Georgina coloured slightly at her deception, which now seemed to have been the act of a different woman and to have happened a long time ago. Her lovely sister had not betrayed her by accepting tonight's invitation. She knew she was in love with Luther, even before Georgina had known it herself. As had the Duchess. She looked from one smiling woman to the other, her heart almost bursting with happiness that she had such wonderful women in her life.

'But this worked out better than we expected,' Olivia continued, and looked at the Duchess, who nodded her agreement.

Her gaze returned to Luther, who was staring at his smiling mother and shaking his head slowly in wonderment. Then he looked back at Georgina, still smiling. 'It looks like we've been outmanoeuvred, my darling.'

Georgina's smile grew even wider, as if she was radiating with a warm inner glow. Not just because they had been outmanoeuvred in the nicest possible way, but because he had called her darling. She was his darling.

Olivia and the Duchess immediately started talking about wedding arrangements, as if they were continuing a discussion that had been started before Georgina and Luther had arrived.

While talk of flowers and dress styles whirled around them, Luther took Georgina's hand and kissed it lightly. 'It seems, my darling, you will be having a wedding fit for a duchess, whether it is what we desire or otherwise.'

Georgina laughed. 'All that matters is that we are in love and will always be together.'

'And all I want now is to be alone with my future bride.'

Georgina nodded. They looked over at Olivia and the Duchess, who had their heads together and were talking animatedly. Duncan smiled at them, then turned away, as if he knew they wanted their privacy. Luther once again took her hand and they quietly backed out of the drawing room. The moment the door closed behind them they were back in each other's arms, celebrating their love in the best of all possible ways.

Epilogue

The Rosemont ball traditionally opened each new Season. It had been the case for the last ten Seasons. The tradition had started because the Duchess saw it as a good way for her sons to assess the new debutantes right at the beginning of the Season, particularly Luther, who was expected to find himself a Duchess of Southbridge before the Season was over.

This year was no different.

Once again the Rosemonts' London townhouse was bedecked with flowers, ferns, potted palms and an array of other foliage. Invitations had been sent out to all the prominent families, particularly to those with young ladies making their debuts, or eligible men in want of a wife. Extra staff had been recruited to cope with the large number of guests, and the best musicians had been hired to provide the music.

But this year there *was* one big difference, and all those expectant debutantes were destined to suffer an enormous disappointment.

At the entrance to the ballroom, the Duke of Southbridge, the Duchess of Southbridge and her two other sons, Ethan and Jake, and their wives, Sophia and Violet, stood in line to greet their guests. But there was an unexpected addition to the line-up: Miss Georgina Daglish, whom the Duke introduced to each guest in turn as his fiancée, the future Duchess of Southbridge.

Reactions varied, from those who merely congratulated Luther and greeted Georgina with politeness, to those who looked scandalised, to some who even appeared affronted. The latter response usually came from the mothers of debutantes who were hoping that this year it would be their daughter who would be the one to capture the elusive duke.

Whatever their reaction, Luther's expression did not change, and he smiled throughout. Nor did Georgina's. If her husband-to-be did not care that some people were scandalised by their engagement, then why should she?

The Duchess also took the opportunity to inform the guests that Luther's future bride was soon to be her business partner. This announcement caused shocked eyebrows to rise further up foreheads and eyes to grow even wider. The Duchess, however, did not remain impassive to these reactions and appeared to relish being the cause of such consternation.

Since her engagement, the Duchess and Georgina had held many discussions on their new enterprise, and had decided that instead of starting one business, they would use their wealth and influence to invest in the businesses of other young women, so they could find financial independence. This was something which gave Georgina immense satisfaction.

Banks were all but shut to women and bank managers would never consider financing a woman into a business of her own, no matter how potentially profitable that enterprise might be. Georgina and the Duchess intended to right that wrong and provide low-interest loans to bright, enterprising women. It was something they were both passionate about and had discussed with as much enthusiasm as the upcoming wedding.

But the Rosemont ball was all about celebrating love, not business, as it had been for the last two years. Ethan's wife, Sophia, and Jake's wife, Violet, were so excited that the engagement was to be announced at the ball. As they had said, on several occasions, the Rosemont ball had played an important role in each of their journeys towards true love, so it was only fitting that the only remaining unmarried Rosemont son should announce his engagement at the ball. They also hoped there would continue to be a Rosemont ball every Season, so they could celebrate their love with the family and mark their happy anniversary.

Once the guests had all arrived, the orchestra began to play and Luther led Georgina onto the floor for the first waltz of the night.

They swirled around the dance floor, and were soon joined by Ethan and Sophia, Jake and Violet, and Olivia and Duncan. Even the Duchess decided she needed a bit of romance in her life, and took to the floor with the widowed Duke of Redcliffe.

It seemed that, now her duties as Duchess were about to come to an end, she had other ideas on how to occupy her time, other than becoming a business investor.

The entire evening was magical. If people did gossip, Georgina did not hear it. She was with the man she loved, surrounded by a loving family.

Lady Dallington had even, finally, come to accept the reality of the situation. Once that had happened, she began announcing to anyone who would listen that Georgina had always been more than just her husband's ward but was more like a much-loved daughter, which meant, effectively, she herself would soon be the mother of a duchess.

While many of the debutantes and mothers who attended the ball were disappointed that an eligible duke was now unavailable, they did have the compensation of attending an additional event on the Season's social calendar—the lavish wedding hosted at Rosemont Estate.

As only one woman became the Duchess of Southbridge in each generation, no expense was spared for the festivities, and the future Dowager Duchess saw it as her final act as Duchess to host a wedding that would be talked about for generations.

Georgina wore a white wedding gown, designed in Paris by the House of Worth, with intricate embroidery, pearls woven into the fabric and a five-foot lace train. Every inch of Rosemont House was decorated with flowers, and several additional chefs were hired to cater for the multitude of guests.

While it had been wonderful to share such a joyous event with so many people, it was the moments she spent with Olivia and her father before the ceremony that had been the most touching, and among the memories of the day Georgina most cherished.

Olivia was her matron of honour, and her father had insisted on walking her down the aisle.

When he was helping her into the open carriage bedecked with white flowers that would take them to the church, he'd turned to her with tears in his eyes. 'You look beautiful,' he had said. 'You remind me so much of your mother. She would be so proud of you. I am so proud of you.'

Then he quickly brushed away the tears that had started to fall. 'If I had been a better man, I would have married your mother. My biggest regret in life is that I never did. Instead, I made two women miserable. I tried to love my wife, but it was your mother who always had my heart.' He lightly kissed her on the forehead. 'The Duke is a wise man to marry for love. And a lucky man to have fallen in love with my daughter.'

Georgina also fought to hold back her tears. 'Thank you, Father,' she said, saying that word out loud to him for the first time since she had become his ward.

'I know the Duke will treat you better than I treated your mother. You deserve this happiness, Georgina— I just wish your mother was here to see our wonderful daughter find true love with such a good man.'

Smiling through his tears, he then helped Olivia into the carriage and kissed her cheek. 'Both my sons-in-law are such lucky men, with enough sense to pick such perfect young ladies to be their brides.'

As they'd travelled to the church Olivia had taken the opportunity to inform her that she was responsible for this wedding, something that had taken Georgina by surprise.

'Oh, yes,' she had said with a proud expression. 'I saw it immediately. Well, not quite immediately. The way you two looked at each other when you first met had me confused to begin with. It wasn't until I met Duncan that I understood that what I had witnessed was love at first sight. That's why I insisted you wear my green gown to dinner. It was so you would drive Luther wild with desire.' At that point she had blushed and looked at her father, who had tactfully acted as if he was fascinated by a passing field full of grazing cows.

Olivia had lowered her voice and continued. 'That was why I insisted you go for long walks each day, so you would meet up with Luther.'

'I thought that was so you could be alone with Duncan.'

'Well, that too, I suppose. I wasn't surprised when you said you had,' her voice lowered further, 'kissed him. And I didn't believe you for a moment when you said you didn't want to marry him. And see, I was right.'

With that she had sat back in the carriage, looking even more pleased with herself, and their father had smiled and repeated that he was proud to have such intelligent daughters.

While the wedding reception was a spectacular event, the ceremony was conducted at the village church, and attended by only family members and close friends.

As if in a dream Georgina had walked up the aisle towards her handsome husband-to-be, who was nervously awaiting her, with his two brothers beside him.

The only part of the ceremony she remembered with absolute clarity was when she and Luther had declared their love for each other in front of the congregation, had been pronounced man and wife, and the bells had tolled out to share their love to the world.

And they had continued to declare their love for each other every day since.

* * * * *

*If you enjoyed this story, be sure to read
the other books in Eva Shepherd's
Those Roguish Rosemonts miniseries*

A Dance to Save the Debutante
Tempting the Sensible Lady Violet

*And why not check out her
Young Victorian Ladies miniseries?*

Wagering on the Wallflower
Stranded with the Reclusive Earl
The Duke's Rebellious Lady

Get 4 FREE REWARDS!

We'll send you 2 FREE Books plus 2 FREE Mystery Gifts.

FREE Value Over $20

Both the **Harlequin® Historical** and **Harlequin® Romance** series feature compelling novels filled with emotion and simmering romance.

YES! Please send me 2 FREE novels from the Harlequin Historical or Harlequin Romance series and my 2 FREE gifts (gifts are worth about $10 retail). After receiving them, if I don't wish to receive any more books, I can return the shipping statement marked "cancel." If I don't cancel, I will receive 6 brand-new Harlequin Historical books every month and be billed just $6.19 each in the U.S. or $6.74 each in Canada, a savings of at least 11% off the cover price, or 4 brand-new Harlequin Romance Larger-Print books every month and be billed just $6.09 each in the U.S. or $6.24 each in Canada, a savings of at least 13% off the cover price. It's quite a bargain! Shipping and handling is just 50¢ per book in the U.S. and $1.25 per book in Canada.* I understand that accepting the 2 free books and gifts places me under no obligation to buy anything. I can always return a shipment and cancel at any time by calling the number below. The free books and gifts are mine to keep no matter what I decide.

Choose one: ☐ **Harlequin Historical**
(246/349 HDN GRH7)

☐ **Harlequin Romance Larger-Print**
(119/319 HDN GRH7)

Name (please print)

Address   Apt. #

City   State/Province   Zip/Postal Code

Email: Please check this box ☐ if you would like to receive newsletters and promotional emails from Harlequin Enterprises ULC and its affiliates. You can unsubscribe anytime.

Mail to the **Harlequin Reader Service:**
IN U.S.A.: P.O. Box 1341, Buffalo, NY 14240-8531
IN CANADA: P.O. Box 603, Fort Erie, Ontario L2A 5X3

Want to try 2 free books from another series! Call 1-800-873-8635 or visit www.ReaderService.com.

*Terms and prices subject to change without notice. Prices do not include sales taxes, which will be charged (if applicable) based on your state or country of residence. Canadian residents will be charged applicable taxes. Offer not valid in Quebec. This offer is limited to one order per household. Books received may not be as shown. Not valid for current subscribers to the Harlequin Historical or Harlequin Romance series. All orders subject to approval. Credit or debit balances in a customer's account(s) may be offset by any other outstanding balance owed by or to the customer. Please allow 4 to 6 weeks for delivery. Offer available while quantities last.

Your Privacy—Your information is being collected by Harlequin Enterprises ULC, operating as Harlequin Reader Service. For a complete summary of the information we collect, how we use this information and to whom it is disclosed, please visit our privacy notice located at corporate.harlequin.com/privacy-notice. From time to time we may also exchange your personal information with reputable third parties. If you wish to opt out of this sharing of your personal information, please visit readerservice.com/consumerschoice or call 1-800-873-8635. **Notice to California Residents**—Under California law, you have specific rights to control and access your data. For more information on these rights and how to exercise them, visit corporate.harlequin.com/california-privacy.

HHHRLP22R3

HARLEQUIN
PLUS

Try the best multimedia subscription service for romance readers like you!

Read, Watch and Play.

Experience the easiest way to get the romance content you crave.

Start your **FREE TRIAL** at
<u>www.harlequinplus.com/freetrial</u>.